Salt and Sky

By Norma L. Jarrett

Published by Norma L. Jarrett

Printed in the United States of America

Visit our website at www.normajarrett.net

First edition published 2016

All quotes from Scriptures taken from the King James Version of the Bible.

Dedicated to my mother and father,

the late Norman and Ethel Jarrett

To my husband Clarence York, My sister and brother, Paulette Jones and Stephen Jarrett, Mary Upshaw (My "Queenie"), My Aunt Queenie Ewing and the rest of the Jarrett, York, Jones and Page family. Friends that span decades and geographic region. Lastly, to Abby McGrath and the Renaissance House of Martha's Vineyard and New York. Mwah!!!

Acknowledgments

Thank You God for allowing me to discover my purpose, to uplift and inspire through writing and speaking. Thanks for the journey *and* the destination. May all that I do honor You and may I never be taken out of Your hand. Thank you to my North Carolina A & T, Thurgood Marshall, Alpha Kappa Alpha family and friends and "seed sowers" too numerous to mention.

There are years that ask questions and years that answer.

—Zora Neale Hurston

Table of Contents

Prologue

Sierra closed her eyes and summoned her sacred place. The tide caressed her feet as the ocean called. The angels and air whispered calming prayers. She was lost again in the shore, floating aimlessly in a pool of serenity. Baptized…again as the salt water elixir washed over her. Cleansing, purifying, restoring. She pursed her lips and kissed the sky. She'd tasted God. He was good. She trusted Him…here, the ocean too vast and infinite not to believe. Whenever life wrung her like a wet cloth, she'd mentally, physically or spiritually sojourn to the sea. Inhaling and exhaling all her dreams. Until the next trial, pain or sudden tragedy.

Sierra wanted to stay in her sacred place. Stay and keep floating. She wanted to run. She wanted to move. She wanted out.

God, heaven would be a home on the vineyard, surrounded by the beautiful waters you have created. My life would be so different. I just know it.

She'd often pictured her life there, her place of promise. A cottage tucked away on the island of Martha's Vineyard. She'd never been, but read about it, saw pictures and watched movies about it. She belonged there. Her soul knew it. She craved a place of simplicity and solace to wash away all her pain. However impossible it seemed, she'd play out the vision in detail again and again. A quaint house by the shore. A tall easygoing handsome husband with an irresistible smile. And a son, the spitting image of his father. A porch with rocking chairs. Days filled with swimming, long walks, cozy nights, laughter and a village of family and friends.

She smiled. *Perfect.*

Seconds later, she sucked her teeth and shook her head. *God, really? So far from my present life.* She sighed. *A financially challenged, single mother, and well…the rest you already know.* Her eyes fell to the table where the envelope she'd ignored for a week remained.

Another letter from the dead. Sierra's fingertips nudged the envelope resting on the table. The no-frills envelope was a stark contrast to Deja Reaux's stationary. She nudged it again and paused before tearing it open.

She really messed up this time. No fixing this one. Sierra winced at the smack of the gavel that sealed her mother's fate. *She's a lot of things, but a criminal?*

The sight of her mother lying in a cell splashed across her mind, but was instantly replaced with her mother's face. Her flawless bronze skin boasted sculpted cheekbones with persimmon blush. Her textured mane wrapped in a regal up do anointed by dangling earrings that danced with her slightest move.

Sierra rubbed her temples as the former image re-emerged. It sliced through her mind like a madman wielding an ax. *Mother. Cell. Jail.* Her curve-hugging dresses and airy bohemian tops traded for a jumpsuit. Numbers replaced the accessories Sierra had designed just for her. *No longer my mother, a business owner, or a person who'd fought her way to sobriety for over six years, but just a number?*

Air from Sierra's lungs hurled itself up and out as she plugged the gusher of pain flooding her soul. What now, God? Pain lurched from her diaphragm as she slid to the floor, her head cupped in her hands. I'll never understand your plan. No matter what they say about you. I'm exhausted. Finally, I surrender.

Chapter 1 – The Best Thing I Never Had

Sierra knew summer. Lazy-day drives in vintage rides, ocean aphrodisiacs and sun-kissed thighs, iced coffee sips at outdoor cafés, tangerine beams that showered her face.

This definitely ain't it. She sighed as her butt shimmied and settled on the train seat. She loosened her scarf and crinkled her nose at the stale cramped spaced. *I hate public transportation.* After cursing January, she reached down in the tote between her feet and grabbed a book. After a few pages in, the bus whipped, thrusting a nearby man into her space. She sucked her teeth and closed her book. He clumsily leaned back.

She pressed her back against the seat and closed her eyes. She visualized the sea, Cape May, Belmar Beach, Asbury Park, any place along the Jersey shore. The ocean was her sanctuary. She could feel it. The feather light mist caressing her face. She inhaled the peace of her sacred place. Her true heartbeat emerged. *My little Gray.* Her son's image warmed her heart. His glacier blue eyes could melt the frost off her soul. *He's the best thing that's ever happened to me.*

The vibrating phone in her coat jolted her to reality. She retrieved it and read the name. Her insides twisted into knots.

She took a deep breath and pressed the button. "Yes, Grayson."

"Hello, Sierra, I'm doing fine, thank you."

"What's up? "Her response to her child's father—familiar, curt and tense.

"You mean why am I calling?"

She silently mocked him before speaking. "Gray-son, what do you want?" She realized her voice was too loud when the woman nearby cleared her throat.

"I'm taking my son to see the Lion King on Broadway this weekend."

"It's not your weekend, Grayson." Her words hijacked the end of his sentence.

"I'm aware of that. However, these are front row seats, and well, I just think it's time that *we*…"

"You and Cassie."

"Yes, Cassidy and *I* spent more time with little Gray—together."

Her words lurched as she replied, "Grayson, you know you do this all the time, and I abhor it."

"Uh-oh, a new word. They teaching advanced English at the fashion school?"

Ignore him.

"Sierra, it could be worse. At least you have a man who wants to be in his child's life.

You know you need the break, a little free time to hang out with Brock. I'm sure dating with a kid isn't easy. Thank God Cassie's understanding."

The best way to respond to a narcissist is not to withhold the response he wants. "BRYCE. His name's *Bryce*. "Her words measured, she added, "And for the record, he knows little Gray and I are a package deal." She coiled her finger around the end of a twist.

"He still trying to do the acting thing? You know Mother sits on the theatre board."

Sierra rolled her eyes. "Yes, Grayson, I know." *Why am I playing this game?* "Anyway, this isn't about him."

"Okay, Sierra, just let me know about this weekend. It's his favorite movie, and well, you'd never get front row seats unless *I* bought them."

She pressed her lips together and closed her eyes. *He bought the tickets before he even asked.*

"Sierra?"

Air gushed from her nostrils like a charging bull. "Okay, Grayson, you can come get your son early Saturday."

"Great. I'll be there around 11 a.m. Sierra, please have him dressed. You know I hate waiting."

You hate having to come in my house. Whatever. "...and Grayson, *don't* change his clothes. I'm capable of picking out a decent outfit for my child." She hung up without prolonging the exchange another second. She pulled out her MP3 player and quickly shuffled. Somewhere between India.Aire, Jill Scott, Mary Mary and a few curse words, Sierra's spirit grieved the day her life collided with Grayson Grier, Jr. She closed her eyes, hoping to silence his voice and current rapid fire thoughts. But Technicolor images of that seemingly innocent day over six years ago emerged.

Chapter 2 – The Year of Grayson Grier

The only exciting thing about Sierra's junior year of high school was getting one step closer to graduation and taking advanced art. She twirled a wavy strand of hair as she scurried past classmates and bumped her leg against a table on the way to her seat. She clenched her teeth and swallowed the pain. Finally, she dropped in a chair, ignoring her throbbing thigh. She tucked her book bag between her feet and glimpsed at the door. She gazed in that direction until she remembered her only friend had dropped the class. Her eyes fell toward the table while she tried to recall an affirmation. *The only time you have a hung down head is for prayer.* Her head slowly rose as her fingers caressed her bracelet. The smooth stones soothed her. *One day pictures of celebrities wearing MY jewelry will appear in magazines. How's that for an affirmation, Zoe?*

The bell rang and the conversations reduced to a simmer. A large Caucasian woman with a thick white braid down her back and dressed in what looked like a large potato sack walked in. Heavy ceramic bracelets and African inspired jewelry adorned her neck and arms. Sierra focused on the teacher's chalky makeup free face as her eyes dotted up and down the roster.

She counted then paused. "Hmmm, we're missing…"No sooner than she said that, the door flew open and Grayson Grier, Jr. slithered inside.

"Well, what a way to make an entrance, Mr. Grier. Gonna still have to mark you tardy."

"Sorry." He cleared his throat, shoving his McDonald's bag in his backpack as he searched for a seat.

“I hope this isn’t a sign of things to come. Just in case you’re wondering, I know your entire family, Grayson. You got a reputation to uphold, Mister.”

Ignoring her warning, he plopped down in the nearest empty seat at Sierra’s table.

Great, she thought. *I was hoping to have this table all to myself.* She certainly didn’t want some pompous fool in her space. When he started tapping the table with his pencil, Sierra cut her eyes at him. He rolled his eyes and continued.

“The person you’re sharing your table with will be your partner for the very first project,” the teacher announced.

Sierra sucked her teeth. Grayson rolled his eyes again and let out an exaggerated sigh.

“It’s one project, ladies and gentlemen. Try to endure.”

At the end of the class, Sierra got up and didn’t utter a word to Grayson Jr. He must have felt the same as he sprinted toward the classroom door.

Chapter 3 – Any Sober Mother Will Do

Sierra sulked all the way home in the rain. The class she'd most looked forward to was now ruined. *Ugh, chained to Grayson Grier Jr. Like I want to deal with some arrogant son of a millionaire.* She marched up the steps and slid her key into the door of the two-story Victorian. *Stubborn as always.* She was just as irritated at the chipped paint as at the temperamental lock. *Finally.* The door popped like a cork on a bottle of aged wine. Once inside, she dropped her backpack, walked a few steps and plunked on the slip-covered couch. She played tug of war with her rain boots while anticipating the wisdom "goddess Oprah" would reveal that day. *What if Oprah was my mother?* She shrugged and looked up. *God, it's not that I don't love my mom. I just need her sober.*

Once she set her feet free, Sierra grabbed the remote and turned on the TV. Her stomach rumbled like two kids on the playground. She rubbed her arms then jumped off the couch, heading toward the kitchen.

"Forget the chic, this is plain old shabby," she mused as she shuffled across the dated linoleum. "All these dust collectors and knick-knacks." She sighed and grabbed a can of soup from the cabinet.

When the microwave stopped, Sierra carried her bowl to the coffee table and sat back on the couch. "O-whoa-O-prah," she sang as the show came on. *I'll clean up and cook dinner right after the show.* She knew her mother would probably be home late, tipsy and with the nerve to expect a spotless house and something edible on the stove.

"I hate alcohol," she muttered, right before she pursed her lips and blew on her spoon. She slurped the warm liquid and sucked in the dangling noodles. “Aw man, I thought she was going to announce the book club pick.”

She flipped momentarily to watch music videos. Her eyes gazed at the chiseled, honey roasted love interest begging the video girl. Something weird happened to her body as Grayson Grier’s face popped in her mind. *What? Why am I thinking of him?* Despite her protests, his handsome face remained. *He is fine.* Visions of Grayson Grier, Jr., of the Montclair multi-millionaire Griers, his butternut skin, steel blue eyes and moist lips persisted throughout the video.

This is ridiculous. After watching TV for about an hour, she started dinner. She wasn’t as concerned about her mother as she was about the leftovers she’d have for lunch. She opened the cabinet and searched for a bag of rice. “I know I brought some from the store the last time,” she said, standing on her toes. She then grabbed the step ladder to check the cabinet above the refrigerator. Her hand felt around and hit a hard glass object. She paused and retrieved the object although she already knew what it was. *Vodka.* She swallowed and closed her eyes. Disappointment hit the pit of her stomach like a thousand-ton anchor on an ocean floor. “I can deal with the beer, not the liquor.” She grabbed the bottle and poured it down the sink. As the nauseating liquid gurgled, she knew she’d pay a price.

What is it about this stuff that would make a person ruin their life over it? I just don’t get it. She reached in the refrigerator for the thawed chicken. As she started to clean and cut it, tears formed in her eyes. Tears for her mother, herself and the hope for peace that drowned in the alcohol.

“I’m tired, God, so tired,” she said as she wiped her eyes with her sleeve.

~~~~~

“Where is it?”
~~~~~

Sierra rolled over and looked at the clock. 2:05 AM blared in its bright red hue. Sierra smashed a pillow against her face. Moments later, she heard her mother creeping up the hardwood steps. "Where could she be coming from this late?"

"You hear me! I told you not to touch my stuff. I pay the bills around here. I don't want anyone moving nothin' 'round here but me. Wake up!"

Sierra threw her body on her stomach and pulled her cover over her head. "What? Mom, it's a school night. I need sleep!" she shouted in response to the loud banging at her door. Her strong tone reduced to a desperate moan. "Please."

"I pay the bills around here, you open this door! I don't know who you think you are!" Her fist pounded like a jack hammer on the pavement. "When you leave this house and pay your own bills, you can touch whatever you want. But it won't happen, not selling that ugly jewelry you make. I know *all* about that dollar and a dream crap. I bust my behind at that shop every day for your lazy behind. You don't 'preciate nothing."

Sierra knew she'd have to go to school exhausted—again. She sat up, opened the door and climbed back in bed. "You can fuss till dawn, Mom, I just don't care anymore." Her voice cracked. "I'm tired, just tired. Don't you get it?" She repositioned her body and pressed her cheek against the pillow. "I hate this," she mumbled as tears began to form.

Her mother put her hand on her hip and looked toward the ceiling. "Did this heifer say she hate me?"

"Mom, why don't you just go to bed like normal people?"

"I'm a grown woman. I'll go to bed when I want." She snatched the comforter and sheets off Sierra. Then turned on the light. "Hey, hey!" she yelled close to Sierra's ear. "I'm talking to you!"

Sierra prayed to herself with her eyes still closed, "Please God. I need to get some sleep. I can't miss anymore school." She curled into a fetal position.

"Oh, I got something for you. Talkin' about some dag gone school."

The slur of her mother's words confirmed the bottle Sierra had emptied wasn't her only supply.

"You get your lazy behind downstairs and clean that kitchen," her mother insisted.

Sierra rolled over and lifted her head. "What? I cleaned it already." *That's the alcohol talking. Hate the disease, not her. Hate the disease, not her.* Sierra rubbed one eye with the palm of her hand.

"Are you talking back to me?" Her mother's eyes had that pocketed look. The skin on her lips was extra pink and moist.

Sierra still didn't move out the bed.

"I *said* get down there and do those dishes right now! I found dirt on the glasses. Get your lazy behind down there." Her mother grabbed a shoe and started beating Sierra's thigh. "Gonna," slap, "talk," smack, "back-to-me!"

Sierra held up her hand in defense. "Okay, okay! I'm going." Her mother pushed her toward the top of the steps. Without time to put on her slippers, the hardwood floor felt extra cold beneath her feet. She eased down the stairs, rubbing her arms as her eyes watered.

"You must think I'mma fool. Do some half-behind job while I work all day."

Once Sierra reached the kitchen, she looked for any unwashed dishes. The sink was empty. "What dishes, Mom?" She tried to sound calm and respectful.

"Start with the ones on the bottom shelf of the cupboard. Then dust when you're finished."

"Are you kidding? This is about that bottle, isn't it?" Sierra continued staring at the sink.

"Don't ever put your hands on my stuff again!" She walked to Sierra and popped the back of her head. "Do you see me touching them stupid books you read, or that ugly jewelry you make? How'd you like if I gave away those books and threw out those stones?"

Sierra held her hands to her side as they formed into fists. She closed her eyes briefly to stop the water from forming. Tears only pissed her mother off. Sierra wanted to swing. She'd hit her once, out of pain and anger, and vowed never to again. She moved slowly, taking down a few dishes. *God, please let her get tired. Please make her go upstairs to bed.* Sure enough, her mother moved toward the steps and fussed all the way to the top. The door slammed, and it was eerily silent. Sierra stopped "washing the dishes," walked over to the couch, grabbed a quilt and passed out.

Chapter 4 – Art Imitation of Life

Over several months, Sierra's junior year went from doom to something magical. Why? Someone besides her best friend Zoe acknowledged her presence. And it wasn't just any "somebody" but Grayson Grier, Jr. Because of that, her life would never be the same. His words, presence, stares ignited every prism of color in her once gray world. But she would never let him know it.

"So what you wanna do after high school?" Grayson rolled the gemstones Sierra brought to class around in his hand.

She shrugged one shoulder and bit the side of her lip before she spoke. "I don't know. Fashion school. I wanna be a jewelry designer, I guess."

"How come you never look at me when you talk?" He waited for her to make eye contact.

"I don't know." She began to sketch on her note pad. But she did know. She'd sneak in looks when he wasn't watching. His perfectly lined haircut and sly smile made her insides warm. She could recognize the slight pimp in his walk in a crowded hall. And he always smelled like Cool Water. She'd went to the department store and smelled the men's cologne until she'd figured out which was his. All this scared her.

He chuckled. "How in the heck are you going to launch this big jewelry line and make millions if you can't even talk to people? My dad says—"

"Who says I want to make millions?"

"Why else do it? My dad says…"

"Oh no, not another Grayson Sr. quote. Save it, my friend Zoe just finished your father's book. She's worn me out for the last week with his quotes. What does your dad really do anyway?" Her eyes momentarily connected with his.

"Let me *finish.* My dad says to never trust anyone who won't look you in the eye. He does a bunch of stuff. Commercial real estate, mergers and acquisitions, investments. He got his start on Wall Street. Then my Godfather Bencil James saw his potential and hired him. And eventually they became partners."

"Well, in some cultures, Mr. Know-it-all, it's offensive to look people in the eye." Sierra folded her arms. "Besides, I don't trust *anybody.*" She paused and purposefully allowed her eyes to lock with his. "So whatchu gonna do with *your* life? You can't even focus on an art project." She turned her nose and eyebrows slightly upward.

"Funny." He slid his hands behind his head and almost fell out his chair.

Sierra laughed. *Mr. Smooth.* "Wait, let me guess. You're headed to an Ivy League school, maybe an MBA with a concentration in finance. Then presto you will be a vice president at one of your father's companies where everyone will kiss your butt and talk about you behind your back." She tried to look away, but his smooth skin and extra white teeth kept her attention.

"For your information, you got it all wrong. I may joke, but I have a plan. I'm gonna be a Morehouse man majoring in computer science. I want to create video games. My dad can't tell me what to do. That's why I'm here instead of some corny prep school. I held my ground."

"Uh-huh. We'll see." She liked his bravado but didn't show it.

"Why are you so serious all the time? I mean when you smile once in a while, you're actually kind of cute." He leaned toward her and coaxed her mouth to a smile with his sheepish grin. "And why do you wear those long dresses and headbands around your braids? You ain't Erykah Badu." He reached for a dangling strand of hair. "Wow, you have that good hair. These aren't extensions."

Kinda cute. A chill raced through Sierra's spine at the sound of those words. "First of all," she slapped his hand away, "these are two strand twists, not braids. Second, it's *all* good hair and three, don't touch me. Furthermore, I don't have to be like everyone else. Conformity is overrated. All the great ones are different. And FYI, life *is* serious. What am I supposed to do, walk around school half-naked like the rest of these girls tryin' to be a YouTube star or make a living on a pole? I don't think so." Sierra resisted the smile that was trying to form on her lips. She turned her attention to her art project.

Air escaped Grayson Jr.'s mouth like a decompressed balloon. "Okay, okay, I get it." He noticed her lips curl. "Uh-huh, I knew I'd get a smile out of you." He brushed the side of her face with the back of his hand. She jumped at his touch. Then he reached toward her horn-rimmed glasses. She held her breath and squinted as he gingerly removed them.

"Vintage," She said as he inspected them with a hint of curiosity.

"Weird."

She snatched them back, and her insides tingled.

Chapter 5 – Teenage Love Affair

Sierra's hands were shaking as she opened the door and entered the foyer to her house. Her mother, when, sober always used the words charming, character, vintage and butternut woodwork to describe their home. But when she was drunk, she called it a dump. Sierra could only hope Grayson Jr. could overlook the sloping floor, knocking pipes and much-needed paint job. She knew it didn't compare to The Grier "compound" as people in Montclair called it. Everybody knew the Griers occupied the mansion perched atop the sprawling property. However, the most any outsiders could see were the sculpted topiaries and the manicured lawn. Sierra had only seen pictures of the house interior in several features in a few magazines. Security was tight. The Griers had their equal share of lovers and haters.

Grayson stood close behind Sierra as she turned the key. "Hurry up, girl, it's cold out here." He rubbed his hands together then blew into them as he stood on her porch. He kept looking around to see if anyone was watching.

"Shh, my neighbors are nosy." Until now, she'd been sneaking off with Grayson after school to one of his friend's house. She blew a loose strand of hair away from her face and tried to open the door again. "There it is." She pushed it and yanked him in behind her.

"You can put your stuff on the coffee table for now, "she said as she walked toward the kitchen. "Want some hot chocolate or soda?"

"Rather have you." He watched as she peeled off her coat and kept moving. "But hot chocolate is cool."

While she disappeared, he walked across the living room looking around, then took a few steps up the staircase. "Wow, look at you. You were a cute little rock head kid." He eyed the photos lining the stairway. "And your hair was actually done. This must be your mom wearing this neon dress." He leaned in closer. "Dang, she had a nice booty." He burst out laughing.

She peeked from the kitchen doorway. "Not funny. Who told you to go all up there? Get down please." After several minutes, she carried in a tray with two cups of hot chocolate and set them on the coffee table. She walked over to him and pulled on his arm. "C'mon, those pictures are embarrassing. "Sierra didn't talk about family. She mentioned her mother's drinking to him once. "Wow, that must be hard" was all he said. They never spoke of it again. "Well, let's um watch BET or something. "She yanked his hand.

"Okay, in your room." He left little room for protest as he took off his varsity jacket and tossed it on the couch, then grabbed the tray of hot chocolate. "Okay?"

Everything in her spirit was shouting no. His eyes focused on hers, and she was slightly hypnotized. Heat rose in her body. She didn't want sex, but loved being held.

"Okay," she said quietly. She was fully clothed but felt emotionally naked. Sierra climbed the stairs, guilt setting in with each step. *But I never have company*, she reasoned. No one else besides Zoë confirmed her life. But now she had a friend...a *boyfriend. Yes, definitely a boyfriend.* Her hands shook as she opened the door to her private space. *It's Friday, Ma's gonna be late, Grayson and any evidence he'd been here will be gone by then.* "Just for a little while." She turned on the TV.

After a few sips of hot chocolate and a few music videos, Grayson reached for the remote to turn the volume down. He pulled his cashmere sweater over his head, exposing his T-shirt.

Sierra's eyes focused intently on the outline of his muscles. "What are you doing? Are you crazy? If we get busted, my mom would kill us both! "Despite her exasperation, Sierra's eyes fixated on the veins protruding from his arms.

"It's not like we haven't done anything before. "His voice lowered. "I got something for you. "He motioned for her to sit closer as he reached behind her pillow. A powder blue box appeared in his hand.

Sierra's eyes grew wide as she focused on the box. "How'd that get there? Is that…?"

"Uh-ha. Pretty slick, right?" He handed it to her. "Open it."

She reached for the box then slid off the white ribbon. "Omigod. This is beautiful, "she said as she pulled out the Tiffany toggle bracelet. "I've never had anyone give me something this nice, or special." Her eyes ogled the bracelet and box. "Tiffany's," she whispered in disbelief. "This is something Zoe would have. I just can't believe it." She swallowed as a surge of gratitude rushed to her heart.

He took it out the box and slid it on her arm. "Perfect." He placed his hand against her face. "You deserve the best. "He leaned in and kissed her softly on the lips. "See, I didn't forget, January 9, I'm just a few days late. Turning 17 is a big deal!" His mouth spread wide, and he beamed with pride. "Happy belated birthday. Now, this more than makes up for being late, right?"

"Huh? Oh yeah. This more than makes up for it!" She assured, her eyes shining with pleasure.

"So now, you know without a doubt you're mine. "His hands cupped her face as he kissed her again nice and slow. That was all the prodding she needed. His hands slid to her shoulders then traveled beneath her sweater.

"C'mon, Gray, please stop," she purred, closing her eyes.

He ignored her and kissed her neck. "You're just so beautiful," he whispered.

His breath was hot against her skin. She swallowed, then bit her tongue to keep the ungodly sounds from fleeing her mouth.

He stood and pulled her body toward the edge of the bed. He knelt, wrapped his arms around her waist and buried his face in her lap. "Sierra, I *need* you. And, you need me."

She could feel the warmth of his body near her most intimate places. *He's right. I need him. We need each other.* Her body overruled her objections. Her fingers massaged the back of his head. After a few minutes of silence, he eased off the floor and gently pulled her from the bed. Once she stood, he slid his fingertips up her sweater and slowly pulled it over her head. All the while, he kept eye contact with her. She started to cover her chest with her arms, but he grabbed her hands. Her eyes stayed locked with his as she stood in her bra and skirt.

Sierra felt safe, secure and unashamed. And instantly, she collapsed into his cavernous chest as his arms wrapped around her tiny waist. She exhaled all the pain, frustration and fear.

"Shhh." He gripped her tighter, then loosened her hair.

"I, I know we've come close, but I promised my mom I'd never get…"

"Sierra, shhh." He gently placed his hands on her face. "I love you, you know that? I really do. I don't care what happens. I'm gonna take care of you. You're my baby." He pulled her close then eased his fingertips down the elastic of her skirt.

Love? His baby? "I know, but we're not…" Her eyes wandered around the room in a panic. She noticed, of all things, the little pink Bible on her vanity. That same Bible she tucked beneath her pillow at night. The same Bible she clutched when her mother yelled and cursed. That Bible was the only God she knew. "Grayson," she whispered, her lips partially touching his.

"Shhh. Sierra, when two people love each other, it's not a sin," he whispered. "Some married people don't even love each other, but say they make love. Now *that's* a sin."

The letters of the word "but" tumbled in her mouth like clothes in a dryer, but never spilled out. She finally gave in. She wanted paradise, and she wanted it in that moment. She removed her skirt and slid under the covers in almost one motion, cursing the unflattering briefs she wore.

Grayson eased under the covers behind her. Their bodies quickly intertwined and gave way to immature moans and permissive affection. Once the threshold had been crossed, they slid into a deep winter slumber. A few hours later, Sierra rolled over and stared at Grayson Jr.'s face.

He's perfect. She couldn't believe how grown up she felt. She'd been so afraid, but the fear transformed into the most beautiful thing she'd ever felt. She stroked his skin with a feather like touch, thankful for his tenderness. She wanted to hold onto the feeling forever. She'd surrendered and had no regrets. *I know this is supposed to be wrong, but I feel nothing sinful or ugly about it.* All she knew was somebody, no—a boy like Grayson Grier, Jr., actually loved her. *Surely God couldn't get mad at that.*

Chapter 6 – The Wages of Sin

Lydia Grier paced the porch then peeked into the living room. Her view was blocked by curtains, but she could at least see what looked like light from a television between them. *Hmmm.* On the porch, she had caught a glimpse of her son's SUV in the partially hidden driveway. *I don't believe this boy.* After about fifteen minutes, her ladylike taps turned to loud pounding fists.

"You hear that? "Sierra's eyes opened. Grayson grunted. "There it is again, someone's knocking. "Sierra went to the window and noticed a black Escalade out front.

As she neared the stairs, she heard a woman's muffled voice and jumped back on the bed. "Grayson," she said, grabbing his bicep, "there's a woman downstairs, and it sounds like she's calling your name, but it's hard to tell."

"Huh, what?" Still groggy, he finally recognized where he was. "Let me see. "He got up and looked out the window. "Shoot! That's my mother's car."

Sierra stared at the biceps that held her moments ago, then snapped to reality. "Omigod. Omigod, what do we do? What time is it? We must have fallen asleep for a while. It's close to eight." Sierra's hands danced wildly in the air as she paced.

Grayson checked his cellphone and noticed his mother had called several times. He grabbed his clothes and sneakers.

"Where you going? You gonna open the door?" Sierra said, her eyes begging for his answer.

He barely finished dressing before he rushed toward the door. He backed up before he rushed to the stairs. "I love you, "he said then gave Sierra a quick peck on the lips.

Sierra smiled faintly. Then looked for her clothes and threw them on. With knees quaking and her heart a flutter, she sprinted after him. When she finally reached the bottom stair, she brushed her hair back with her hands.

"Grayson Napoleon Grier, Jr., get your behind down here before I beat the black off you!" His mother's voice was muffled outside the door.

Once Sierra came down, he walked over and threw open the door. "Mother!" He'd never seen her act that way and wanted to save her and himself from further embarrassment.

She pushed past him and marched inside. "I've been calling and calling you on that cellphone. You know we were supposed to meet your father and a client for dinner. What on earth is wrong with you?" She placed her hand on her hips, waiting for his answer as she glanced around the room.

"How did you know where to find me?" He asked, scratching his head. He noticed his shoes were still upstairs.

"Your so-called friends, everybody has a price. Remember that. We'll be late for the 7:30 dinner reservations but forget it. You can't go dressed like that. I'll drop you at home and meet them. She rolled her eyes and snatched his arm. "Get your coat and shoes. Your father's furious." She folded her arms. "I swear," she eyed him up and down, "you got better sense than this." Her eyes shifted toward Sierra. "And I pray you didn't do anything stupid." She shook her head. Her bronze-layered bob swirled as she punched each word.

Grayson almost forgot Sierra was there. "Mother, stop!" He wrestled away from her grip then straightened his posture. He looked toward Sierra, who was holding his shoes in her hands. "Um, Mother, this is, um, this is um…"

"S-i-e-r-r-a, "Sierra said slowly as she extended his sneakers toward him. Her face was tight. Her forehead creased.

"Who?"

"Sierra, ma'am. My name's *Sierra*, "she repeated slowly to the woman she'd only seen in pictures. She hadn't imagined meeting her future fantasy mother-in-law this way.

"Well, *Sara*," Lydia Grier looked at Sierra like a pair of manure-stained shoes, "I trust you were both doing homework?" She nodded until Sierra mirrored the motion.

"Ah-um." Sierra looked at Grayson, expecting him to say something, anything, her arms prickling with goose bumps.

"Mother. Um, Sierra is my g-g-g-girlfriend." He gasped for some air. By this time, he'd grabbed his shoes and slipped them on. He neglected to tie them up.

"What? Don't be silly. I thought Cassidy Kimble was your girlfriend. You know the one you took to the movies two weeks ago."

Sierra balled her fists as all available air escaped her soul.

Grayson's head snapped toward Sierra. "Mother, you asked me to keep her company while her dad was in town doing business with Dad. You were entertaining her mother, and I didn't have a choice. It was a favor, and you know it!"

"Grayson, you have the audacity to raise your voice? Boy, you're too young to know what you're doing. Oh, this is silly." She waved her hand at him. "We need to go. And you just earned yourself a sit down with your father, mister! Charmaine, it was nice to meet you." She pulled the belt to her fur-trimmed coat and turned toward her son.

Grayson looked at Sierra. Her eyes begged for his voice to soothe the sting in her spirit. His shoulders slumped in resignation. He grabbed his jacket off the couch. *I'm seventeen and you can't tell me what to do* were the words swirling in his head, but "Sierra, I gotta go. I'mma talk to you when I get back tonight. I promise" were the words that came out.

"Boy, let's go." His mother's posture and tone were unequivocal and final; she marched dismissive steps toward the door, never looking back.

Sierra's heart felt like it had been rung like wet laundry, but the worst was to come. She heard a stumble as the Griers were about to step onto the porch. "Please God no, I promise, don't let this happen. Not here, not now," she prayed. Unfortunately, God must have given her the hand. Her mother's voice outside the front door confirmed her fear. *For once, God, let her be sober.*

"What the…?"Maxine Sanders' and Lydia Grier's eyes met as she burst out the door.

Mrs. Grier raised her leather glove to her mouth.

"What? Who decided to have a party and didn't invite me?" Maxine gurgled.

Sierra's head fell down and her eyes closed tight. *Please, God, please spare me.*

Lydia Grier shook her head and glanced at Sierra. "Poor child," she said as her eyes softened.

"I know this ain't the fabulous Griers up in *my* house? Um, um, uh!" Maxine stomped for emphasis and laughed.

"Mrs.

"*Ms. Sanders*." She waved a wobbly finger at Lydia Grier.

Sierra's eyes watered as her arms went limp.

"Ms. Sanders, I came to pick up Grayson, my son. He and your daughter, well, I'll let her explain. But rest assured, he won't be back here again." She pulled her clutch toward her chest. She was about to walk away but paused. "With all due respect to you and your daughter, don't you think we have enough single mothers running around here?"

"Is that right?" Maxine's body swayed with her words. "Well, let me tell you sumtin. If

You think yo' son is too good for Sie, Siera, Sierra, you fooling yo' self. Y'all ain't no better than anybody else." She poked Lydia Grier her on the shoulder as she balanced herself. "And another thing! Just 'cause you got that fat mansion on that hill don't mean nothing in my book." She moved in closer to her face. "...and my book's a bestseller!" She squeezed Lydia Grier's face together with her hand.

Sierra sat on the stairs and commenced to rocking back and forth. She tried to block out their voices but couldn't. She wrapped her arms around herself for comfort.

"As for your precious son, I ain't stupid. He been sniffing around Sierra for a while. Every shut eye ain't sleep, and every goodbye ain't gone." By this time, she was standing so close to Lydia Grier they could have kissed.

Lydia stood in shock, trying to ignore the smell of alcohol that made her feel as though she needed a shower. "Excuse me?" She shot a look at Grayson. "This is ridiculous."

He shrugged. "I tried to tell you. I, I'mma man, you can't control me!" His words cranked up like a choking engine, finally churning out.

His mother slapped him upside the head. "Boy, please!" She practically yanked his arm out his socket. He relented as they marched toward the door and to the car.

Sierra finally stood up straight. She didn't move until she heard both car engines start and tires screech.

Grayson Grier, Jr? Of all people. Maxine was tipsy, but the possibility of her daughter messing around with Grayson Sr.'s son hit her brain like a fallen brick. "Sierra, Se-rah, didn't I tell you? If you bring some baby in here, I was gon' whip your tail?" Her mother gurgled.

She walked over to her daughter, wielding her purse like a weapon. Sierra lifted her hand to shield herself.

"Swinging at me?" Maxine almost lost her balance.

"No, no, no." Sierra turned to run toward the stairs. Before she could reach the third step, her mother grabbed one of her legs and partially dragged her down. Sierra stumbled and fell back down to the floor. "I hate you," she screamed, tears streaming down her face. "You b—"

Before she could finish the word, her mother snatched her by her top and smacked her face. The sting remained as Sierra instantly grabbed her mother's neck to choke her. When her mother's eyes appeared to almost pop from their sockets, Sierra let her go. She stared at her hands then backed up toward the stairs. She paused momentarily as her mother gasped for air. Then turned and ran to her room. She dropped on the bed, out of breath, then jumped up to lock the door. Sierra slumped to the floor as her head fell against it. Her entire body trembled at the realization that the same hands that had tried to choke her mother now captured a puddle of tears. She eventually lay on the floor, delirious with grief as the pain of rejection gnawed through her heart and punctured her soul.

Chapter 7 – Gray Skies Are Just Clouds Passing By

"Well, whatchu gonna do?" Zoe sat with her arms wrapped around a ruffled pillow. After her friend didn't answer, she walked over and played some music from her tablet. "Love, love Nia Allen, her voice sounds like heaven." She swayed to the words of the sweet gospel song.

"Who?" Sierra smirked. "Forget that. Zoe, focus." She sucked her teeth. "What do you *think* I'm going to do?" she asked, annoyed at her friend's naiveté. "How can I take care of a baby? Look at me? I'm the most exhausted seventeen-year-old in life ever! I can barely take care of myself. This isn't an MTV reality show, it's my life!" She jumped off the bed and walked the pattern of the big flower rug. She looked up at the quote filled notes all over the mirror. *Ugh! So irritating.*

Zoe watched her friend's footsteps trace the floor. "Well, maybe we can talk to my mother when she gets home." She grabbed a scrunchie and smoothed her relaxed tresses into a ponytail. "We usually talk about everything. Well, not *everything*. But most things."

Sierra fought rolling her eyes, but knew her friend meant well. "No, Z.I can't." She took a deep breath. "Look, I appreciate it. Having you to talk to helps." Her eyes fell back to the floor. "But it doesn't solve a thing. I tried talking to God, but I don't know. It just isn't working. Not like we were close in the first place. Best I could do was muster up a prayer or two. Man, did I blow it this time." She pulled on the ends of the scarf wrapped 'round her neck.

"Stop talking like that. Anyway, I'm always here for you. I'm not going *anywhere*. But, you gotta talk to someone else soon." Zoe stood and folded her arms. "I'm not equipped for this! I mean this is like Oprah or Iyanla heavy duty stuff. "She rubbed the back of her neck with her hand.

Sierra continued to circle the rug. As she tapped her index finger against her chin, she said, "I can't tell my mom. We ain't even speaking. From the time I got my period, all I've heard was, 'You better not bring no babies in this house'." Exasperated, she dropped back on the bed. "It's April. Graduation's around the corner. How could I let this happen?"

"W-e-l-l, what's up with Grayson?" Zoe dropped down beside her.

Sierra shrugged one shoulder. "He knows and it's not like he's cut me off. He still takes my calls. Says he loves me." She grabbed a pillow and played with the fringe. "But it's not the same. I can just tell."

"I bet it's not. And love, please. My auntie always says love can't pay the bills. You deserve more. We need a commitment, some financials!" Zoe slapped the back of her right hand against her left palm. "Brother needs to pay up! We gots to call Maury."

"Uhh, Maury—no, I don't think so. Seriously, Z, what do you think the boy's going to do, plan our wedding? Oh yeah, we'll be featured in *Essence*. Puleeaze." She sucked her teeth. "His mom, the grand dame of Montclair is trying to ship him outta here fast. He's going to Morehouse." Sierra bit the side of her lip. More silence. "It's a mess, huh?"

Zoe turned her lips to one side. "Maybe." She shrugged. "In the words of Oprah, 'We gotta turn these wounds into wisdom'." She landed a soft playful punch against her friend's arm.

"No offense, but I'mma need you to chill on the quotes today, okay?" Sierra wanted to hit her for real.

Zoe sighed. "One day you'll understand the power of words and worship." She turned up the volume on her iPod, closed her eyes and swayed.

Sierra was way too confused to let any music settle in her spirit. The whole exercise was irritating. "Zoe, I know you mean well, but this isn't working for me. I don't know, seems like God's so in love with you and constantly pissed at me."

Zoe dropped her hands, deflated. "Sierra, God's not mad at you. We are *both* his daughters. He loves us both the same."

Sierra folded her arms and sighed. "I'd like to believe you, but look at my life compared to yours."

Zoe's smile faded. *God, this is tough. I want her to know you so bad. But after all these years, nothing's changed. I'm getting nowhere.* She wrapped her hand around Sierra's. "Look, I don't have the answers. But God does. Wisdom is a promise. He can't renege on his Word." She smiled so wide Sierra thought she'd gotten some major revelation.

Sierra shook loose from her friend. "Zoe, I don't have time for the sky to open up and rain down some divine epiphany." Sierra threw her hands up. "I messed up, okay? *I'm* messed up. Always have been, always will be." She blew a loose wavy strand from her face.

"Sierra, stop it! Your words are keeping you in bondage. The more negative your words, the harder this'll be." Zoe jumped off the bed then paced the floor. "Lord, we need you. Your sheep know your voice. Speak! Tell us what to do!" She paused and closed her eyes. Then opened them instantly. "Thanks, Father." She raised her hands.

Sierra wanted to roll her eyes but she stayed still.

"God is going to send a counselor. Oh thank you, Holy Spirit!" She looked up.

Sierra pulled away at first. "The holy who? I thought He *was* the counselor. This is stupid." She jumped up and turned away. "I just can't believe I was so stupid." She slapped her hand against her forehead. “I traded a Tiffany’s toggle bracelet, a silly blue box and ‘I love you’ for a kid.”

“Darn it, Sierra!” Zoe blurted. “You know you had no business with Grayson Grier, Jr.!” She sucked her teeth and folded her arms.

Sierra turned to face her. “What? So, this is all *my* fault? Oh, I forgot. It’s *always* Sierra’s fault.” She threw her hands in the air. “You have no clue, sister! You and your Cosby, Sisterhood of the Traveling Pants, Disney Channel life!” She pointed toward Zoe. “You have two parents, a freakin’ dog and you vacation *every* summer. What would you know about struggle?” She gasped for breath and forced her tears back. “You know where I vacation? On my front porch with a glass of Kool Aid!” She paced back and forth “I’m *raising* an alcoholic mother, cooking, cleaning and trying my best not to have a nervous breakdown! You have no idea what it’s like to be me!” She slapped her own chest. “No idea.”

Zoe winced. She started to raise her finger in protest then lowered it. She kept still as she’d never heard Sierra yell like that.

“So don’t you judge me, Zoe Newsome, don’t you dare judge me!” Sierra fell back on the bed. She hid her eyes with her palms as she released her tears.

Zoe felt her friend. They were connected at the heart. After a few moments passed, she tugged on her friend’s arm until Sierra finally eased up and hugged her. “Sierra, I’m sorry, it’s not all your fault.” She sighed. “But a big situation calls for a big God.” Zoe pulled away to check Sierra’s expression. “Trust me, okay?” Her eyes widened. Zoe rubbed her palms up and down her jeans as she stared upward. “Wait! I got it! My youth pastor! She’s a counselor.”

Sierra met her eyes at the sound of her enthusiasm. “I don’t know, Z, I don’t know. Those people in your church are all bougie. It’s not one of those come as you are situations. I mean, I don’t want to bring you any shame.”

"It may seem that way but just trust me on this. Our youth pastor always talks about forgiveness and second chances. She's really cool. You came to my church a few times before. Didn't you feel welcome?" She kept eye contact, waiting for a sign of agreement.

"I guess, we were much younger, and it was only Vacation Bible School. Your church is much bigger now, on television and stuff. Besides, this is *way* different." Sierra wiped her face with her sleeve. "I can't talk to a stranger, and church is the last place I need to show my face."

Zoe grabbed her hand and held it. "Sierra, God isn't gonna give up on you that easily. Just promise you'll go." Her face pled more than her voice. "If it backfires, you can stop speaking to me forever."

Sierra pressed her lips together as her shoulders dropped. "Okay, and please. Would I ever stop speaking to you? You are my sister, "she said, wiping tears.

Chapter 8 – Tear-Stained Glass

Sierra sat on the cushioned bench. Her legs shook so much she heard them knock through her tights. Her heartbeat sped up as soon as she'd stepped inside the building. She finally placed her palms on her thighs and lost herself briefly in intricate patterns of purples, blues, and deep red hues. Although her heart gradually slowed, she still felt like a guest in a stranger's house.

"Sierra?"

She jumped at the sound of the pillow soft voice and the hand at rest on her shoulder. "Yes, yes, ma'am." She looked up then eased from her seat as the woman in a Black cashmere sweater and camel pencil skirt greeted her.

"Apologies, I wasn't trying to startle you. I'm Angela, Angela Martin. We spoke on the phone? So nice to meet you." She gave Sierra a hug then stepped back.

Sierra felt warmth that extended beyond an embrace or sweater. "Would you like to come back to my office?" Her face illuminated from a smile.

She nodded and grabbed her tote bag. Once there she noticed all the pictures and quotes that decorated Angela's office. A beautiful melody filled the room.

"You like it? 'I Choose to Worship,' one of my favorites. Do you have one? I mean a favorite song." She tucked one side of the hair of her chin-length bob behind her ear.

Sierra shook her head. Her eyes continued to roam the room.

"Let me turn this down a bit. Music helps me work. Just feel like angels abound the atmosphere. She cleared her throat. "So, Sierra how *are* you feeling today?"

"Um, okay I guess." Sierra's eyes met hers for an instant. *Her smile is so warm. Maybe I can trust her a little.*

Angela walked from around her desk and in the chair across from Sierra. "You can relax. I'm sure Zoe told you I'm the youth pastor. I talk to lots of young people about...well just about everything. They love to visit and chat."

"You look pretty young yourself." Sierra instantly realized she may have said the wrong thing.

"I'm not *that* young, but I'm not an old woman either." Angela chuckled. "Why don't you tell me a little about you?"

"Um, not much to tell, I guess." Sierra shrugged. "I'm a junior in high school. I, I, kinda like books, art and music." The words scrawled from her mouth. "And I make jewelry."

Angela searched her eyes. "Anything else you want to share?"

Sierra shook her head slowly. "No, um ma'am, not real-ly." Her legs shook.

Angela leaned back. "Well, I'll tell you a little more about me." Her plump cheeks burst from her smile. "I'm married with two children, a girl, five and a boy, well young man, fifteen. I like to decorate, write and love music, too– all kinds and I love the Lord."

Sierra forced a closed-mouth smile. *She and Zoe been sipping that same Jesus juice.*

"Sierra, wow that's such a beautiful name." She paused. "Just so you know, whatever we discuss today will stay between us. Okay?

Sierra was distracted as she stared at the two large framed documents on the wall. "Wow, that's a lot of school on the wall."

"I guess so. Maybe not too much, "she said, now looking toward the frames. "I realized I loved helping people. So I figured I'd get licensed and education to be the best. And because I wanted to work in ministry, I went to seminary. It's all a part of my *passion.*" She winked.

Sierra's eyes widened. "Wow that took lots of time and dedication."

"Well, it was worth it. How about you? Thinking about college?"

Sierra swallowed. "Mrs. Martin, I don't want to waste your time. I don't know how I'm going anywhere because of well, a situation. I, I know Zoe told you." Her shoulders dropped in resignation.

"No, not really. She didn't give me specifics. Why don't *you* share what's on your heart? You can tell me a little or a lot. I'm just going to listen, okay? I'm here just for you." She folded her hands and smiled.

Sierra bit the side of her lip momentarily then spoke, "Mzzz. Martin, I'm not a fast girl or promiscuous. I tried so hard to do what I was supposed to. I did whatever my mother told me. I tried hard. I mean really hard every day, but I messed up…bad." She sighed. "It was my first time. I thought he loved me and well, I just needed somebody." Her words poured out like honey from a jar.

"Okay, okay. Sierra, you need to stop beating yourself up. We don't always make the best choices every time. Don't get me wrong, sometimes there are consequences. But you don't have to figure it out all by yourself." She looked Sierra straight in the eyes.

Sierra's facial expression didn't change. "Yeah right. I'm pregnant. I sinned big time and I'm going to Hell. In the meantime, I don't know what to do with a freakin' baby. My life's ruined." Her words were a mix of confusion and panic.

"Sierra, let's get one thing straight, God hasn't crossed you off His list, sweetie." Angela smiled faintly and grabbed Sierra's hands. "Here's the thing. I can pray for you, but I can't tell you what to do. I'm here to listen. You've been on what seems like a long and lonely road, but God is here, lean on him." She moved closer and wiped Sierra's tears.

Sierra's shoulders dropped at her touch. She shook her head. "Mrs. Martin, I'm just tired. I'm so tired. And nobody understands. I keep trying to explain. I'm hurting in so many ways." She shielded her eyes with her hand.

Angela paused reached over to her desk for some tissues, then handed them to Sierra.

After a few seconds, Sierra could not help but grab and hold her. "Sorry, "Sierra said as she pulled away and held the tissue over her face. "Sorry."

"Sierra, sweetie," Angela said, "you're gonna have to stop apologizing for everything. And you are not *sorry*. Be careful what words you use. Words have power."

Sierra took a deep breath and nodded. She laughed a bit. "Zoe says that all the time. She has like a gazillion quotes." She blew her nose.

"Wow, is that a smile? Sweetie, you are strong, but all of us need God and a little support. We just can't do it by ourselves. Living gets tough, even when you think you're doing all the right things. God's our helper because he knows we can't fix everything."

Sierra's reserve of tears poured out over and over again.

"What is it? Did I say something wrong?" Angela's eyebrows knitted as she held her breath.

"I don't know what it means to have *any* help. My real father died right after I was born.

I have no memory of him. My mother, well, she acts like *I'm* the mother. She depends on me for so much. I love her, I mean so much. But when she gets angry, it so painful." She lowered her voice. "When she drinks, it's tough. I know she has pain, too." She covered her eyes and pressed her fingertips over her lids.

Angela felt her chest cave at this revelation. "Oh dear, it makes so much sense. You've truly been on this road alone. God led you here to me." *God kept showing me in my prayers that a young woman would come broken from a generational curse.* "Sierra, this isn't easy. You are too young and bright to let this stop you. You have your whole life ahead of you. It isn't over! It may not seem like it, but he's gonna to give you beauty for all these ashes."

Beauty, ashes? Sierra looked puzzled. "I don't know what any of that means. I just know I don't want to hurt anymore."

"It's going to be a process, but I'll be here for you. But—" She bit her lip. "First thing you're going have to do is tell your mother. I know you don't want to, but you don't have a choice." She patted Sierra's knee. "I feel that so strong in my spirit." She saw the horror in Sierra's face. "I can come with you."

"NO! No, Mrs. Angela." Sierra startled herself at the volume of her voice.

"Okay, okay, sweetie, but I have a strange feeling she's waiting on you."

"She's going to be so angry. If she puts me out, I have nowhere to go."

Angela kept her eyes on her as she quietly prayed for God to guide her next words. "I wouldn't say this if I didn't feel it. She won't put you out. God's going to go before you. He's showing up in the midst of all this. You just watch."

Sierra felt light as a calm washed over her. "I did tell Him I was sorry, you know. God I mean. Like a thousand times."

Angela knew behind Sierra's armor was a hurt, confused little girl. "Sierra, you are forgiven. It's done. Stop condemning yourself." As much as Angela wanted to take her home and love on her like the child she was, she had to trust God to do the work. She sighed. *Boundaries.* "Know what? I'm going to give you my phone number." She reached and grabbed her card from her desk. "Call me anytime you want to talk. No matter what time of day or night. Okay?"

Sierra nodded, still sniffing, and grabbed the card. She felt a little better. "Mrs. Martin, "she said as she stood.

"Yes, sweetie."

"I'm scared. *Really* scared."

Angela hugged her tight. "I know." She spoke quietly in her ear, "When you feel the fear just repeat, 'God does not give me the spirit of fear, but of love, power and self-control'."

Sierra studied her face. She decided she could trust her, a little. "Well, I feel better than I did before I walked in this building." Before she turned to leave she glimpsed at the silver photo frame perched on the desk. "This your family?" She smiled on the inside.

"Oh yes." Angela's face lit up.

Sierra picked it up the frame and studied it. "Mrs. Martin?" she said as she gently placed it back on her desk.

"Yes."

"Why do you care what happens? Don't you have your own life to worry about?"

The woman pressed her lips together for a moment then smiled. "Well, because that's what God commands us to do. And besides..." she paused, "years ago when I was a teenager—I *was* you."

Chapter 9 – Light of the Sun

Sierra slept like she'd been hit in the head with a brick. She dreamt about her graduation. And awoke to bladder pressure that felt like a dam about to burst. She slid from the covers as the April ran splattered against her window. She eased out the door and wandered down the hall. Her bare feet cooled to the touch of the uneven floor. She took several steps, then paused at a faint noise from her mother's room.

She eased backed then peaked into the door. *Gospel?* Her brows furrowed as she peered through the slit again. Her eyes enlarged when she saw her mother on the floor. Sierra couldn't tell if she was singing or praying. Normally, at this hour she was passed out if she'd made it home at all.

She felt like an intruder but couldn't peel her eyes away. However, her bladder was about to give way. She tipped passed the door, silently cursing the creaky floor. Once in the bathroom, she sat on the toilet, sighing of relief, then closed her eyes. *God, please tell me this isn't a joke.* She eased back down the hall to her room and floated back to sleep. Partly convinced it had all been a dream.

~~~~~

Maxine Sanders awoke at exactly three a.m. on Sunday. That day marked the beginning of her deliverance. An inexplicable presence engulfed her like two sculpted arms. The constrictive force was heavy and thick. She slid under the covers and mumbled to God.

After a few minutes, she jumped from the bed and fumbled with the old radio atop her dresser. She searched for anything that sounded spiritual. One thing she knew for certain. The devil hated worship. She rushed back in bed, pulled the covers and curled into a
~~~~~

ball. Maxine whispered the few scriptures she knew. *Lightness can't dwell with dark...resist the devil and he will run.*

As the music filled the air, her spirit calmed. She fell back and shut her eyes as a wave of peace washed over her. Music from a childhood hymn encircled the air. *If it had not been for the Lord on my side, where would I be?* She didn't remember much of God from those days in Louisiana, but she vaguely recalled the few times she and her mother were in church. She visualized the seersucker pinafore and patent leather shoes she'd begged to wear. She could feel the sizzle of the hot comb and smell the Royal Crown hairdress her mother used to tame her massive curls. Her mother cursed and combed. Maxine refused to cry because the pristine braids and satin ribbons were worth it.

The rest, she knew. However, Maxi hid those memories in the pitch black parts of her soul. The many times her mother left her alone. The night her mother was shot at a club. That day the one relative she knew refused her because a child "wasn't her portion." The melodic elixir consumed all the unpleasant thoughts and excruciating pain.

The lyrics sliced her spirit like a hot knife through butter. Soon her body poured out the bed and onto the floor. She eventually knelt and placed her head on the bed. Her soul lay bare, her flesh involuntarily stripped.

She whispered, "God, I've failed. I have failed you, my child, myself." Her vintage chenille spread soaked with tears. The remorse, regret excavated from her inner man with each confession. Healing and redemption covered her wounds like salve. "Jesus, please remove this taste. Take it. I want to hate the taste and smell of alcohol. I'm *begging* you." She kept her head on the side of the bed. Exhausted, she finally whispered in the creator's ear, "Please make me whole."

~~~~~
~~~~~

Sierra wrapped her arms tighter around her body when she heard the sound of footsteps. The floor creaked once, and the door to her bedroom screeched. A few soft steps and her bed sunk as her mother's body settled beside her. Sierra flinched when her lips pressed against her cheek.

"Sierra, Sierra…baby, wake up." She gently nudged her. "We need to talk."

Sierra opened her eyes slowly. She turned and stared blankly into her mother's face.

"Just listen to me." Her mother's eyes watered. "This, um, it's my fault. I've made lots of mistakes. I wasn't there for you." She sighed. "And I've made some really bad choices." Sierra squinted and swallowed. "What I'm trying to say is," she paused and brushed Sierra's hair from her face. "I'm not gonna let you down." She shook her head. "Not this time. I mean with the drinking. It's going to stop. And, it won't control us ever again. I'm gonna get help." Her lips quivered. "So I can be a better mom," her head dropped, "and the best..." she slowly looked up and swallowed, "grandmother." Her lips formed a smile as tears dampened her face.

Sierra's eyes grew wide. *How does she know?*

She placed one of her hands against her daughter's face. "A mother knows her child."

Sierra's hands trembled as she reached to wipe her mother's tears. For the first time in her life, she felt her mother's sincerity. Besides, she was willing to take the chance because she needed her more than ever. *God, I'm going to trust you...just this once.* She grabbed her mother and held on tight, praying it wasn't all a dream.

Chapter 10 – Don’t Need No Appointment

After a short train ride, Maxine Sanders was full steam ahead on her mission. She was never a person to mince words and couldn’t wait to allow the boiling volcano in her spirit to erupt. She crossed over a few streets and paused to look up at the skyscraper. **GRIER ENTERPRISES**. Her stomach turned at the sight of the imposing letters outside the building. She was swept into the revolving door and quickly marched into the regal lobby.

She charged past the security desk, and the guard jumped from behind. “Scuse me, lad-y.” He almost tripped as he rushed toward her. The thin fifty-something man recognized her just as he stepped to block her path. “Maxi?”

She walked around him and continued to walk briskly. “Wait,” his reedy body caught up. He held his hands up. “You just can’t–”

Once again she burrowed through his weak blockade. “Darn it, Woody! You know you owe me.” She edged ahead of him. Woody was a reformed crack head from her neighborhood. He once tried to rob her shop. She didn’t press charges because she felt sorry for him. Grayson Grier, Sr., put him to work as part of his fake non-profit community outreach.

He grabbed her arm. “Now, now, Ms. Maxine, you know I can’t mess up. I’m beggin’ you,” he said in a quiet but firm whisper. His bug eyes pled even harder. “C’mon now.” He moved with each step she took like they were a synchronized pair.

“Woody, look I don’t have time for you today, now move!” She finally gave an obligatory pause in her steps. “Okay, okay. Call *him.*”

“Him who?” His eyebrows knitted.

She sucked her teeth. "Grayson. Grayson Grier, Sr."

"Oh, no, no…Ms. Maxine, please." He held his hands up and shook his head like a bobble toy.

She adjusted the burnt red shawl draped across her shoulder. "Either you *call* him or I'm going up."

"Okay, okay." He walked toward the security desk. When he turned his back, she ran and jumped on the elevator.

Once inside, she watched with laser focus as the lighted numbers changed at each floor. The elevator stopped on the third floor, and she ignored the polished employee whistling as he joined her. She clinched her teeth at the sound.

"How about that weather?" he said, his voice chipper as he clutched his folder.

Her feet remained planted and her body stiffened in silent rebellion. The man quickly reverted to his phone, scrolling through the screen. He slightly rocked back on the heels of his wing tip shoes. His whistle turned to a hum.

Once he reached his floor, he shot out. She continued to the eleventh floor and continued her mission. She almost ran over the petite receptionist as she rounded the corner and passed the floor to ceiling glass windows of the conference room. *I know he's up here somewhere*. Seconds later, she heard footsteps behind her.

"Ms. Ms. …" She ignored the mealy mouth voice of the lady trailing her steps.

She stopped when she reached a door. *Grayson Grier, Ra*fter a quick glimpse of the sign, she heard another voice.

"Maxi, I know you didn't come all this way to see my newly decorated office." She looked to her left in the direction of the cavernous voice. He turned toward his secretary and smiled. "It's okay." The woman paused, sighed then sped off.

Grayson Grier, Sr. opened the door to his office suite and stepped aside as Maxine strode in. He walked passed her directly toward the panoramic view of New York. He stood for a moment basking in view of the skyline. "So, Maxi, to what do I owe this distinctive pleasure?" He turned quickly to face her.

"Grayson, spare me. You know *exactly* why I'm here."

He spat a laugh then eased around his Cherrywood desk. He slowly leaned against it, folding his arms.

Maxine had to work overtime to ignore how handsome and dapper he looked. He was fit and fine. Fifty-three looked good on him. *Time is usually good to people with money.* His rimless glasses framed his familiar speckled eyes. His wheat colored goatee with flecks of gray framed his supple lips. *That daily five mile run he was so anal about paid off.* In that instant she recalled lying across his bare chest many mornings when he'd jump up to hit the treadmill. His coppery skin was smooth as the monogrammed sheets they used to lay on.

"Okay, let's talk." He began to reach inside the jacket of his tailored gray suit. "How much?"

His bluntness jolted her to attention. "I don't want any more of your money. That was the past." She shifted the weight of her body to one side and placed her hand on her hip.

"Still the same stubborn prideful Maxi. What are we gonna do with you?"

"Please, kill the Eddie Murphy Boomerang routine. This isn't about me." She sucked her teeth and smirked.

Grayson Sr.'s eyes caressed her every move, shifting at her slightest gesture. He wanted to see more of her dress; he imagined how the fabric hugged her ample hips and framed her bosom. He licked his lips before he spoke. "Care for a drink?" He walked toward a large wooden trimmed mirror and adjusted his bow tie.

“I don’t drink…anymore. I quit.” She cleared her throat in response to his raised brow.

“Well, I’m working on it—counseling.” She began to remove her voluminous shawl that kept the March winds at bay. “And when did *you* start drinking?”

“I don’t, it’s for my clients.” He paused, his eyes meeting hers. “Counseling, that’s big. Proud of you. Hope you’re serious this time.” He stepped toward his desk and lifted the lid on his humidor. “Max, I’m busy.” He retrieved a cigar. “What’s this about?” He waved it like a wand as he spoke.

She rolled her eyes then reached in her purse. “Grayson, you might be able to buy half of Manhattan, Montclair or the entire East Coast, but my daughter and *your* grandchild are not for sale.” She pulled a check from her purse, tore it up and let the pieces drift to the floor.

He sat on the end of his desk. “Okay, the whole rhyming thing…cute.” He raised his brow. “You do realize this is your fault.” He slid the cigar under his nose, savoring the aroma. “And it’s a little too late to play the doting mother.”

She walked closer to him and looked him dead in the eye. “*Screw* you.” Her nostrils flared as she spat the words.

“You already have.” The corners of his mouth curled upward.

Maxine hesitated, nothing she could say. *The truth will set you free, but first it’ll piss you off.* “You know, I wonder what your friends at Montclair Pinnacle of Praise would think? Mr. board member…funding abortions.”

She walked around the office as her words lingered in the air like a stench. His eyes tiptoed along. He tried not to be enticed by the sweater dress that wrapped her curves and hugged her bosom just as he’d hoped. She was thick with a tiny waist, a deadly combination in the past. When she turned to face him, he was all but drooling. *Nothing's changed.*

He cleared his throat. "Maxi, you know I'm a realist. Your daughter, my son, well neither are mature enough for a kid and you know it." He sat on the edge of his desk and shrugged. "That check would have covered your daughter's education and then some."

She walked toward him. "It's not about the money." She stepped closer, "But you're right about one thing. Some of this *is* my fault, and I'm gonna do something about it. I plan to be there for my child *and* grandchild. It's the Godly thing to do." She was standing right in front of him now.

"Since when do you care about what God thinks?" he said quietly as a familiar hint of lavender and almond oil sauntered by his nose.

"Since I, I...never mind!" She paused as she coaxed the words scrambling in her brain into a sentence, "You know you've got a lot of nerve with *your* selective Christianity." She stood a little taller and pulled back her shoulders. Her eyes fixed on his. Let me be clear. "The day I let *my* daughter lay on a table to have somebody cut a living being out of her is the day you do the same. You can't ever know what that feels like." She fought back long forgotten tears. "Forget it! You can keep your money and the curse attached to it. And I PRAY your son doesn't turn out to be the spineless hypocrite you've become." She threw her shawl over her shoulder and bolt through the door before he could speak another word.

Chapter 11 – Doors of the Church

Maxine remembered the grand bargain she'd struck with God to get the demons off her back that night. She knew a vow to God was serious. That's why she rarely made them. But Maxine was proud of herself. She'd kept her commitment to finish rehab, but the real work was only beginning. The other promise proved more difficult. Church. Real church. Her weekly self-guided Bible studies were no longer enough. So here she was. Up on a Sunday morning rummaging for the right dress with half her clothes piled atop her iron bed.

"Shoot, if it's not too tight, it's showing too much cleavage!" She tugged on her sweater dress, then snatched it back over her head. She headed back to her closet for another contender, a green Diane von Furstenberg wrap dress. *Darn, I'm not going to make it to the 11 o'clock service either.* She hastily put it on. *Hmmm.* She did a half turn in a mirror. She grabbed a pin and cinched the top enough to camouflage her chest. *Sigh. This is gonna have to work.* Maxine grabbed a yellow leather clutch bag and slid on her heels. "Sierra," she yelled, "Ready?"

Sierra had been ready with no wardrobe issues. All she owned was already loose and blousy, easily doubling as maternity wear in her first trimester. She wore a black long skirt and a loose fitting sweater. "Yeah, I'm ready." *I guess.* "What do you know about this church?" Sierra said as she followed her mother downstairs.

"Not much, this lady from the grocery store mentioned it several times. She seemed nice. Back then I used to run the other way when I saw her. She'd corner me every time, talking 'Jesus this' and 'Jesus that,' 'praise the Lord...God is able'. Used to get on my nerves," she said as grabbed her light trench coat from the closet.

"Well, I'm not crazy about anybody's church house. Especially now, this town's so small. What will people say?" Sierra said as they stepped out on the porch.

Maxine struggled to lock the door. "Sierra, who cares? We're gonna meet

Jesus not the people in the pews. And the Bible says not to forsake the fellowship with the saintly."

"Huh?" Sierra said.

"We gotta go to church, worship with other people." Maxine jiggled the lock for several more seconds. "Finally!" She said, momentarily dismissing her daughter's protest. "Besides you can't even tell you're pregnant under all that fabric. You're all stomach and your face hasn't even filled out." She grabbed her daughter's hand and kissed her on the forehead. "Look, change is always difficult. I don't know much about religion, but I do know evil is stubborn. We need all the weapons we can get. C'mon, now we're already running late."

~~~~~

Sierra walked toward the manicured church lawn. She only looked up enough to keep from tripping. When they reached the top of the stairs, her mother opened one of the heavy wooden doors. After they both stepped in, they stood on the blood red carpet. The usher looked at them, her watch and smirked. Maxine waited for a signal to move toward a seat. The choir was near the end of a song and announcements followed. *At least the music's good*, Sierra thought. Maxine grabbed Sierra's hand as they waited. Another couple stepped in. That same usher asked if they were together, then pointed toward the usher a few feet away. Off they went toward the front. "Mom, did you see…"
~~~~~

Maxine placed her two fingers over her mouth to silence Sierra, then slid off her coat. The usher turned her attention toward them and finally walked over. She discreetly motioned toward the top of Maxine's dress. Maxine looked toward her chest. Her pin had popped, exposing major cleavage. The usher sighed. "Follow me," she whispered and extended her gloved hand toward the balcony stairs.

Maxine followed the woman wondering how the pin she'd so strategically placed had come apart. She tried to ease her coat back on but reached the top before she had the chance. The usher rushed them into the aisle of the pew as prayer was about to start. The couple at the end shifted so Maxine and Sierra had to climb over them to the empty spaces next to them. The lady her grabbed her husband's arm and slid closer. Once seated, Maxine tried to focus on the sermon. However, she couldn't help notice the loud *amen* from the lady seated next to her. Especially when the Pastor spoke on modesty quoting 1 Timothy2:9, "…women should adorn themselves in modest apparel." Once the sermon was finally over, she and Sierra wasted no time. They bolted out the church doors. Once they hit the last step of the front stairs, Sierra paused.

"Sierra, what's wrong? C'mon let's go." Maxine plastered a fake smile as the crowd moved past.

Sierra noticed several of her classmates a few feet up the walkway. She lowered her head as her feet shuffled. She looked out the corner of her eye as she passed and couldn't help notice the whispers and giggles.

"Wonder where Grayson Jr. is now?" One of the young ladies said loud enough for her to hear.

Sierra's heart dropped to her shoes, but she kept moving.

Once in the car, Maxine tried to camouflage her deflated spirit. *God, are you sure you live up in* that *church?* Maxine thought, feeling no better than when she'd left the house. She started the ignition and held her hand on the steering wheel. “I don’t think we’ll come back here again,” she said looking forward.

Sierra let out a sigh of relief. “Thank, God. No pun intended.”

They both laughed. Maxine placed her hand over her daughter’s belly, then smiled.

Sierra mustered a smile that quickly disappeared. “Mom, if we can’t find God in the church, where we gonna find him?”

Maxine placed her hand back on the other side of the wheel and put her foot on the gas.

“I don’t know. Guess we keep looking till we do. Maybe if we try hard enough, He’ll find us, “she replied, feeling like Thelma and Louise about to make their getaway.

Chapter 12 – Mother, May I

Maxine Sanders kept her promise. Six years after Sierra had given birth, and she was still sober… with help of course. She hadn't officially joined a church, but Sunday mornings she was a faithful member on the front pew at "TV church." T.D. Jakes, Joel Osteen, Charles Stanley or Joyce Meyer, she was Bible ready and prepared for worship. In her mind, living room worship was the best. She even kept her notepad nearby for sermon notes and paid her tithes online where her spirit led. Occasionally she had a group of ladies over for Bible study.

Her boutique Deja Reaux, on trendy Bloomfield Avenue, was turning a decent profit. Vintage clothing and eclectic décor were suddenly hot. Everything that was old was new again as the economy crawled back. She was very meticulous about the clothing and furniture she sold and even did some interior decorating. She'd found her passion. Creativity was the one thing she and her daughter shared. Despite the rocky start, she was finally moving forward.

"Sierra, I'm gonna need you to help me at the shop today. I want to show you some things about keeping the books. It would give me some backup and well, you just need to learn all parts of the business. And since you plan on creating a jewelry line, it's good practice." Her mother grabbed some coconut oil from Sierra's dresser. She sat on Sierra's bed and started to moisturize her legs and arms and ran a little through her hair.

"Mom, I don't have time, I got a huge design project. Considering how long it took me to get into the fashion school, I've got to give it my all. It's competitive. She paused to glimpse her mother's expression. *Guess it's now or never.*" Mom, "she smiled wide, "I kinda need a favor.

Can you keep your grandson tonight?" She whipped her hair into a messy top knot. "Got a date with Bryce." She avoided eye contact on purpose.

Maxine rolled her eyes and sighed. "How do you know *I* don't have plans myself?" She jumped up and placed the jar of oil back on Sierra's dresser.

Sierra paused from inspecting her hair and faced her mother. "You mean with Ray?" Sierra waved her hand. "All he's gonna do is bring some of those artery clogging ribs from that shack he calls a restaurant while you sit on the couch and watch old Sanford and Son reruns. Little Gray will be in bed before nine. He can rub your corns after that. That's the most action I know he's gonna get." Sierra let out a cautious chuckle.

"Funny, very funny. I'm not that old. Wait, I'm only forty-seven. That's not old at all! I'll babysit, if you come early and work all day at the boutique tomorrow. You can finish your project there." Maxine shot a glare at Sierra until she got her intended response.

"All right, all right." Sierra sounded like she was back in high school." As long as Amber, your perky part-timer doesn't bug me. Dang she can work a nerve spouting and laying hands on the mannequins. And I promise I saw her rubbing oil on the computer and speaking in tongues." Sierra sucked her teeth and rolled her eyes as she pulled a scarf from her dresser drawer.

Her mother chuckled. "She's sweet. Say what you want, that girl knows some Jesus." She popped Sierra on the butt.

"*Whatever*. I know Him, too, but I don't have to talk about it 24-7." Sierra wrapped the scarf around her head and tied a knot in the back. "Anyway, something about her grates my nerves."

"Sierra..."Her mother sighed. "Never mind. Just be thankful she's there to help out. I don't pay her that much. She practically volunteers."

“Mommy, “Little Grayson burst in, “see my drawing.” He handed Sierra a piece of paper. “Ta-daaaa!”

Sierra grabbed it, thankful for her son’s timing. “OH, wow that’s beautiful! You’re soooo talented and creative, just like your mommy!” She rubbed his sandy brown curls then kissed him on the forehead.

“Gramma, I made one for you, too,” he said with his expectant eyes gazing upward.

“Aww, that’s my baby!” She bent down and almost sucked the air out of his cheeks with a kiss. “C’mon, I’m gonna make you some breakfast.”

Sierra finished getting ready and followed the smell of eggs and sausage down the stairs.

“Did you hear what I said about the store? It’s important, “her mother said, still facing the stove.

“Mom, I gave you my word.” She kissed the top of her son’s head, fixed a plate and sat at the table.

Chapter 13 – Date Night

Sierra waited patiently as Bryce returned from the restroom. Date night at Cuban Pete's was an upgrade. He got a check from a small part in an indie film. Her mouth was salivating at the thought of her coconut fish.

"So, tell me about this last audition," she said as he sat. She slid over and shifted her body to face him in the booth.

"Um, the usual." Bryce placed a napkin in his lap. "Man, seems like the same dudes show up every time. Everybody's bringing their A game. I keep telling my agent to look for parts that aren't necessarily ethnic, like one of those Leonardo DiCaprio or Ben Affleck roles." He dipped a Queso Frito in some sauce and devoured it.

Sierra was half listening as she stared at her man licking his fingers. Her eyes drank his strong jaw line and other features that looked chiseled from a chocolate block. *How could any casting director pass on my man? He's perfection: glistening locs, pearlescent teeth and confidence. It's all good and all mine.* "Mmm."

"Sierra, you listening?"

She sat up taller. "Yeah, yes, I heard you. Think you got this one?"

"Your man put it down, but you never know." He drank a sip of tea.

She was about to say something, but her mouth dropped open at the sight in the entryway. *Oh no.* She slightly eased down in her seat. *What are they doing here?*

"What's wrong?" Bryce looked at her, then toward door.

"Girl, you trippin' sit up." He rubbed his chin as his brows furrowed. His back straightened from his more relaxed posture. "You're with your man."

In less than two minutes, her son's father was strolling over with girlfriend in tow.

"Sierra, how are you?" His voice low and assured.

"Sup, man," Bryce interjected before Sierra had a chance to respond.

"Oh, pardon my manners – Brian, right?" His mouth coaxed into a half grin.

"Bryce," he said then mirrored his expression.

"And this is my lady, Cassidy." He glanced at her then fixed his eyes on the two of them.

Sierra shifted in her seat and leaked a smile. *They can't be matching? Boy, do they look stupid! What's this, a J. Crew commercial? Everybody wanna be Barack and Michelle? Bye, Felicia.*

"Nice to meet you." Bryce nodded toward Cassidy.

Sierra watched waiting for "silent partner's cue" to speak. She was physically pretty, but couldn't pry her mouth apart with the Jaws of Life. Sierra sipped, trying to recall whether her curls cooperated that day or not. Then realized she didn't care. *Messy ponytail piled atop the head day.* She refocused at the sound of Grayson's voice.

"So, we just left an art exhibit. What are you two up to?"

"Just left the movies." Bryce visibly massaged Sierra's hand.

"Ah," Grayson said as he nodded. "I had my mouth set for Tassot De Chevre at Saveur Creole's, but the lady loves the Flan Cubano. Whatever the lady wants, she gets." He laughed as his eyes quickly scanned the restaurant.

Silent Partner continued smiling. Not even a full smile, a bit like Mona Lisa. Sierra had nothing bad to say about her, but couldn't understand how she had the same stupid expression all the time. Her whole situation was predictable. Shoulder-length hair layered and blown out to perfection as if she had the same hairdresser since twelve. *Definitely a twin set and pearls kinda girl. I bet Mrs. Grier loves her.*

Just when Sierra was about to listen to whatever Grayson Jr. was saying, she caught a flash of light. Silent partner had raised her left hand to brush her hair, one of her other few tricks.

A RING? Before she realized it, the words "Grayson, Cassidy…you two engaged?" splattered on the table, with no way to stuff them back.

Silent partner woke up. "Yes, yes, we are!" She shoved Grayson's hand out the way and presented the evidence. "I thought Grayson told you."

As she proceeded to articulate every detail of the proposal, Sierra knew Bryce could read her mind. Grayson Jr. stood in false humility, basking in his shower of glory.

"And I've already started planning. I had a private appointment with Amsale's last weekend and found my dress on the first visit. I mean who does that? What are the chances? It's supposed to be an *experience*. Unbelievable, right?" Her face burst into a sunbeam.

Bryce elbowed Sierra. "OH, wow, that's great," she said. "Congratulations you two."

"I knew from the moment we met she was the one." Grayson Jr. gazed in her eyes. Sierra quickly gulped her water, coughing as she placed the glass on the table.

"Wow."

"I was going to tell you, but it just happened." His easy tone explained with a hint of sincerity. He locked his arms back with Silent Partner.

Uh-huh, I bet. "No worries. It's all about you two," Sierra said through clenched teeth. "Wish you the best." She pressed her lips together forcing any further sentiments back in her mouth.

They were just about to walk off when she heard silent partner, who had never spoken so much in her life whisper something to Grayson. She raised her eyebrows and nudged him, "Go on."

"Well, um, Sierra. I mean I really didn't think I needed to ask, but Cassidy wanted to know if little Gray could be in the wedding. I mean she wanted to see if it was okay with you." He almost sighed.

Really God? This is really the icing on the cake. "Um, sure, of course, Grayson. Of course. And no, you didn't have to ask, but it was a mature and considerate thing to do." She glared at Grayson Jr. "Cassie."

"Yeah, this is going to be fantastic!" Silent partner clapped her hands together.

"Yeah, great." Sierra chirped.

"Well, guess we'll let you guys get back to your date." Bryce mustered with finality.

"Oh yes, of course." Grayson agreed, eager to get on his way. He winked. "Sierra, we'll talk soon."

"Right." She nodded and took another long sip of water.

~~~~~

"I could care less about the engagement. Those two mindless wonders are meant for each other. It's just I don't know, little Gray talks about her—*a lot. Ms. Cassie's so nice, Ms. Cassie's so*
~~~~~

fun..."Sierra sneered as they turned the corner toward Bryce's apartment building.

"Well, could be the opposite. She could be a *horrible* stepmother."

Omigod, stepmother? Her eyes inflated.

Bryce saw the panic in her face. "Babe, let's keep it one hun-ed. You a little jealous?"

"Of Cassie? Puleeaze. I don't want him. It's not about her it's just about the whole family. You can have your manufactured happily-ever-after and fakery but don't try to make me feel less in the process. Grayson's always done that. Now they're a team." She paused before walking up the concrete steps of his apartment building. "I just don't want them taking over my son. I mean I can't compete. He gives little Gray the most expensive toys, front row seats...to everything! I buy him what I think is a great birthday gift; Grayson flies him to Disney World. And his parents *never* say no. He swoops in with his cape on every occasion and saves the day! Now he's got Lois Lane!" Her hands moved wildly as she spoke.

As they stood on in front of the steps, Bryce turned to face her. He placed his hands on her shoulders. "Babe, you're exaggerating."

"Really?"

"Okay, maybe not. He *is* the first grandchild. Besides, I'll bet Cassie will be spitting out kids in no time. Her kind usually does. They have a master plan and leave nothing to chance. She can't let you have the spotlight."

She sighed. "They're all a trip. They didn't even want... never mind."

He stepped up the stairs then faced her. She looked into his eyes. He placed his hands on her face and pulled his lips toward hers and pressed against them. She melted at the warmth of his kiss.

When their lips pulled away, he let his forehead fall against hers. He grabbed hand. "It's gonna be a'ight."*This is why I never wanted to date a woman with a child. If she wasn't so darn gorgeous and sweet...why didn't I keep walking pass the coffee shop that day?* "Come up, we can talk."

"I don't want to be bothered with your roommate. He can't take a hint, third wheel and proud. Who wants to sit up and look at his big block head and listen to his corny tech talk?" The fact that her boyfriend didn't have a place to himself or a car suddenly irritated her. *This aspiring acting situation ain't cute at ALL. So tired of living broke.com.*

He laughed then hugged her. "Babe, he's outta town. Met some woman online and they started dating. Hope I don't see him on an episode of Catfish." He chuckled again. "C'mon, you know you want to come up. I got some cheesecake from Gina's Bakery."

"Will you go upstairs so that boy can stop whining?" An old man sitting on the porch a few feet away interjected. "All that begging. In my day I ain't begged no woman for nothing."

"Rufus, who you talking to out there?" A woman peaked out the window on the first floor. The man waved his hand. "Can't a man sit out here and enjoy some peace?" he mumbled.

Bryce shook his head. He grabbed Sierra's hands, and she followed up the steps.

"Okay, for a little while," she said. *After all, this is a date.*

"That's what they all say," the old man chirped. He grabbed a flask from his jacket and took a swallow. Then waved his hand.

Once inside the apartment, she dropped on the couch. He sat next to her. "Just so your baby's daddy won't ruin the rest of my night, I'll let you vent for another five minutes. Then it's a wrap." He grabbed both her hands and kissed her knuckles.

"Funny." She finally looked up at him. "I'm not tripping. And I told you not to use that ghetto phrase. Ugh. He is the father of my child, my co-parent."

"Anyway, bottom line. *You're little* Gray's mother, no one else. He knows how much you love him. Don't get caught up in the Griers. Just do the best you can and let God bless the rest. Kill that fear 'cause what you fear most happens."

"Okay, Mr. Iyanla Fix my Life. We all know it ain't that easy. I mean these people own Montclair and half of New York. Grier Enterprises, The Grier Report, The Grier Scholarship Fund, The Grier Estate…I'm sick of it!"

"Well, maybe, just maybe if Sierra Sanders gets out of her own way and let God do his part, you wouldn't feel so powerless. Besides, you can't punish people for their success. They ain't bad people…"

That's what you think.

"They do a lot for the community. I'm proud to see a successful Black family at that level."

She turned away and put her head on the arm of the sofa. "And FYI, I do have faith. I just don't run around talking about it." She sucked her teeth. "You sound like Zoe…never mind. I see the Griers have you brainwashed, too."

"Sierra, I'm just sayin', you can be hard on people, including me." He sighed. "Stop giving your power away to these people. Fact is, they're getting married. Cassie's going to have a part in your son's life. I'm sure Grayson isn't doing cartwheels at the thought of some other man spending time with his son either." He grabbed the remote.

Sierra thought about his words. *Grayson Jr.'s so self-absorbed Bryce probably doesn't phase him.* "Whatever. I'll try not to make it bigger than what it is."

"And besides, your time's coming."

Her eyes and smile widened. "Really?" "Yep, right after I land a part in a major motion picture."

Jeez. "I think I'll have a piece of cheesecake now."

Chapter 14 – Expect the Unexpected

Sierra decided to repay her mother for babysitting so much lately by thoroughly cleaning the house. Over the last six years, her mother had more than fulfilled her grandmother role. Sierra knew it was in part to make up for all the pain her drinking had caused. With her son at his father's and her school work complete, her day was cleared for the tasks at hand.

Sierra had already done the dishes, dusted and mopped the kitchen floor. Her mother's room was next. She stood in the doorway. *Hmm, Mom needs some major organization.* She almost didn't know where to begin, eyeing the pile of mail and spread of folders atop her desk. She walked over and began gathering the envelopes to put them in some order then noticed a several letters from the IRS. She really wanted to respect her mother's privacy but couldn't help but open several. She mouthed as she read the words.

Sierra put the paper down as fast as she'd picked it up. She changed her mind about the desk and moved around the rest of the room. *Mom's got it under control.* Even when her mother used to drink, the bills somehow got paid.

The vacuum cleaner drowned her thoughts. After she'd finished her mother's room and the laundry, she took a break. That turned into a nap. When she awoke, she jumped up and took a shower. She put on her terrycloth robe and began drying her hair. After about ten minutes, she thought she heard the doorbell. She shut off the dryer and peaked out her bedroom window.

Shoot. "He's early." She threw on underclothes, an oversized T-shirt and leggings. Then sprinted downstairs.

"Okay, okay." When she opened the door, Grayson Jr. was standing there with Gray in his arms. "He wasn't feeling well, so I brought him home a little early. He doesn't seem to want anybody but you when he gets sick. I tried to call, but you wouldn't pick up your cell."

"I was vacuuming earlier then I got in the shower." She felt her son's head. "Oh, poor baby." She ran her fingers over his damp curls. "Take him upstairs please, and put him in his bed."

"Okay, no problem." Without hesitation, he carried his son upstairs. When Grayson Jr. returned downstairs, he made himself comfortable on her couch.

"Uhhh, nobody said you could sit down." She eyed him from the kitchen as she fixed her iced tea.

"Yes, Sierra, I am a little thirsty, I'd love a glass of your homemade tea." He rubbed his throat with his fingers.

She rolled her eyes upward. "Want something to drink?"

"Please." He flipped through the short pile of coffee table books and grabbed one from the bottom. "Love Basquiat. So tragic but his paintings are worth a mint." He mused, thumbing through the pages. "There's an exhibit going on in Brooklyn."

Sierra seethed as she poured a second glass of tea. She silently prayed for strength then headed toward the living room. *No drama, no drama.* "I'd thought you'd be rushing off. Shouldn't you be knee deep in wedding to dos?"

"Nope. Was told all I had to do was show up and look good. Which shouldn't be hard." He winked, his arms outstretched along the back of the couch. "Although, I have to admit, it's looking more like a production than a wedding. Actually sitting here is a welcome distraction." He looked in her eyes and smiled.

"Uh-ha." She handed him his glass and sat in the wing back chair near the couch. "Well excuse me if I don't feel bad for you." She brushed her hair behind her back.

He took a sip of his drink and sat it on the coffee table. "So."

"So what?" She quipped.

"How you feel about it? I mean, the wedding, Cassie. You know." He turned his body slightly toward her.

"What am I *supposed* to say? Your funeral. You like it, I love it." She shrugged then sipped on her drink.

His mouth crawled to a grin. "Cassie's a good girl."

"You trying to convince you, me or the both of us? Besides, takes more than that to make a marriage."

"How would you know?" He raised his brow.

"Look, Grayson, what do you want from me? Am I supposed to cry, be hurt? Our chapter ended a long time ago. I got a man and I'm happy for you." She crossed her legs.

He paused a few seconds. "So, what's up with you and ole boy? Bruce."

"It's Bryce." She rolled her eyes. "You know it's Bryce."

"Whatever." He reached for his glass and took a large swallow.

"We've been committed…over a year." She glared at him with intent to arrest further inquisition.

"Umm." Grayson Jr. nodded then leaned back. "He's not right for you. An actor?

Too unstable, one of you has got to have a real career."

"I'm working on a *real* career, and everybody's not looking to get married. It's not that important."

"Right. Well you know we got connects. I can hook you up with a job when you finish school."

She shot him a look but didn't respond.

"So, you feeling dude? He must be gettin' it in." He eyed the way her leggings outlined her toned calves." I can see why. You never wore tight pants when we were together. You lookin' good these days. Must be working out." His moistened his lips.

Amazing how all that proper English goes out the window around me. "What?" Her eyes squinted. She walked over and snatched his glass from the table. "I think it's time for you to go." She paused, waiting for him to obey her command.

"Why you getting all serious? You know I'm just playin'." He jumped up and swooped her in his arms. He paused, before planting a feather light kiss on her neck. "I miss you." He buried his nose in her flesh, inhaling the scented oil on her dewy skin. "Sierra, I know you miss me. *Umm*, you feel *so* good. Smell even better." His grip tightened.

Initially paralyzed, she struggled to free herself. "Grayson, are you crazy?" The hard plastic tumbler fell to the rug on the floor. He pulled her tighter with one hand and grabbed the back of her hair with the other. He placed his lips over hers until she went limp. He eased them toward the couch as the weight of his body forced them down. Her eyes closed and he smiled. His kisses turned firm, then softened as he raised her arms above her head. When her body stopped moving, he positioned himself more comfortably. He brushed the inside of her arms with his lips, as she moaned.

"Grayson, I, I," she whispered as all resistance escaped her limbs.

A few seconds later they both moaned, escaping to a place far from the present truth. His hand traveled up her shirt and began to fumble her bra, but she grabbed it. "Stop it. Grayson, stop it!" She pushed hard. "STOP IT!" She freed her arm and slapped him. He finally sat up. He was breathing heavy as he wiped his mouth." I can't believe you."

She stood and moved several steps back as she smoothed hair back into place. Their eyes locked for a moment as her heart raced.

"Mo-mmy." Little Gray groaned from the top of the steps. She looked toward the stairs then at Grayson Jr.

"C-c-c-oming, Gray. Mommy will be up in two seconds." She yelled quickly. "You need to go." She placed her hand over her forehead. *My God, what just happened?*

Grayson Jr. stood and straightened his pants. He kept his eyes on her. He wasn't convinced they were done.

She walked over and opened the door. "Go." After a bit of hesitation, he eased toward the door. "Grayson, don't *ever* try this again," she said through clenched teeth as he slithered by. Reality slapped her to the present. He wasn't the seemingly tender young man who'd stole her heart. He'd changed. Sierra slammed the door and leaned her back against it as she wiped a tear. She closed her eyes as her body trembled. A wave of shock, satisfaction, then regret led to stark revelation. *He's different now.* But she couldn't help to think, "Grayson Jr., her first everything, the man she'd spent hating for over the past six years, still wanted *her*."

What scared her most?

The tiniest possibility she felt the same.

Chapter 15 – Nuptial Healing

Maxine watched her daughter fold clothes, dress mannequins and color coordinate racks of clothes in her boutique. She admired Sierra's creativity and focus. Her daughter hummed, losing herself in the tasks. She seemed peaceful, but her mother knew better.

"Sierra? Honey, you okay?" She looked up from tabulating receipts.

Sierra lightly jumped in response to her mother's voice. "OH yeah, I'm fine, Ma." *I'll be perfect once this stupid wedding's over.* Even Zoe was going. Her father was Grayson Sr.'s fraternity brother. *Ugh. This is all such a joke!* She slammed a bunch of hangers in a bin.

Her mother jumped at the crashing sound of metal and plastic. "Sierra!"

"Sorry," she said as she paused, then slid some of the clothes on the rolling rack to make room for more. She couldn't get the image of clueless Cassie and Grayson Jr. standing at the altar out her head. She couldn't stomach silent partner basking in all her wedding glory, in light of what had just happened. *Poor silent partner.* She continued tagging and organizing the items on the rolling rack. She stepped back, satisfied with her inventory tasks. She looked over at her mother who was still sorting through receipts. *Now's as good a time as any to ask her.*

"Mom."

"Yes, sweetie."

Sierra walked closer to the counter. "I need to ask you something."

"Ask away." She kept tapping her adding machine with the end of her pencil.

"The other day I was cleaning your room. And, um, saw the stack of letters from IRS. "Are we okay?"

Maxine removed her reading glasses and sighed. "Sweetie, I know you meant well, but please don't go through my mail. We're fine. Don't you see all this business coming through here?" She smiled. I'm on a payment plan. It's under control." She waved her glasses for emphasis. "You just need to focus on getting through school."

"Well, you *would* tell me if you had some issues or needed more help…right? "She searched her mother's face for clues. "I mean I can help more, Grayson's child support…"

"No!"

Sierra jumped a little in response to her tone. Her mother began to rub her temples.

"Mom," Sierra said slowly, "talk to me, it's not all right, is it?"

Her mother sat down on the stool behind the register. "Sierra, I said its fine. I've have the best accountant he's on it. It's was a stupid error the wrong accountant made years ago. I'm not gonna let anything happen to my business or us."

"Ok, if you say so. But, I'm here to help. We're a team..." She watched her mother's facial expressions for any other clues.

"Sierra, you're only job right now is to finish school and raise your son. Enough about this, can we talk about something else?" She sighed then made eye contact with her. "I know you don't want to, but I think you should reconsider attending the wedding. The less time my grandson spends around the Griers alone the better." She began punching numbers on her adding machine again.

Sierra tilted her head and frowned. "Mom, seriously? Besides, I can't recall the last time you were in the same room with those people. You avoid them like the plague, just like me. Honestly, I'd rather drink cyanide. Besides, his grandparents may not care for me, but they treat Gray like royalty. There's no role at that type of wedding for a baby's momma." She folded her arms and cringed at the sound of the phrase *baby's momma*. "I mean, the thought of finding something to wear, the paparazzi photogs, and all that fakery overwhelms me. It's a production, not a wedding." She fumbled with the end of her fishtail braid. "I'd just fade into the background anyway.

Her mother came from behind her counter then placed her hands on Sierra's shoulders. "Baby, don't let them intimidate you. You're beautiful, gifted and a great mother." She grabbed her face. "As Amber would say, 'you're the apple of God's eye'! Trust me, money or not, those people have some serious issues. All that blings isn't the real thing."

Sierra nodded. *You can say that again.*

Chapter 16 – The Grier Men

Grayson Grier, Sr. slid his cardkey in the door to his penthouse suite. The Bose system floated Chris Botti through the room. He cut on a light and surveyed the space. A few half-empty bottles of Scottish Diva, DeLeón Tequila were left on a marble counter, and several premium beer bottles littered the floor. Trays of catered leftovers and a hint of Cohiba cigar smoke lingered. *Those fools know better than to tear up this room.* He crept past the white leather couch to the master bedroom as he glimpsed the skyscrapers through floor to ceiling windows. He eased into the bedroom and sat on the edge of the bed. He leaned down toward his son's ear. Before he spoke, he stared. *My seed. He's a man, not the boy from high school.* He silently wondered if he'd pushed too hard. Whether 25 was too young to get married. He wanted his son to take the best part of him not the worst.

"Son, get up." The lump on the other side of him purred. After a failed response, he leaned in again. "Gra*yson*, get *up*." He playfully smacked him in the back of his head. This time the body next to his son moaned and shifted beneath the Egyptian cotton sheets. She raised her body slightly and looked around. When she met the eyes of Grayson Sr., she smiled then dropped back on the pillow. A few seconds later, his son's head shot up like a periscope. Grayson Jr. opened his eyes, blinked, then snuggled his pillow again.

"Dad, c'mon, man," he croaked. "Frat shut it down last night. Only had two hours of sleep."

"Uh-huh. Don't put it all on them." His father half-joked.

Grayson's eyes flew open like a shade on a window. He sat up and rubbed the bridge of his nose. He stared at the woman that lay next to him. A thick mass of auburn hair grazed her partially exposed back. A sheet covered her tan tight body from the waist down. "Man–." He scratched his head, unable to recall most of the night's events. His eyes darted to the nightstand littered with empty condom wrappers. He slid against the tufted headboard, scratched and swallowed. "Man, I need some water." He closed his eyes tight momentarily then opened them. "Phew."

"I guess I'm not gonna get any sleep, "the woman quipped, still turned away from them. She finally sat up then eased out the bed. They both watched her naked body as she walked toward the bathroom, unfazed by her audience.

"Son, get up. I need to talk to you for a minute." His father grabbed a hotel robe and handed it to him. He struggled to put it on. Then they both walked toward the spacious living room.

"Dad, just a sec, I need some water." Grayson Jr. reached in the refrigerator and grabbed a bottle of Voss water, then dropped down on the couch.

"No son, this way." Grayson Sr. nodded toward the balcony of the penthouse suite. His son slowly got up and followed. "You see that?" His eyes gazed out to the buildings darting the skyline.

"What?" Grayson Jr. squinted at the various buildings in the distance.

"We're blessed, son. Not a cloud in the sky. Perfect day for a June wedding. His eyes peered out. You can see Grier Enterprises from here and more property over there."

His son shook his head and yawned. "Right, Dad."

"You know how I did it? I worked smart, hard and maintained self-control." He pulled a cigar out his sports jacket and held it. "The mistake most of our people make is they don't want to do the work. They sit and pray all day like opportunity's gonna fall from the sky. Don't get me wrong, you need God but you have to work. Our people are just lazy sometimes. Listening?"

His son scratched his head. "Uh, yeah Dad," he said, distracted by the after party happening in his head.

"And when success comes, own it. People try to make you apologize for success. Most of the time it's the broke ones. Nothing wrong with winning." He made sure he had his son's attention. "And those same haters are just waiting for your fall." He turned his eyes toward the skyline then, back to his son. "Be wise as a serpent, innocent as a dove. Don't give them the satisfaction." He wet the end of the cigar with his lips.

"Dad, it's too early to get this deep." Grayson Jr. yawned, then smacked his lips. "Man I'm hungry."

"Son, I'm not going to always be here. You have to pay attention. Otherwise, you'll let the little things trip you up. When you're up this high, there's nowhere to go but down. So you make sure *everything*'s vetted." He looked toward the bedroom. "*Everything*. And make good intentional choices. For example? Cassie—good, Sierra—bad. Don't get me wrong, I love my grandson. But that girl had your nose wide open. You made something that was supposed to be temporary permanent, and we have to pay for it. You were young and stupid. Boy, if I'd had known—"

"But you didn't because you were too busy. Dad, look, I get it." He rubbed the crust out his eye.

"Yeah, I hope you do. Just know the difference between a jump-off and a wife."

Grayson Jr. watched his father's lips as they moved. Maybe there was truth to his words, but they were competing with the drumbeats in his head. He sighed. "Dad, I get it, but I wouldn't exactly call the mother of my child a jump-off. Our son is going on seven. You need to respect his mom."

"Okay, maybe she's not. But Cassie has grace, intellect. She's not loud and mouthy like a lot of women. She's a little slack in personality," he raised his shoulders, "but that's not such a bad thing. Too much sass will come back and bite you in the—" He pointed the cigar toward him. "You get the point."

"That's exactly why I'm marrying *Cassie*." *Anything to shut him up. There's got to be a jackhammer inside my head.*

"Mmm-hmm. And you need to start a family right away. Kills me every time we got to send little Gray home. I don't like the idea of other men spending time around my grandson. A son needs his father."

Grayson Jr. looked his father in the eye. "Sierra's not serious with anybody. Little Gray knows who his father is," he said, wishing he could swat his father away like an unwelcome fly.

Grayson Sr. raised his brows. "Okay, but what if Sierra decides to get married one day?

She may not be for you, but she is a beautiful girl. And women like that know how to use what they have to get a man."

Seriously? "Sierra has never kept me from my son," he said, a hint of offense creeping into his voice. "And…she's not like that."

His father stared at his son's face as his forehead creased. "You still have feelings for her?" Hypocrisy gnawed the inside of his own stomach.

"Naw, no Dad, I'm just sayin' Sierra's a decent…person. She's got a good heart."

His father put his head down for a second then looked his son in the eye. "Look, all I'm saying is, no more random crumbs." He slapped his son on the back. "We clear?"

My son's not a random anything. Grayson Jr. swallowed his thoughts. "Yeah Dad."

Chapter 17 – The Big Break

Several months after Grayson's wedding, Sierra still couldn't shake what had happened between them. She was mentally replaying the incident when her son plopped beside her on the couch. "Mom, I'm hun-gry."

Sometimes I wish I could just disappear. She looked at his face and saw his father. Anger abruptly washed over her like a cold bucket of water. She didn't speak for several seconds.

"M-o-m-my," he said as he pulled on her arm. "I'm hon-gry! I want breakfast."

"Gray, Gray…okay!" she finally expelled.

Sierra jumped from the couch and pulled down the cereal box, then slammed the cabinet door. She pulled out the milk, set it on the kitchen table. She mumbled a few curse words then reached back in the cabinet for a bowl. Several others fell out and crashed to the floor.

"Ugh!" She paused and closed her eyes and rubbed her forehead. Her son walked over and pulled on her shirt. "What Gray?" she said calmly.

"I'll clean it up, Mommy."

She opened her watering eyes, reached down and gave him a big hug." I love you. You know that?" She finger-combed his sandy brown curls.

"Yeah, Mommy." He chewed on a few pieces of dry cereal. "I know dat!"

The doorbell rang. "Great! Little Gray, stay away from this mess on the floor." She walked to the door and looked out the peephole. "Bryce?" she mouthed, trying to recall if she'd brushed her teeth yet.

"Hey baby," he said as she opened the door. He breezed past her. "I came to take you out."

"You could have called. Wait, I need to–" She was about go back in the kitchen.

He grabbed her hand. "No, no, baby, this can't wait! I need to say this now, right now." He pulled her toward him and planted a warm kiss on her lips.

Hmmm, no, this couldn't be…he mentioned getting engage— "Wow, babe, what's going on?" She searched his face for clues. "Wait, please, please, just one sec. I need to finish getting little Gray his cereal." She rushed back to the kitchen and poured the cereal in a bowl. Then gave her son a kiss atop his curls. "Now finish before you get up." She bounced back to the living room.

It wasn't more than two seconds before he called "M-o-m-m-y!" from the kitchen.

Sigh. "In a minute." She yelled back then focused on Bryce. "Okay, okay, what's going on?" Her big brown eyes begged.

Bryce grabbed both of her hands. "Okay, okay…sweetie, I got the part!"

"Which one, you've auditioned for a million?"

"*The* part! The med school series. They want me to fly out to L.A. next week! "He grabbed her. "Aw, babe, this is it, I feel it! "He held her tight and swayed then kissed her lips.

She pulled away, her stomach mixed with equal parts joy and personal disappointment. "Wow, that's great!"

"What's the matter, aren't you happy?" He placed his hands on the sides of her face.

"Yeah, I mean, I'm really happy for you, Bryce." She smiled. "But, just thinking, well, what about *us*?"

"Babe, c'mon. This doesn't change us. The timing couldn't be better! You're almost finished with school. When you're done, I'll send for you." He looked in her eyes.

"What does *that* mean? I'm just supposed to pick up and *stay* with you?" Her eyes pled for a better answer.

"Babe, seriously? Don't ruin the moment. We need to celebrate, get little Gray."

She bit the side of her lip. "Do you mind if I drop him by the shop? I really need a little break. Okay?"

"Yeah, all right. I was thinking we could go to Leela's? Maybe take a carriage ride around the park? Or maybe a quick trip to the beach. OH man, I can't explain to you how good this feels!"

She smiled at the mention of the beach. Just hearing the words made her heart light. She relaxed as she watched his face explode in excitement. *This is his moment*. "Babe, I, I'm really proud of you. I vote for the beach!" she countered with new enthusiasm." I didn't mean to put a damper on things, you really deserve this." She wrapped her arms around his neck and planted a kiss on his lips.

Bryce looked in her eyes. "No, *we* deserve this."

~~~~~

"S-i-e-r-r-a." Maxine was shaking her head.

"But Mom, this is really important. Bryce got a part and he's leaving for L.A. and, well can we just have some alone time? "She begged.

Her mother straightened a rack of blouses then moved about the store with Sierra at her heels. Sweetie, I'm happy for Bryce, but I can't keep watch on Gray *and* work. Why can't you understand that?" She moved to a table and rearranged several bowls of colorful
~~~~~

bracelets. “Look how busy we are.” She smiled at a customer walking by.

“But Mom…”

Finally, her mother stopped to face her. “Sierra, every time you want to ‘celebrate’ something with Bryce, I have to babysit.” She sighed. “This is it, Sierra. I’m here to support you, but I let you guilt me into doing a lot more of my share.” She paused to squeeze her temples. “You better be lucky Amber’s coming in soon.”

Yeah, Amber always saves the day. Sierra planted a kiss on her mother’s face. “Thanks Mom, I appreciate it. I love you.”

Chapter 18 – Salt

Sierra leaned over the rail as sea mist lovingly kissed her face. Bryce watched the subtle breeze tease her hair and the ocean beckon her soul. *If only she were this peaceful all the time.*

She turned to face him then leaned her back against the rail. "Umm, can't you just smell it? The salt, the sea. It's the air I breathe."

He smiled at her and shook his head.

"What?" She twisted her mouth to the side.

"You, you're just so…"

"Poetic? Melancholy?" Her big eyes peered into his.

He smiled. "Yeah, I guess. I just never met anybody more in love with the ocean than you." He brushed a loose hair away from her face then gently rubbed the back of his hand against her cheek. Gonna miss you."

She looked down for a few seconds then up. "You too." She fell into his chest. He held her and stroked the back of her hair.

"C'mon." They took off their shoes, and she grabbed his hand. They eased down the sand to the tide. The gentle tide washed over her feet. She inched her strapless sundress above her knees then let it fall. She turned her face upward as the sun bathed her face. Her face turned upward as the sun warmed her face.

Bryce walked behind her. He wrapped his arms around her waist and nuzzled behind her, the gentle tide dousing the bottom of his linen pants. "Whatchu see out there?"

She sighed and paused. "It's not what I see. It's what I feel."

"Okay, whatcha feelin'?"He kissed her cheek.

"Serenity, peace. Most people look for God in a building. Not me. Traditional church is just a building with a bunch of messed up people. This is where He lives. I can just feel it." She wrapped his arms around her. "If you close your eyes, and listen, you can hear him. If you pick up a shell and listen, he whispers. And heaven? It *has* to be near the ocean. That place where the salt meets the sky."

"You're so sure, huh." He mused.

"Yes."

"Why are you so sure?"

"It's the *only* place that I feel safe."

~~~~~

Maxine was thankful for her business, but it had its challenges. In spite of that, she was proud of something she owned. She had a steady clientele and was known for high end vintage and décor. Hers was a hard fought independence. Most days she counted it a blessing. Other days she'd wished she'd taken the easy way out. *Why of all times did I let my conscience kick in? They owe us all.* She glanced at the door. Her part-time help was running late. She tried to assist the customers while keeping an eye on her grandchild. Frustrated, she finally sent him to the makeshift break room with cookies and his computer.

"Yes, ma'am, can you give me a few more dollars off this Chanel belt?"

Maxine resisted the temptation to suck her teeth. She walked over to the young lady with brunette tendrils, dressed in a peasant dress and cowboy boots. "No, I'm sorry this is the final price. It's in mint condition, a great vintage piece," she said, examining the belt.

The young woman spent a few more minutes inspecting the buckle while Maxine dashed back to the register to check out a customer. Before she knew it, a line of five people had formed.
~~~~~

Where is Amber? On cue, her part-time employee came rushing through the door as usual.

"So sorry, Ms. Sanders, so sorry. Food pantry at church! "She got behind the counter. "I'll take over. "She promptly assisted the next customer.

Maxine was halfway to the stock room when she heard a loud crash. Some of the customers stopped in their tracks, others kept shopping.

She ran to the door. "Little Gray!"

~~~~~

Sierra lay in Bryce's arms. There were people around, but it seemed as if no one else was there. The tide had almost lulled them to sleep as they reclined on the beach. It was the end to a near perfect day.

"Babe, I know you don't ever want to leave, but we have to get back. My roommate's going to be calling soon about his car."

She took a deep breath and rolled on her back. He jumped up, reached down and pulled her up. He grabbed and hugged her. She didn't want to let go. She grabbed a handful of his locs and held them tight. She inhaled the scent of his skin and rubbed her face against his and finally let go.

Just as they reached the boardwalk, Sierra's phone went off. "Mom?" she said after answering.

"Sierra, I don't want you to panic. I'm at the hospital with little Gray." Her voice was calm and fatigued.

"Mom, what happened?" Sierra's body stiffened as she looked at Bryce.

"Your son decided he wanted to climb on the ladder in the back of the store and fell. We're in the emergency room right now."

"Omigod! He okay? I'm leaving right now."
~~~~~

"Gray?" Bryce uttered before she could explain.

She nodded. She began walking in the direction of the car. Bryce followed. "Okay, we are about an hour and twenty minutes away. We'll get there as fast as we can!"

"What? What's going on?" Bryce asked as their pace quickened.

"Little Gray took a fall at the shop. He and my mom are at the hospital."

"Hospital? He okay?"

"Not sure. I just have to get there. "Her eyes were focused ahead.

"Okay, baby wait, hold on." He grabbed her arms and halted her steps. "Look, I'll get you there as quick as possible, but I, I'm not going to be able to stay. I hope that's okay. I'm not even finished packing, and well, we stayed much longer than we'd planned. I'm mean, you understand, don't you?"

"You're not gonna stay?" Her face softened.

He grabbed her hands. "Sierra, please don't do this now. You have to understand. I can't afford to miss this flight in the morning. I have so much to do. Promise, we'll talk and see each other tomorrow before I go." He grabbed the back of her head and kissed her on the forehead.

"But, I need you!" She whined.

"Baby," he took a deep breath, "this time it's about me. I really need to you to understand. No, I'mma need you to grow up. You're his mother, handle this." He sighed. "Sweetie, I'm here, but you're being selfish."

Sierra's heart dropped. "Grow up? I'm being selfish?" Her eyebrows knitted. "If you haven't noticed, I've been raising a child for close to seven years. I get it, it's a convenient excuse. You want to break up before you leave. *Whatever.* Just get me to the hospital."

They finally reached the car, and she stood outside the passenger side with folded arms.

He shook his head. "Unbelievable, are you serious right now? Let's just get to the hospital."

~~~~~~

"I can't believe you're just now calling me." Sierra winced as Grayson Jr. went on a tirade over the cellphone. She eyed her mother a few feet away with two coffee cups. She waved her hand, signaling she'd be there in a minute.

"It was an accident, Grayson. Little boys get into things," She said, trying to convince him and herself it was a minor incident as she walked in a small circle.

"Again, why didn't you try to call me earlier?" His voice was loud enough for any person passing by to hear.

"For the record, I DID call you. I also had you paged at the country club. Can't you get a signal on that cart?" She quickly realized her voice was too loud when the nurse at the station cut her eyes.

"That's not the point. How did this happen, weren't you watching him? Cassie, be quiet I'm trying to get the information! I can't drive, talk on the phone and babysit you, too!"

Jeez...what a prize. "Grayson, listen. He's fine, they just finished the x-rays and are going to put a cast on his arm. Okay? "She crossed her fingers.

"He broke his arm? Little league's about to start!"

"You didn't clear that with me."

"Sierra, never mind, I'm parking. Tell me exactly where you are."

Sierra uttered her exact location and hung up. Her mother walked over and handed her a coffee. Sierra rubbed her forehead.
~~~~~~

"Mom, I'm so tired of him. I hate that this happened. He's always looking for some reason to put me down like I'm so incapable of raising his child."

They both walked toward the nurse's station then sat down and waited on little Gray. "Don't worry about it, sweetie. Gray is fine. It could have been much worse." Sierra nodded then took a sip of coffee.

After several minutes, Sierra heard Grayson Jr.'s voice. "I'm his father!"

She handed her mother her coffee then shot up. "Grayson, Grayson!" Sierra said through clenched lips as she rushed toward him.

"Please tell this woman I am little Gray's father! This is ridiculous."

Do I have to? Sierra's stomach churned at the sight of Grayson and Cassie. *Matching golf outfits? Argyle…Really? He can't even golf!* Cassie took off her cap as they walked and allowed her newly extended hair to fall. "Grayson please, don't make a scene. Hi Cassie."

Cassie gave a polite smile.

Sierra walked toward her trying to decide on the way whether to shake her hand or give her a slight hug. Finally, the awkward hug won. *Who puts on perfume to golf?*

"Look, Grayson, I can understand your concern, but it was a minor accident. I take full responsibility."

Maxine had quickly walked over toward them. "Hey, little Gray is back there and doesn't need to hear everybody argue. He's okay."

"Well, better be glad it wasn't something worse, like a concussion or something." He marched passed them into the room where his son was waiting his brand new cast.

He better be glad I've been delivered. Maxine held her tongue. She brushed her hands down her maxi skirt, then opened and closed her fists.

"Daddy! Mom Cassie!"

Sierra's eyes got big as saucers in response to her son's mistaken identity. "Oh-uh-ah ..." Her nails dug into her mother's arm as her hand grabbed it tight.

Her mother clutched her arm. "Not here."

Chapter 19 – Beginning of the End

"Can you believe it? *Mom* Cassie?" Sierra sat in Bryce's apartment as he waited on his Uber driver.

He was quiet as he peeked through his blinds.

"Bryce, did you hear me?"

Her pause prompted his response. "Sierra, I'm about to leave for L.A. for one of the biggest opportunities in my life. Can we take a five on the baby daddy saga for the moment?" His tone was void of emotion.

She froze at the words "baby daddy." Then calmly spoke. "You're right. I'm really sorry." Her shoulders dropped.

You're always sorry. Bryce turned to face her, sighed and hesitated before he grabbed both her arms. "Sierra, I really care about you and little Gray. I know you're concerned. But things have a way of working out. So can I just have this moment? Please?"

"I didn't mean it. I mean to be so selfish. You've worked so hard for this, and I'm glad I could be a part of this major breakthrough. "Her eyes fell toward the putty colored carpet. *God, can I do anything right?* She released her hands then placed them around his neck. She quietly sang *No matter how far I go*…lyrics to "their" song. She watched his face.

Finally, a smile crept across his face. "Don't know what I'm going to do with you." She grabbed the bottom of his face with her hand and pulled him in for a kiss. Just as their lips touched, a horn blew outside the window. Bryce jumped. "That's the driver!" He reached down for one of his bags.

She grabbed the other one. “Wait, look Bryce,” She rushed toward him and grabbed his hand before it opened the door. “Stop for just a second.”

He paused and turned to face her.

Sierra looked in his eyes. “Baby, you’re gonna make it. I just know it. I, I, I’m praying for you.”

“Did you just say the word ‘pray’? Now, that’s *my* baby. I need a faith walker, somebody that’s got my back. We gotta be that power couple!”

Sierra smiled, quieting her insecurities.

He grabbed the door. “Now, we better get out of here before my ride leaves me!” She walked past him, and he locked the door behind them. “I’m coming, I’m coming,” he shouted, as he rushed the both of them down the stairs. “Right, here…right here!” He wildly raised his hand as he brushed past her.

When he got to the curb, he faced her. “I hate goodbyes.” Water formed in her eyes. He pulled and held her tight against his chest, his hand raking her hair. “I know you love me. Love you, too.” He kissed the side of her head, her forehead then finally kissed her lips.

His touch was warm, sweet…familiar. “Now that’s more like it, “Sierra said as their lips parted.

The driver pressed his horn for several seconds. “Awww, c-mon…what is this, Love Jones?” his raspy voiced blared out the window. “We got places to go!”

Bryce turned toward the car and held up his hands. “All right, man, chill! Okay, babe, this is it.” He winked then released her. “The next time you see me will be on the red carpet.”

“Better be.” Sierra turned away then heard the car door slam. She walked up the street then turned a few seconds later. As the car disappeared down the street, she pressed two fingers against her heart. The space felt tender, like the car had stolen a piece of her with no guarantee of return.

Chapter 20 – Graduation

Sierra stared at her reflection with approval. Her posture, more erect and assured. The one person she thought of was Angela, the counselor she'd talked to in high school. Angela didn't stop their relationship after high school. For her, encouragement was for a lifetime, and she had spent the last several years doing just that for Sierra. Those initial seeds she'd planted were never forgotten. She couldn't wait to put on her cap and gown. *Maybe people in this town will finally respect me.* She wore her hair loose and flowing. Her curly waves extended to the middle of her back. She even took the time to make up her face, including eye shadow *and* mascara. Sierra was about to apply her same "barely there" lip color, but grabbed her red. Her face flushed with happiness as she lined her lips. "There! I finally *feel* grown!" She mused with a half turn.

"You look pretty, Mom-my." Her son had snuck in with a few toys in tow.

She turned around and gushed at how adorable he looked in his blue blazer, white shirt and khakis. "Oh, thank you, my handsome son!" She reached down and gave him a hug and kissed the top of his hair. "Love you!" *He's the best thing that's ever happened to me.* She released him and grabbed a tissue from her dresser.

"Mom, you're 'posed to be happy," he said as he commenced his two toy action figures to a battle. "I will destroy you…"

"I'm *supposed* to be. The word is 'supposed'." She took a deep breath. "Never mind. You're right. I am supposed to be happy." She gently dabbed the tissues to her eyes, then leaned down to plant a kiss against his cheek. "You're such a big boy!" She knelt and adjusted his bow tie. Then grabbed her cellphone for a picture. "Gray, look at Mommy." He was preoccupied with his suspenders. Her son looked up and flashed an instant smile.

"Okay, Mommy, that's it. Just one picture." He refocused on his action figures.

"Oh no, Gray, you'll get dirty. "Her phone began to vibrate.

"Bryce, where *are* you?" She held her breath for the answer.

"Sierra! Hey sweetie, I'm *so* proud of you."

"I know, babe, but where are you? Are you meeting us at the auditorium?"

A few seconds passed. "Sweetie, I tried, but I, I'm not gonna be able to make it. My publicist scheduled an important meeting, and I just wouldn't be able to get back in time. I've only been out here a little over a month and well, I just can't up and leave."

"Since when do you have a publicist? Bryce, the show is not even on the air yet, and it's like this already? You promised!"

"Sierra, I know you're disappointed. If there was *anything* I could do, you know I would. Babe, this was one of the hardest decisions I had to make. I wouldn't have missed this for the world. Everything's been moving lightning fast since I got here. It, it was beyond my control."

The doorbell rang.

"Did my flowers get there yet?"

She held the phone and took a deep breath. "No, but that's probably the delivery now. Bryce, I..."

"Sweetie, please, I'm gonna have to go. I can't talk long. We said this wouldn't be easy, remember? I promise I'll make it up."

She heard a bunch of noise in the background. "I know, but I worked so hard. Maybe it's selfish, but I wanted my man, one of the most important people in my life, to be here. I can't help what I feel." She leaned against the dresser and cradled the phone as she folded her arms.

"Well, how about I get you a plane ticket to LA?"

"*Really?* Really?" She stood upright and bounced on her toes.

"Yep. We'll talk about it in a few days. Text me pictures! Love you, babe."

Sierra opened her mouth as Bryce ended the call. She looked at the phone as her chest deflated. "Love you, too."

~~~~~

"Omigod! I thought it was flowers from Bryce, but this is so much better!" Sierra ran over to her friend Zoe and grabbed her. She about squeezed the air from her petite body. "My sister, my friend." Tears immediately fell from her eyes.

"I wanted to surprise you!" Zoe broke from their embrace. "Oh, c'mon on now, you can't mess up this gorgeous makeup."

"I just can't…" She held her hand over her eyes. "This was the best." Sierra finally looked at her mother then back at Zoe. "Mom, can you believe this?" She grabbed her friend's hands and stepped back. "And she's gorgeous! All right, Ms. Georgia Peach!"

"Me? Look at you? Look at this hair!" She pulled a few strands of Sierra's hair and allowed it to float back to her shoulder. "Girl, you know people pay for this kind of hair, right? And your makeup is perfection! You look fabulous, chick!"

They both laughed and gushed like school girls.

Zoe suddenly gasped as her eyes fell on Sierra's necklace. "You made that? It's gor-geous."Zoe eyed the mother of pearl and onyx creation.

"When you leave, it's yours!" Sierra grabbed Zoe and hugged her again.
~~~~~

"So, I *can* keep a secret," Maxine interjected with pride.

"Wow, this *almost* makes up for Bryce." Sierra hugged her mother.

"He's not coming?" Zoe's eyes widened.

Before Sierra could answer, little Gray ran in the room. "Aunt ZZZZ!"

"Little Gray! Come here. That's my big boy." Zoe knelt as he landed in her arms for a generous hug.

Sierra's heart was full of equal parts joy and sadness. She smiled at how much love Zoe poured out on her Godson. "So, when are you and Marcus going to get of that career train and start a family?" Sierra asked.

Zoe released little Gray. "Well…" She rubbed her belly as she lit up the room with her smile.

"Noooo!"

"Yes!" Zoe confirmed. They both squealed.

"Oh, congratulations, sweetie." Maxine hugged them both. "Okay, ladies, we need to get this show on the road because my baby's graduating today!"

~~~~~

"Nobody puts baby in the corner!" Sierra barked.

"That's easy, duh, Dirty Dancing!" Zoe kept focus on the humongous collection of vintage DVDs in her parents' media room.

Sierra was still stunned her best friend flew in for her big day. After the festivities it was nice for the two of them to hang out like old times. It took the sting out her disappointment with Bryce. Soon, they'd be in the midst of an old school movie marathon, like back in the day. Sparkle, Dreamgirls, The Best Man and Brown Sugar DVDs littered the floor. While Zoe finished scanning the shelves of movies, the popcorn machine was in full operation. Sierra
~~~~~

flipped through the cable channels as the smell of hot butter filled the air.

Just like old times. Sierra leaned back against the headrest to relax. "Girl, I used to come over here just to get peace. I used to pretend your parents were mine, and we were real sisters. "Before she got too melancholy, she changed the subject. "Wow, your parents are living it up now that you're out the house." She looked around at the roomy den now transformed to a media room.

"Really, I can't keep up with them. But they can do a drive or fly-by to Atlanta in a minute! They can't wait to be grandparents." She stacked DVDs on the nearby table.

"Girl, how many movies you think we're gonna watch?" Sierra continued flipping channels. "Ooh, I love the E-channel, especially the Fashion Police." She turned up the volume. "I'm such a celeb junkie. Love the host. Look at that dress. Must be a premiere."

They watched as the correspondent thrust a mic toward a young actress.

"So what are you wearing?" the correspondent asked.

Sierra squinted. "She looks familiar, but don't recognize the girl she's interviewing. That dress is a Zac Posen, I know it. Really pretty." Sierra threw some popcorn in her mouth, her eyes still fixed on the screen.

"Yeah, seen her popping up recently," Zoe echoed.

Sierra's forehead creased. "Ugh, what is her name? This is bugging me!"

"I think she's that model-turned actress from that new Girlfriend-like series, *Sunday Brunch* on Bravo." Zoe finally dropped in her chair.

"Is that your date in the background?" the correspondent asked.

Sierra imagined herself in a designer gown, arm in arm with Bryce one day.

"Yes," the young actress replied, gushing. "He's starring in an upcoming drama series." She waved him over toward the camera. "This is Bryce Wayman."

Sierra's eyes bulged. She jumped up and screamed while knocking the entire bowl of popcorn on the floor. "Omigod! Did she say *Bryce Wayman*?"She put her hands on top of her head. Her eyes grew large as saucers. "No, can't be. I'm gonna *kill* him. How could I be *so* stupid?" She slapped her forehead.

Zoe froze as she stared at the huge flat screen. "Omigod. Bryce? Noooo. That *is* him." She looked at her friend, trying to grab the words circling her brain. "Sierra, I, I, I'm so sorry. Gosh, he cut his gorgeous locs." She placed her hand over her mouth.

Sierra paced across the carpet. "This is a wrap!" She threw her hands up. "What did *I* do to deserve this life?" she yelled. Zoe winced. "One disappointment after another." She stopped in front of Zoe and pointed at her face. "Even you, Zoe. *You* let me down. Never wanted to say it, but there it is. You hurt me, too!"

Zoe's eyes focused. "Me? What did I do? I've *always* been here for you. Through everything!"

"*You* left. There I said. And you changed." Sierra's voice grew louder. "I'll never forget how you acted when I came to visit you at Spelman. You and your *sorority* sisters. You acted like you were ashamed, all stuck up. Besides, you were supposed to be with me at fashion school, not Spelman. *You* reneged on our plans. You didn't have the guts to tell your mother you wanted to go to design school!" Sierra dropped to the carpeted step and covered her eyes.

Zoe stood and stepped in front her. "I'm sorry you felt that way, and it wasn't intended to hurt you. But it's not fair for you to group all this together. I haven't changed, I've *grown*. Spelman was *my* choice. Yes, I love to sew and design clothes, but you know how excited I was once I went to visit. I knew in my spirit that's where I belonged. The history, the sisterhood, it's hard to explain. You're still my sister, my best friend. I've always had your back."

"Whatever, Zoe. You always thought you were better than me anyway. Well, guess what? I'm not your pity project anymore. You and your college friends can go on with your perfect lives." Sierra knew immediately her words were a mistake. She watched Zoe's eyes narrow and her chest rise and fall.

"Sierra," Zoe paused. "Sierra, I've been for you so much it's made me sick. For your information, my life isn't perfect. I'm blessed, but blessings come with responsibility. I'm a newlywed, I have a good husband, but marriage is not easy *and* I have a baby on the way. Half the time I can't tell you any of my problems because we're too busy fixing yours. I spent my hard-earned money to come here for your special day. And you have the audacity to whine, complain and go on a rant?"

Sierra stared at the one person whom she called a friend, feeling doubly betrayed. But she couldn't form words to speak.

"I have prayed and walked you through some of the darkest moments of your life. And I've had enough! I'm in a new season of my life and," Zoe paused to take a breath, "well, I have to take care of me." She put her hand on her hip. "Sierra, you may not understand, but at some point, you're gonna have to walk this thing out with God alone."

"Walk *what* out?" Sierra had calm, measured words.

"Life. God...salvation. Nothing comes easy. We all have our turn at the wheel. As long as you keep making everybody responsible for your happiness, you'll run them off. It's called co-dependency. I hate the break the news, God's not gonna give you anything, including Bryce until He's got your full attention. And for the record, Spelman was *God's* plan. For once I wasn't spending all my time saving Sierra. For once I was supported and surrounded by positive women who held *me* up. He sent me to Atlanta to meet me husband. I love you, Sierra, but I have nothing else to give you right now."

Sierra trembled. She paused before she spat her pain-soaked words. "Zoe, fine. Thanks for your friendship. Sorry it was such a burden and you were that miserable." She wanted to feel bold, but all her gut was saying was she was about to lose her friend.

"Sierra, can you please." Zoe paused. "This woe is me attitude will push anybody away." Zoe regretted her last words as soon as they fell off her lips.

Sierra blinked and mentally gasped. "Thanks, Zoe. Thanks a lot." She spoke soft and pointedly. "I appreciate you coming. I promise, from now on, Sierra will be responsible for Sierra." She rushed to the door. As much as Zoe wanted to follow, God spoke loud and clear, "Let her go."

Sierra marched with defiance until she stepped out the house. She wanted to hear Zoe's voice call her name, but she knew this time she wouldn't. When she continued to walk, the reality of what just happened set in. She lost her boyfriend and best friend on the same day. Her chest caved. She continued up the block as two fresh wounds pierced her heart. She walked and walked…but refused to cry.

Chapter 21 – Broken Glass

"Mom!" Little Gray shot into the kitchen.

Sierra sighed. "In a minute," she replied, her teeth clenched. She grabbed one of several glasses off the counter to finish loading the dishwasher.

"Mommy!"

She abruptly turned and knocked a glass off the counter. "Little Gray, look what you made me do…get out of here! Go to your grand…"

Before she could finish her sentence, her mother rushed in. "Sierra! You've been yelling at this baby all day. What's wrong with you?" She removed her reading glasses and placed her magazine under her arm.

"Sor-ry, I couldn't find my tablet so I could play my game, "little Gray said, his eyes large and apologetic.

Sierra brushed past him to get the broom. "Move, Gray, so you won't step on all this glass."

"Gray, go upstairs. Grandmommy will help you in a minute." Maxine kept her eyes on Sierra.

"Mom. Mom, I didn't mean it," little Gray pled, still gazing up at his mother.

Sierra placed the broom against the counter and knelt. "I know, baby." She looked him in his eyes. "Now go upstairs like Grandma said." She walked him around the splattered glass then grabbed the broom, purposefully avoiding her mother's glare.

"You wanna to tell me what's wrong with you?" Maxine asked, her hand placed on her hip.

Sierra rolled her eyes up toward the ceiling. "Nothing, Mom, I got this." She continued sweeping the glass into a dustpan.

"Well, *nothing* has you acting mighty ugly right now." Maxine kept her eyes on her daughter.

"Ma, just leave it alone." She dumped the remaining glass in the trash.

"No, I'm not gonna leave it alone. You been slumping around about to bite everybody's head off. It's about Bryce, isn't it? Maybe you wouldn't take it out on everybody if you'd answer the man's calls."

Sierra tugged on the scarf that held her thick hair at bay. "Okay, Ma, yeah, I'm ticked off. But when did *you* become such a relationship expert? When's the last time *you* had a man?" She rolled her eyes, then turned to put the broom back in the closet. "As a matter of fact," she continued, marching back toward her mother, "when did you become qualified to give advice about *anything*? The fact that I can't keep a relationship is *your* fault. Yeah, I said it. As a matter of fact, our address *should* be 2500 Dysfunction Street." She stormed toward the living room.

Maxine paused before walking behind her. She grabbed Sierra's shoulder. "Look at me. I said *look* at me."

"What, Ma? What do you want from me? Credit for cleaning up your life? Fine." She clapped her hands once. "Congratulations. But you still screwed up mine." She threw her hands up and let them slap the sides of her ripped denim jeans. "Of *course* I can't communicate with a man. Of *course* I'm clingy. Of *course* I'm needy. I'm co-dependent! Never mind, forget it!" She headed for the door.

"Sierra, I deserve that. I'm glad you didn't hold back." Her mother shook her head. "I'm not sure what I can do. I can't change my mistakes. I've said I'm sorry a thousand times. I don't have a man because I feel like I don't deserve one. I sacrificed the last decent relationship I had. Why? He was always on me about you. How I spoiled you, treated you like you were still ten. But I didn't care. I'm trying to be here for you and little Gray now. I can't make up for everything, but I'm trying."

Sierra was silent. She just stood there taking deep breathes and tapping her foot.

"You know," her mother folded her arms, "do you think you're the only woman who's ever fallen in love? Been hurt? *Puleeaze.* If you want Bryce, you could have him. You're just afraid you're gonna mess it up. Trust me, I've been there." Maxine's heart burned at the thought of her greatest love, biggest mistake and most guarded secret.

Sierra looked her mother in the eye. "He said he'd never lie to me, ever." Her lips quivered. "I'm not afraid, Mom." She swallowed. "I'm broken."

Chapter 22 – Salty

It took a little over two months after Bryce and Zoe left Sierra's life for her to begin to release some of her anger. Bitterness bound her body and refused to let go. Bryce's calls ceased after several weeks. Zoe hadn't called at all, and Sierra declared them both dead. She resolved to do what everybody thought she couldn't–stand. She focused on her son, jewelry making, and finding a real job. In between she helped out at Deja Reaux.

Sierra inspected the images on the computer screen and clicked a few pages. "There, finished!" She smiled, proud at the completed work. She walked from storage/office area into the floor of the store. "Mom, can you come here for a minute?" She noticed her mother chatting with a customer. "Mom, can you come back here?" She said, unable to contain her excitement.

Her mother ended her conversation and briskly walked toward her daughter. "Why are you acting like something's on fire?"

"Just come back here." She held back the long velvet curtain. "Look!" Sierra pointed toward the computer. "My website! You like it?"

Her mother looked at the computer screen. "Wow, that's beautiful. You did this yourself?"

Sierra nodded. "And a Facebook page!" Sierra tapped on a few keys. "I'm trying to do all I can to get my collection out there. I mean the pieces are selling at the boutique, but that's not enough.

"Huh…isn't that something, "her mother said, looking at the computer screen. "Well, now that I know you have these extra talents, what is it going to cost to get a website for the store?"

"That's what I'd *thought* you'd say. Voila!" Sierra typed in an address and proudly displayed their new store website.

"Oh Sierra, this is beautiful!"

"Ma, are you tearing up?" She placed her arm around her mother's shoulder.

"No!"

"Well, I'm taking a break, I think I've earned it. I'll run and grab us some lunch."

"Yes, you do. And your timing's perfect. I'm famished. See if Amber wants something on the way out," her mother said, still smiling and gazing at the screen.

~~~~~

Maxine hummed on her way back to the store floor. She straightened a few racks and watched as the postman came in to deliver the mail. Her heart instantly dropped.

"Oh shoot." She watched as her regular carrier Gabe came in the store. "Hey Gabe."

He walked toward her and handed her a pack of several thick letters and had her sign off on the certified letter slip.

"Hey Maxi, you have a good day now." He stared at a female shopper on the way out. She didn't need to guess what was in the letters. She rubbed her forehead with one hand as her heart began to beat faster. *Just when you think things are going good.* She placed her hand on the side of her hip. *Not today, Satan.*

~~~~~

While Sierra waited on her order, she watched a couple and their children laughing and full of joy at a nearby table. A little boy was perched on the man's lap and pulling off his glasses. The woman was glowing as she held her daughter. Sierra sighed. *God, will I ever have that?* She suddenly missed her son who she was sure was having the best time at a birthday party.

On the way back, she made a quick stop at the drugstore to glance at magazines. She paused to glance over the glossy pictures touting the who's who of society feature. She flipped a few pages and stopped cold. Mr. and Mrs. Grayson Grier, Jr. *Ugh!* She couldn't deny they made a handsome couple. She recognized Cassie's dress from a Tracy Reese collection. Sierra could spot designers. She always visualized her jewelry in their shows. *Lord, the foulest people seem to live the best lives.* She stared closely at Cassie's face. *I guess she is pretty. Maybe it's the weave.*

All of a sudden, she didn't feel guilty about kissing Grayson. All of a sudden, she felt he owed her that and more. All of a sudden she felt like Cassie stole her life. *C'mon Sierra, would you have really been happy as Mrs. Grayson Grier, Jr.? Bryce was supposed to make up for how he threw me away like a bucket of trash. The way he betrayed me. He was supposed to make everyone see I was worth something.* Her eyes watered. She immediately closed the book, leaving it and her heartache back on the shelf.

Chapter 23 – Red, White and Broke

Maxine rubbed the back of her neck while she waited on a response.

"Ms. Sanders, there's nothing else I can do. You may want to try to contact a tax attorney."

I hate this place. I hate the long wait, the rude staff, that stupid voice recording announcing the number for service... "Now serving the next loser who can't pay their taxes and needs to beg for mercy..." I hate the walk back to the cubicles void of all privacy. Why can't I be part of the one percent? "But sir, I've done so well up to this point. Besides, I never really owed all that money..."

The man behind the desk had no expression. He waited for a break in her run of sentences so he could speak.

"I even had another accountant review, but it was too late for an amendment ...you all, well whoever applied my payments to the wrong year and it looked like I hadn't paid. But they fixed that." She pressed her palms against her black slacks.

"Ms. Sanders, I would love to help you, but my hands are tied." He swiveled his chair to face the computer again. His nose wrinkled as he scrolled further down.

Please God, give me some sign there's a chance. She looked behind the desk of the IRS agent and saw a Bible lying open with yellow highlights. Behind him was a series of children's drawings and a family photo. Maxine allowed the weight of her body to fall back against her chair. She closed her eyes shut for a second or two. "Sir, it's been a rough road. I've rebuilt my life *and* my business. I just can't afford to..."

He raised his finger toward her as a sign to stop talking. He finally looked in her direction. He rubbed his thumbs together. He relaxed his shoulders and leaned toward her. "*Ms.* Sanders, let me see what I can do. You have to keep in mind, I have to answer to somebody. Try to understand."

"Yes, sir, I know." She felt strange calling a man that appeared close to her same age "sir."

Please Jesus, please. I know he is a man of God.

"Maybe we can set up another installment agreement. Can you at least pay what you owe from the last year?"

If I could do that, I wouldn't be here, Einstein. "I, I don't know…that's still a lot of money," she said, deflated.

"Well, see what you can do, and I'll see what I can do on my end." He gave a half smile. "Let's make an appointment for next week at this same time and see where we're at. In the meantime, we will stay any liens or other actions."

"Thank you, thank you. I appreciate it."

As Maxine walked out the office, she knew what her options were. *I'm just going to have to put my pride aside.* If she wanted to save her business and her home, she had to go to the only person she knew, and it was going to kill her. In that moment she wished she had one friend, someone she could be extremely transparent with. Although she'd been attending bible study for months, she wouldn't dare get this personal.

Chapter 24 – Loft Talk

Maxine couldn't decide whether to knock or use the key she retrieved from front desk. She slid the key in the slot and the little green light blinked. Entering, she was relieved to be alone. She paced as she bit the side of her thumb, then paused and closed her eyes. *God, is this my answer?* She removed her trench and rested on the King size bed. She tried to ignore the plushness of the cotton duvet. All she wanted to do was lay back and pretend she was on an exotic vacation. But she sat, rubbing her forehead. *What am I doing?* She was just about to jump from the bed to make her escape when the door eased open. Her back straightened.

Seconds later, Grayson Sr. slithered in. He closed the door behind him and momentarily lingered his gaze on her presence. He took several steps toward her. "Maxine, I'm really glad you called." He was dressed down in a button down shirt, blazer and slacks.

She shook her head slightly. "Grayson, please don't get confused. It's business."

He put his hands up, "I got it. You look, um beautiful, as always." He walked over and kissed her on the cheek. "I can say that, right?"

Normally, she'd pull away. *It's just a kiss on the cheek. Can't be ugly asking for favors.* When he planted the soft kiss, her insides warmed. She immediately spoke up. "Grayson, let me get straight to the point."

He removed a cigar from inside his blazer and held it between his fingers.

"It's a non-smoking room." She moved away a few feet and looked out the sliding glass doors.

"Maxine. I own the place. He wet the end of the cigar with his mouth as he kept his eye on her.

She turned quickly toward his direction. "You didn't smoke until after you married her."

His mouth crawled to a smile. "You know me better than anyone else."

She immediately moved toward the gray tufted couch and eyed the clean lines of the room for the first time. She sat down and placed her head in her hands.

"Maxi, hey, it's me. Tell me what's going on?"He sat next to her, and then placed the cigar back in his pocket. He removed her hands to search her eyes.

"Don't make this more difficult." She bit her lip and looked toward the ceiling.

"Maxi, look at me," he insisted. His brow furrowed. "Hey, where's that tougher than leather woman from the deep Bayou?"

"Grayson, how'd I get here? I mean we *both* had dreams." She finally looked him in the face. "But I'm still struggling."

"Yeah, from the *deep* country." He took a deep breath.

She looked around the room. "But, you, you made it." She brushed a ringlet of auburn hair from her face then tucked a loose hair in her updo.

"Yeah, I guess you can say that." He took a deep breath. "But at least you have your integrity."

"Ha, that's a laugh." She wiped tears forming with the sleeve of her blouse. "I'm an alcoholic. Haven't had a drink in at least five years, but AA still calls me an alcoholic. I tried doing things the right way, but I just can't seem to get over the hump." She shook her head. "When I think I'm getting a breakthrough, I find my behind right on the floor."Her eyes fell to the carpet.

"Don't be so hard yourself." His finger lifted her chin. "You're your worst enemy. You are strong, and you have a lot to be proud of." He shook his head. "Maxi, it's your pride. You don't have to struggle like this. You can have whatever you want." He moved in closer.

Maxine shot up. She adjusted her clothes. "No! Not that way. I made a vow to God. Repentance does *not* mean repeat the same sin. Your help always came with a price. I don't know why I thought this time would be any different." She uttered in a low voice, "And this, this feels wrong. Sorry, I'm sorry, but I, I gotta go." She walked over to the bed and snatched her purse.

He jumped up, grabbed her from behind and pulled her toward him. He buried his nose in her hair. He held on tight and inhaled her scent. "Maxi, sorry. Please, please don't go."

She felt a burning sensation against her neck. *Please God, give me strength.* She wrangled from his arms. "Grayson, no." Once free, she turned to face him. "I need money, but not this way."

He took a deep sigh. "You know I can't help myself." He looked at her face for any sign of weakness. Then swallowed. "Okay, all right. What do you need?"

She looked in his eyes. "It's really that simple, huh? Who are you kidding? It's never been that simple with Grayson Grier, Sr."

"Maxi, *how much*?" He grabbed and held her hands.

She looked away and took a deep breath.

He let go and placed his palms on her face. "Look at me." He waited until their eyes made contact.

She took a deep breath; her eyelids gently bounced. "Grayson, it's serious."

Her voice unintentionally soothed him like pillow talk. "Maxi…how much?"

“Fifty-thousand,” she admitted as her shoulders dropped. “I messed up, it was interest, and I missed some payments, but I’m trying so hard. It’s like drowning. Just when I think I get ahead…”

“That’s all?” He grabbed her hand. Then pulled her toward him again and whispered near her ear, “Done.” He walked her toward the bed and they both sat. “Wasn’t that easy?”

For you.

He rubbed her back. “The Maxi I know doesn’t fold, she fights!”

She sucked her teeth. “I thought once I left Louisiana I wouldn’t have to beg for anything again. But here I am, begging you for crumbs. I’m forty-three, and you still have to clean up my mess.”

“You’re not begging.” He rubbed her leg. Maxine didn’t move, but her insides were bubbling over. After a few seconds, she placed her hand over his and removed it.

He moved in slowly to kiss her. His cologne eased around her like a soft caress.

The devil sure knows how to do it. Before she knew, it she was down on the bed with him stretched alongside her. His hand untied the bow of her Chiffon blouse while he planted whisper soft kisses around her neck and ear.

“No,” she firmly yet quietly uttered, then pushed him away. “I can’t do this. I, I *won’t* do this.” Her voice trembled. “Grayson, you chose to marry *her*, remember? You didn’t love her, you loved me. I was there for the worst times. You didn’t marry her. You married status, comfort…good breeding. And you knew it almost killed me. I, I never touched a drink until…” She turned her face from him. “Never mind.”

“Maxi, I never promised I’d marry you. I promised to be there for you. I promised to take care of you and I did. Let’s face it, you wouldn’t want this life. Would you? This world, well it wasn’t what you wanted it." His hand swept across the room. "It's not made for you. And well it's a part of me."

Her forehead creased. "Do you hear yourself? *This world?* Her eyes widened, and she shook her head. "You can't be this messed up. The moment you met Lydia, no Bencil, you were in. You didn't even have the guts to tell me about the engagement. I had to hear it from him."

He paused and thought about his next words. "That's *not* true. It wasn't that easy or simple," he said slowly.

"Well, it sure felt like it. All Bencil had to do was plant that seed."

"Look, Bencil," he tempered his words, "Bencil helped me become the businessman I am today. I owe him a lot. But I'm my own man. I make my own decisions." His throat tightened.

"Are you sure that's it? He's got some kind of stronghold on you." Her words sped up. "But, it doesn't matter. Whatever it is has nothing to do with me." She composed herself. "You know, I may not have been your arm piece, but I have peace at night." She shot from the bed with resolve.

"Maxi, it's not what you think." He hesitated. "It's complicated," he quickly added.

"It's complicated? It's complicated?" She rolled her eyes. "Negro, puleaaze, that's a Facebook status."

He stood and moved close to her face. "Look, I *hustled.* And yeah, Bencil and I managed to amass wealth our kind rarely gets. Money, power and respect. I'm not going to apologize for it." He abruptly turned and walked to the wet bar. He poured himself a glass of cognac.

Before she could remind him he didn't drink, she watched him throw his glass back. "I do a lot of things I never used to," he said as if reading her mind then slammed the thick etched glass on the counter top.

She folded her arms. "What happened to the Grayson I knew? Was all this worth it?" He looked away and rubbed his forehead. "How can you ask that question? We came from *nothing.*" He poured another glass of cognac. "Yes, Maxi." He thought some more. "Yes, Yes!" he screamed. "It was *all* worth it! I won't ever be hungry, homeless, and dirty, scared or emasculated again. It was worth it even though it cost me the woman I lov–" He closed his eyes for a few seconds. "Look, you want the money or not? I have to travel in the morning."

She rubbed the back of her neck, literally feeling tension and knots. "No Grayson." She swallowed. "I apologize for wasting your time. But, I thought, well this is my answer." She threw on her trench on her arm and walked toward the door.

"Maxine! Where you going?" He rushed toward her. "I said I'd give you the money." He snatched her arm.

She pulled away. He grabbed her and pushed her back against the door. He reached for her lips with his fingertip, and she jumped at his touch. She felt his breath near her lips. He kissed her.

She opened her mouth as her body went limp. After a few moments, she snapped to reality as she wrestled against his weight. He pressed harder against her and pinned her arms against the wall. Finally, she finally bit his lip and kneed him in the groin. His legs buckled. She watched as coughed. While still hunched over, he spat an expletive. Her eyes grew wide. *He never called me out of my name.*

He coughed with one hand over his groin area. "Bencil said you were gonna drag me back down in the gutter. He knew."

"Bencil?" Maxine's eyes grew wide. "You know what? Both of you can go to straight to hell. I'm outta here." She threw open the door and slammed it with such force it shook the hallway.

She rushed around the corner and pressed the elevator button quickly. Once in the elevator, she leaned against the wall as tears fell. *Okay God, what now?*

Chapter 25 – Identity Crisis

Grayson Jr. slid into the bed shirtless in drawstring pajama bottoms. His wife used to love the muscular indentions of his extra defined chest. She would long for the smoothness of his cocoa brown skin and the brush of his supple lips against her neck. And those eyes could gently seduce her into just about anything. These days Cassie made sure she was under the comforter and turned away before he got into bed. Grayson reached over and pressed his lips against her neck. He figured a good romantic night with his wife would keep him straight in Vegas. When she didn't respond, he knew it was going to be one of those nights he'd have to work for it.

"Babe." Grayson reached up her silk nightgown. She jumped at his touch.

"Your hands are cold."

"C'mon, babe." He brushed her hair away and kissed her earlobe.

She finally rolled over. He took it as a sign and pressed his lips against hers.

Soon, she slid her arm through his and pulled herself closer. He knew exactly where to touch her in a way she couldn't resist. She ignored the taste of brandy that laced his mouth and doused his breath.

He rolled atop her. "Sierra," he whispered into her ear.

Cassie's body froze. She couldn't even blink. She wanted to pretend she hadn't heard it. But she did. She instantly punched her palms against his chest in protest. "Grayson!" she yelled, slapping his bulging pecs.

"What, what are you doing?" He asked, the weight of his body pressed against her.

"Get the off me!" Finally, she was able to free herself.

He rolled over and sat up. Then scratched his head. "What's wrong? Are you crazy?" His heart raced.

"What's wrong with *me*? What's wrong with you? I'm NOT Sierra."

He scratched his head. "You must be crazy. I didn't call you Sierra! Are you out of your mind?"

"Grayson, uh-ah. Not *this* time…that mind game is not going to work with me! I'm your wife…not your baby's momma, or whatever chick you've been with. I'm your wife, and I deserve respect." She took the framed photo of the two of them from the nightstand and threw it across the room before running from the room, slamming the door behind her.

He didn't try to go after her.

I really messed this up this time.

Chapter 26 – Get Jets

Grayson Sr. lowered his head as he stepped inside his jet. He used to pause to inhale the leather interior of his once prized possession. But today he simply slinked past his business partner and dropped in his seat.

"'Bout time." Bencil immediately went back to reading his Wall Street Journal.

"Look, you know I'm always up before you getting my run in. Besides, you can't leave without me. I own the plane."

"Half. You own half the plane," Bencil uttered, and turned a page. "Tried to call you last night. Just to check in."

Grayson leaned back. "Early night," he quipped, and then shut his eyes.

A few seconds later, his son rushed in, his overnight bag in tow and mirrored Ray Bans atop his head. "Hey," he uttered as he walked toward the back. After putting away his bag, he slid in a seat and pulled his shades over his eyes.

Bencil cupped his hands over his mouth like a megaphone. "Okay, maybe you all didn't get the memo. Private party, The Bellagio. *My* birthday. I'mma need you tired fools to get some energy 'cause you bringing my spirits way down!"

Grayson Jr. rolled his eyes behind his glasses then peered out the window. *Old behind.*

"Whatever, man." Grayson Sr. grabbed a pillow, placed it behind his head and turned away.

Bencil shook his head. *Tired.* "Y'all better find something before we touch down in Vegas, especially you Godson. It's a wifey-free weekend."

Grayson Jr. grinned. "Right." Then slid his headphones on. Wife was a word he didn't want to hear, especially after the cold sendoff he got that morning. Cassie was boiling, and this Vegas trip wasn't going to help.

~~~~~

Bencil walked into the elegant foyer of The Bank, the hotel's nightclub. He slowly navigated through the clusters of people stopping every few minutes to talk. He finally reached Grayson Sr. and his Godson clad in custom tuxes and flanked by other guests.

"Man, y'all have been holed up over here all night," he said as he signaled for another drink.

"You're the man of the hour. Long as you're having a good time," Grayson Sr. replied, raising his glass, "that's all that matters."

"Yeah, yeah." Bencil was instantly distracted by a woman passing by with robust cleavage and wearing a sequined mini-dress. Their eyes locked. She tossed her hair, then walked over and whispered in his ear.

Grayson Jr. shook his head. "Happy Birthday, man!"

Bencil nodded. "It will be."

Grayson Sr. watched as Bencil continued to flirt with every woman in his midst. "Welp, guess you gonna be a bachelor for life," he said to Bencil. "Don't see how you keep up. Gotta get tired of this." Grayson Sr. sensed a headache coming on. All he could do was picture the nice suite he left upstairs and how he'd like to be buried deep in the Egyptian cotton sheets and comforter ordering room service.

"Of what? Fine women and fine liquor? And did I say fine women? All shapes, nationalities, hair textures and colors."

"I guess. Honestly, I'm talking about all of it. It's time to retire, man. We've made enough money for three lifetimes."
~~~~~

Bencil's eyes narrowed. "Man, you've been drinking too much? Real estate market's in the toilet and the economy barely has a pulse. That stock market's got to come roaring back." He sipped his drink. "I'm allergic to being broke." He looked him in the eye and raised a brow. "Besides I say when."

Grayson Sr. adjusted his bow tie and cleared his throat. He grinned and softly punched him in the arm. "Man, don't be so serious. I'm just staying, nothing wrong with slowing down. Here we are almost two decades after my wedding, and you still running these streets."

Bencil leaned over and whispered, "We both know Lydia was necessary."

"Man, don't start. I'd already made us both a grip when you introduced us." He gritted his teeth and smiled as a few people passed by.

"True, but she gave you the one thing you were missing…status."

Whatever. Grayson Sr. wanted to be mad. He wanted to tell him exactly how he felt.

But he knew this was a man that bought and sold his freedom. As much as he thought he was free, the secrets they shared would tie them together forever.

And Bencil knew it.

Chapter 27 – Keep Your Frenemies Closer

With her husband away, Cassie decided to take a quick trip to the city. Once in Manhattan, she walked for blocks. She spent hours with her personal shopper at Barneys but failed to walk away with a purchase. She knew something was wrong. Before she knew it, she found herself on a bench in Central Park. To her surprise, it was the most relaxed she'd been in a while. It was one event, dinner or commitment after the other. All about Grayson Grier, Jr. and his family.

She removed a pocket sized journal from her purse. Moments later, the grumble in her stomach forced the pages shut. *Wow, no wonder. It's been hours since I ate*, she confirmed after glancing at her timepiece. She threw the journal in her purse, destined to the concrete jungle in search of a meal.

She walked a short distance then stopped dead in her tracks when she saw a young woman turn the corner. *Naw, couldn't be.Sierra?* She rushed across the street and turned the corner just in time to see the woman step in a sandwich shop. She sped up. *Wait, what am I doing?* She paused a few feet from the door. Then she went in. She figured this was as good a time as any to talk to the woman her husband might still be in love with. A deli wasn't her choice at the moment, but it would have to do. *Probably have salad on the menu.*

She popped into the doorway and had to maneuver through a few people blocking her path. She finally spotted Sierra toward the rear of the place, her back facing the entrance. *So I wasn't seeing things.* She eased up to the table. "Sierra," she blurted a bit too loud.

Sierra jumped and spilled a little tea on her blouse. *Oh no, can't be.* She slowly turned around. "Cassidy?"

She walked over. "Cassie's fine." She stood there for a minute, waiting for Sierra to offer a seat.

"Ma'am, can I take your order?" The waiter rushed over. Sierra sighed. She shook her head and rolled her eyes. "Go on," she said, nodding toward the wooden seat at the table.

After Cassie ordered, she sat quietly, somewhat waiting for permission to speak. *I can pretend to be anyone's friend to get what I want.* "So, isn't this something? What a coincidence."

Sierra bit into her sandwich. "What?"

"You, me running into each other like this?" Cassie faked a smile and let out a nervous laugh.

"Yeah, I guess." Sierra crushed a few saltines and sprinkled them over her soup.

Silence.

Cassie looked around and started to whistle. "Soooo, what are you doing in the city today?"

Sierra winced. "Uh, can you spare us the whistle?"

"Right." Cassie placed the napkin on her lap. "Whistling in public, bad manners." She strummed her fingers on the table. "I was saying what brings you to the city."

"I was on a shopping spree. Don't you see all my bags?" Sierra rolled her eyes again.

"Oh, ha...you were being funny!" Cassie hit the table with her hand.

Sierra bit her sandwich and chewed for a few seconds. Then put it down. "Okay, Cassie, what do you want? We barely say two or three words to each other." She wiped her mouth with a napkin. She continued to devour her sandwich. Famished, the last thing she was expecting was a lunch date with Cassie. Emily Post left the building a long time ago. "If you must know, I had an interview today." *Which went horrible by the way.*

The waiter returned with Cassie's salad.

Sierra's eyes widened. "Is that *all* you're going to eat? Of course, never mind."

"I guess so." Cassie bit the side of her lip. "You know what? I'm gonna get a dessert. I guess I can walk on the wild side!"

"Wow, you're such a rebel." Sierra kept eating.

"So, how'd the interview go, who was it with?" *Like I care?*

"A firm that produces fashion shows." She bit on her pickle and chewed, loud.

"Well, that's something. Um, forgive me, but I didn't know you were into fashion."

Sierra paused. "Hello, that's why I went to F.I.T.I design jewelry, but I have to start somewhere. And for your information, the interview sucked, which is why I'm about to inhale this piece of chocolate fudge cake."

"Oh, I just thought you worked at your mother's store."

Give me a break.

"Okay, Sierra, I was just thinking. Neither one of us are going away. I mean, I'm little Gray's stepmother and you're his mother. Anyway, I think he's latched on to me, and I think I'm pretty great with him."

Omigod, I just want to stab myself. Can someone get me out of here? Sierra stopped eating. "Cassie, I'm a cut and dry kinda girl…and your point would be?"

"I just think we should try to get to know each other a little better. I mean spend some time together…just you and me."

Sierra took a sip of her drink. She didn't say a word for several seconds.

Cassie grew nervous. *Say something, Cassie. A compliment, yeah that's good.* "You know, you have beautiful hair. It's so thick, healthy and…" She cleared her throat.

"Real."

"Um, yeah. I guess, real." Cassie shifted as she remembered she forgot to call her hairstylist to freshen her weave.

I'm hip to your whole keep your enemies close game. You're worried about the wrong person. "Look, I get what you're saying, but things are fine the way they are." Sierra shoved a forkful of chocolate cake in her mouth. "And let's be honest. We don't have much in common." *Besides your husband.*

This isn't going well. Cassie's eyes roamed around the room. "Sierra, I have to say. I am proud of what you've been able to do despite all that's happened in your life. I mean you're a survivor." She nodded. "Yep, I'm sure it's difficult, single mother and all. But of course, with the Griers, I'm certain it's a big help."

Sierra raised her brow. She let her continue, bracing herself for more crazy talk.

"And, you know having to practically raise yourself. I mean you're just a walking testimony!" She stuck her fork in a cherry tomato and placed it in her mouth.

Sierra cleared her throat and leaned back. "I guess you could say that. I'm sure Grayson Jr.'s told you a lot." She smiled then leaned forward and clasped her hands. "Like how we spent most of our senior year in high school together; or how I probably know the real Grayson Jr. better than anyone else; oh, and how he'd said he didn't want any other woman to have his first child." She locked eyes with Cassie. "Did I tell you he was my first? Oh and how we both loved to eat *real* food and I could make him laugh. Did he tell you all that? Yep, the good ole days." She smiled.

Cassie sipped her water. "Uh, well. The past *is* the past."

"Maybe." Sierra glared.

Cassie adjusted the napkin over her sheath dress.

"Who knew you'd get married. Especially when he told me his job was just to entertain you when his parents came to town on business." Sierra chuckled. "Yeah, those were some good times." She stuck her fork into the last bit of cake and slowly chewed.

Cassie was steaming like a pot of hot grits. "Okay. Real talk. Are you still in love with Grayson Jr.? Because I think you are."

"I knew you had a little street in you. Seriously, Cassie, I don't want your husband." She waved the fork at her. "He's the father of my child. That's it. It was a huge mistake, but the best gift came out of it, my son. Besides, Grayson was not the man I thought he was. You don't have a thing to worry about. Put your insecurities in check."

"Sweetie, I'm not worried. I wanted the truth. You'd never be able to walk in my stilettos. You ain't about this life."

"Thank God. Besides," she leaned in, "who'd want to wear a pair of over-priced uncomfortable shoes? I prefer function over fashion any day."

Cassie quickly glanced at Sierra's shoes. "Obviously." She slid her chair out. "I think I better go."

Sierra watched as Cassie stood, grabbed her purse and marched to the door. *Finally, I can have a moment of peace.* She looked at the table full of plates and half-eaten food. *I know she didn't stick me with the bill? Forget it. You can't put a price on peace of mind.*

Chapter 28 – The Dead Has Risen

Maxine had a long day. She hadn't tried to figure out anything since her last meeting with Grayson Sr. a couple of weeks ago. Instead of going straight home, she decided to take a short drive to one of her favorite restaurants. As she turned the corner, tears welled up at the enormity of her situation. "Why couldn't I have just taken that money from Grayson?" She said. "He thinks I'm gonna cave, but not this time. God's got to make a way."

Once she parked, she headed a few feet up the block. She kept looking over her shoulder, feeling a weird presence around her. Once inside the restaurant, she noticed several couples seated at tables throughout the dimly lit room. *When did this become the couple spot on a Thursday night?* She was tempted to do takeout but wanted to wind down a bit. Once seated, she placed her order, then sprinted toward the restroom.

When she walked around the other side of the bar, she instantly recognized a man standing there. *Great. Definitely not in the mood to see him.* A few steps away stood one of the big mistakes of her life. *Gee, God, we're batting a thousand.* She started to turn around, but it was too late. She continued walking, hoping he wouldn't see her.

"Maxine," he said once she eased past.

She stopped and slowly turned around and looked into his face. "Hey, uh, what are you doing *here*?"

"Can't a man enjoy a meal?"

"Not a dead man."

"You got jokes. Can I join you?"

She looked around. "Well actually, I was headed to the restroom and um…"

"Go ahead, I'll get us a table toward the back," he said, reading her mind.

She closed her eyes for a second then opened them. Instead of answering, she turned and went to the restroom. *I certainly don't need this, and I definitely don't want a scene.* By the time she returned, he'd been seated with a place setting for two.

"So, what brings you to this neighborhood?" *Must have been watching me the whole time.*

"Oh, just had to take care of a little business today." He winked.

She looked around. "Hmm." Her phone had gone off several times, and she looked to see who was calling. *Sierra.*

"Well, aren't you going to answer it? Somebody's real pressed. Who's checking for you like that?"

"Your daughter."

~~~~~

Maxine got in her car. She was barely able to eat her food because of the company she kept during dinner. All she'd wanted was to clear her head and sit down for a decent meal, alone. *Lord.* She bowed her head over the steering wheel. *Father, I'm tired. I know you have me in the palm of your hands. You've kept me this far. But there's some roots that need to be plucked. I know you said mustard seed faith will move some mountains, but these mountains keep coming back.*

It seems like I'll never escape my mistakes. They say if you don't pull up your roots, you'll have to deal with the problems for years, sometimes generations. I don't want that for me, my daughter or my grandson. God, I just want freedom. I want all the strongholds in my life to be broken. I don't seem to know how to do that. I know
~~~~~

this looks bigger than me, but it's not bigger than you. I just don't know how to get my permanent deliverance. I don't need to tell you there are powerful people who think I'm a threat because I know things. But I don't care. I just want to be free to live my life. I don't need much. Matter of fact, you can have it all, God. Just give me my freedom. I want my daughter and grandson to know you can love God and win. I keep telling myself, Maxi, you are the salt of the earth. I keep telling myself everyday I'm to be the light, but God it looks so dark.

She opened her eyes. As she turned on the engine and backed out, she felt a little lightheaded. She turned on her radio and the most soothing music filled the car. As she drove toward home, she felt a peace that wrapped its arms around her like a warm blanket. Her eyelids grew heavy. Suddenly after about ten minutes on the road, her vision blurred then everything went black.

Chapter 29 – No News Is Bad News

Sierra paced the floor. She glanced at her cellphone. *1:15 a.m. No sign of her.* Her hands began to shake, her stomach felt queasy. Since her sobriety her mom never stayed out this late. She was usually home by ten at the latest.

Sierra collapsed on the couch. "Think positive, breathe." She wrapped her arms around her upper body and rocked. She grabbed the TV remote and turned up the volume to drown out her thoughts.

She surfed the channels and paused on a Christian station. She gazed as the imposing figure stomped the pulpit. His booming voice filled the room as he wiped the beads of sweat from his forehead with a handkerchief. His eyes were wide and exaggerated as he whooped up the congregation. Sierra could barely make out the rest of his words with all the shouting. He finally stood there silent as the worshippers raised their hands, screamed and danced. Then he slowly waved his hands for them to get quiet.

"You see, when you get close to real deliverance, everything, I mean everything goes crazy. Family, job, friends. Turns upside down. That is a prime time for doubts to creep in. Doubting turns into disappointment. Disappointment turns into bitterness. It happens to the best of us. We stop believing. The Bible tells us that we are to be the *salt* of the earth. And if we lose our saltiness, we won't be good for anything.

"But here's the other good news. We are also the light of the world. And sometimes it may look bleak, but you can't hide a city on a hill. You've got to stand. You got to fight, but you won't be by yourself. Stop running. The battle is not against flesh and blood, but in the spirit. There will be a time when you say enough! I'm tired of going around these same mountains. I need to be free."

He patted his forehead with a handkerchief. Then lowered his voice. "Some of y'all just think you are free. But you've been accepting the same generational cycles. But, here's the thing. You've got to want it bad enough. 'Cause it's gonna get heavy." He had to catch his breath. "Do you want it bad enough?" He yelled.

Sierra jumped.

"God is not a respecter of persons. He doesn't favor others over you. You are special to him, but you've got to give him everything. Time to get delivered but deliverance costs. It doesn't come free. Stay in the word. Stay in worship, that word and worship are the "salt" you need to preserve your strength and your spirit. And that yoke destroying anointing costs!" He stomped his foot and wiped his forehead with a handkerchief.

Sierra sucked her teeth. *Haven't we paid enough, God?*

"Do not be discouraged. He sees you, and he will restore you."

He had Sierra's attention. *How and when, God? Sign me up. I've been waiting. Cause I'm exhausted.*

~~~~~

Sierra had passed out on the couch. It was 3:00 a.m. She sat up thinking it had all been a bad dream. Her heart raced as she rushed to her mother's room. Her spirit sunk at the sight of her empty, half made bed. She came back downstairs and dialed her mother's number once more. *Darn you, answer the phone. No answer.* It went to voice mail. Just when she was about to call the police station, there was a knock at the door. She swallowed then walked over. She peeked out the window where two officers stood on the porch.

The phone rang. "Hello," she spat from her parched throat.

"Ms. Sanders? Sierra Sanders?"

Her stomach contracted in a tight ball. "Yes, this is she."
~~~~~

"I'm Officer Adam Tyson...are you related to a Maxine Sanders?"

"Yes…"

Chapter 30 – That Mountain

Grayson Jr. continued banging on the door until he heard the knob wrangle.

Sierra opened the door, turned her back and didn't speak. She was still in night clothes, her hair half done in a ponytail. The house was a mess.

"Daddy!" His son rushed to him with a dirty face and hands. Little Gray smeared chocolate on his father's khakis as held his pant leg.

"Sierra, I've been blowing your phone up. What's going on? Have you packed Gray's bag?"

She turned to him. "Look, um, I need a favor. I'm going to need you to keep him a little while. Something's come up. No questions, okay?"

Grayson Jr. frowned. "Huh?"

"I'll have to explain later. No lectures please. Just take him." Sierra looked away.

"Not before you tell me what's going on." He noticed she'd been crying and her hands were visibly shaking.

His son was still tugging on his leg. "Look, Dad, I got a Band-Aid. I was brave.

He knelt down and looked at his finger. "What happened?"

"Just a small cut. It was an accident. He's fine."

"Sierra, how did my son cut his finger?" He looked around. "And this house…" He shook his head. "Never mind. You know, my son has had one too many 'little accidents' lately." He walked toward her. "For some reason, you've been slipping lately."

"My mom," she looked away, "it's serious." She bit her lip and paced the floor. She paused and looked at her son now on the couch. "Little Gray, you want to go up and find some toys to take with you? I'll call you in a minute."

Grayson studied her face then pat his son on his back, "Yeah, Gray, go upstairs. I'll come get you when where ready to go, buddy, okay?"

As he shot off, Grayson Jr. watched as him run-up the steps. "Okay, now what happened?" He massaged the bridge of his nose.

"It's my mother. She's at the police station. She walked over and eased down on the couch. "Apparently, there's been a bad accident. They took her to the hospital first, but she's been released, and she's in the county jail. DUI."

His eyes grew wide. "What? I mean, she was hurt?" He sat next to her and touched her on the arm.

"Got banged up but apparently okay, physically that is. Grayson, the other driver was hurt pretty bad. She may not make it." Sierra jumped from the couch. "She promised…no more drinking!" Sierra shook her head. "Just doesn't make sense. She hasn't touched a drop of alcohol in over six years."

He rubbed his forehead. "No, it doesn't." He walked toward her and grabbed her shoulders. "Look, I'm really sorry, but you're gonna have to pull it together. I know how you get, I mean when your mother used to drink. You can't just check out, my son hurt himself."

"*Your* son? *Your* son? Grayson, *our* son is fine." She pulled away.

He stood there and took a deep breath. "Sierra, yes. *My* son. Never mind." He shook his head. "Always some kinda drama with your family," he mumbled.

"Right, Grayson. *I'm* the drama. My life wouldn't have been such a struggle if you wouldn't have abandoned me!" Tears welled up in Sierra's eyes. "So stereotypical."

"Sierra, what do you want me to do? Life happens. We were young and…well, I offered you more money, and we both know it's your mother's fault. She wouldn't let you take it."

Sierra could feel her insides boiling with regret. *I should have taken more money. After the way he treated me?* He owed me. "Sierra? Sierra?"

"Yes!"

"I'm gonna have to get out of here." He looked at his watch. "Gonna miss my fraternity meeting."

"*Fraternity meeting*? Are you serious? So sorry to inconvenience you. My mother almost killed someone and is locked up. I don't know where to begin. I thought I was through fixing her mess! I don't even have money for an attorney. At least a decent one!" She shook her head as she bit her lip.

"Okay, okay." He grabbed her arms. "Calm down. Having a meltdown isn't the answer." He closed his eyes then opened them. "I can handle the lawyer. I'll call my dad. He'll know the best person to call. Or at least get a referral."

She walked slowly toward him. "You should have never left me."

He sighed. "Sierra, this isn't about us. It's about your mother right now."

"It's not about us?" She looked directly in his eyes. "You weren't saying that the day you threw yourself on me right before your wedding." She wiped her eyes with the sleeve of her top.

He reached for his phone then paused. "Sierra, that, that was a mistake. And right now, there're bigger things to focus on. Gray's coming with me."

"Grayson," she whispered, "I need you." She grabbed part of his shirt and pressed her face against his chest. "*Please.*" She buried her nose in the fabric.

He hesitated but slid his arms around her and held her. Her body was warm, and soon, his was too. He wanted to keep holding her. He wanted his lips to touch hers. Their embrace felt so natural, like coming home. "Sierra, c'mon. Stop it! This is just gonna confuse things," he whispered then gently pulled away. He swallowed as he quickly pressed a button on his phone.

She pulled away and folded her arms. "You know, I'm not the only one who needs to grow up. Can't you do anything without *him*?"

He ignored her and waited for his father to answer.

~~~~~

"Son, listen to me. Don't do anything else. Once you get Gray packed up, come straight here. I'll take care of the rest."

"But Dad, Sierra. I'm not sure I should leave her here." He lowered his voice although she'd gone upstairs. "She just seems unstable. More afraid actually. She doesn't even want to go see her mother."

"She'll be fine. First things first. I'm going to call an attorney. And like I said, don't talk to anybody and come straight here. This town is small."

"Why would anybody want to talk to me?"

~~~~~

Maxine stood awaiting the judge to speak. She was calm and assured. Grayson Sr. had hired the best attorney. She was sure she'd be home soon to sort out the rest of this mess. It was all a big misunderstanding. They had to realize that.

"Bail is denied." The judge's gavel slammed. "This concludes the court's business."

"What? What just happened?" Maxine immediately turned to her lawyer with wide-eyed disbelief.

"Maxine, please calm down. Although it's been a long time, it's still your third DUI." He removed his glasses.

"How many times do I need to tell you, I didn't have anything to drink that night? And the other two DUIs were over 10 years ago. I have been sober for over six years straight! I can't stay in here. I worked too hard on my sobriety. You need to do something!" She looked over at Sierra, her heart racing.

Sierra was in momentary paralysis. "Mom!" She finally uttered. "Mom! What just happened?" She looked around in a panic. "I don't understand. I don't know what to do!" She rushed to grab her mother, but the bailiff ushered her out.

Chapter 31– “Step” Up

“How much longer are we going to have to do this babysitting duty?” Cassie asked. “I love my stepson, but he’s been here for two weeks.” She looked in the mirror, admiring the way the vibrant florals of her maxi dress looked against her golden skin.

“Cassie, we’re not babysitting,” Grayson Jr. said from the other side of the large master bedroom. “This is my son. As my *wife*, you should be supportive. I’m having a bit of a crisis here.”

“No, Grayson, you’re not having a crisis, your trifling baby’s momma is.” She rolled her eyes and placed her hand on her hip. “Never mind. What about the Henley’s party in the Hampton’s? I’ve been looking forward to this all summer.” She stood there with her arms folded.

“We can still go. We can take Gray, or you can go by yourself. “He stared at the television as he scrolled through the channels; he knew his answer would tick her off.

“What? Why can’t he just stay with his grandparents or with the nanny? I mean I’ve been looking forward to this trip for weeks. And I’m not going by myself. I RSVP’d for two. She stared at the back of his head, waiting for him to respond.

Why is everything so much work with her? He looked up from the television. “You know what, Cassie? You’re being selfish and I really don’t want to have this conversation right now. I don’t even like the Henley’s. I’m going downstairs to get something to eat. Then I’m going to read to my son.” He walked over and looked in her eyes. “And just maybe, if and when you decide to have sex with me, you’ll have a kid and find some compassion.” He walked off.

"You're right, I wouldn't understand because I didn't have a child out of wedlock. Excuse me for saving myself for you!" she yelled in disgust.

Grayson stopped in his footsteps. He turned around and gave her a steely look. "Yeah, the jury is still out on that one."

She walked over and slapped him so hard her hand hurt. She hated fights, violence, anything confrontational. She shocked herself.

"Look, I get it," she said after a few seconds. "You have a son, but you are way too caught up in his mother's drama. You should have known the dysfunction you were laying up with before you got her pregnant." She was tempted to grab a book off a shelf and throw it at him. "That's what you get for slumming."

He inched closer. He balled his fist but kept his arm pinned to his side. All he could hear was his father's voice. *Never hit a woman*. "Cassie, you don't know her *at all*."

She flipped her fresh sewn in. "You're *defending* her? Give me a break." She fumbled with the solitaire diamond necklace. "You know what? I don't need this." She walked over to her nightstand and grabbed her purse. "I'm outta here. Don't wait up."

He tried to grab her arm, and she snatched it away with force. She turned back to face him. "Grayson, you married *me*. Don't forget that. I took those vows seriously but I'm *not* a door mat." She brushed past him and out the door. A few minutes later, he heard the garage go up and walked toward the window. He watched as she screeched out the driveway.

"She took my Porsche? Oh, she done lost her mind!"

Chapter 32 – Noir

Cassie had spent most of the day with friends. Actually Kensie and Bra were more like close associates. Since her marriage, she'd pretty much alienated herself. It was also becoming increasingly difficult to tell who was authentic over who wanted to be in the Grier circle. But tonight she didn't care. She just wanted to laugh and forget about her life. They coaxed her into hanging at a club. Earlier, she cried on the way to Kensie's loft, but hours later, she was relaxed and ready to let go. She and her girls were seated in VIP, compliments of the Grier name, on a plush sectional. They were chatting, kicking back and taking in the room's sophisticated vibe. Cassie's phone had been ringing for hours, but she ignored it. Her husband never liked her out alone, especially with single women. He'd die if he knew she was in a night club.

"Wow, can't remember the last time the three of us were out." Bre's head slightly bobbed to the music. She crossed her legs and surveyed the room.

Cassie felt her outfit paled to her sequin mini and chiffon blouse. Her trendy red lipstick against her skin and dark wavy bob caught plenty of attention. Kensie's pixie cut and flawless makeup was stunning. She was definitely out the loop on club gear.

Before they could get good into their conversation, a waitress sent over a bucket of

Champagne. "From the gentleman." She nodded toward the bar.

They all looked in that direction. Bencil was leaning against it with a raised glass.

"Oh, God. That's my father-in-law's business partner." Cassie cringed. "He's always pushing up on some young thang. Nice, but kind of creepy."

"Oooh, he's a little too old for me." Kensie quipped and reached for the bottle. "But I love a man with good taste." She eyed the label.

Bre's mega lashes batted. "Bencil? Bencil James? I could work with his age for that kind of money."

"Sorry, no amount of money in the world would make that man attractive to me," Kensie said. "What, he's like sixty? He's got a crater face and his head's shaped a little like a dome. Besides, I have my own money."

"We know," they both said in unison.

Bre noticed him walking over. "Shh, girl, he's coming this way." She adjusted her posture. "Hmm nothing a good dermatologist couldn't work with."

Kensie rolled her eyes.

"Ladies." Bencil smiled as he stood waiting for an invite join in.

"Please join us," Cassie nodded toward the sofa, "and thanks you for the champagne."

While Bencil called himself entertaining her friends, Cassie kept replaying her argument with her husband. She regretted storming out, but that slap felt good. She needed a release. Despite her friends having the time of their lives, the venture reaffirmed her hate for clubs and that she wasn't missing a thing. She sipped on alcohol out of boredom and admitted she missed her man. She'd give anything to be home with him watching Netflix. Instead she spent most of the evening listening to Bencil's tired mack on her friends.

~~~~~
~~~~~

"You didn't have to walk me to my car. I valet parked," Cassie said as she dug in her purse for her ticket. She realized how hard the champagne had kicked in when she got a little off balance. "Finally!" She pulled the ticket from her wallet.

"Yes, I did. You need somebody looking out for you." He stood next to her. "Are you sure you're okay to drive?"

She smiled at a small group of women that walked by. "Um, yeah I think so."

Once the car pulled up, she walked toward the driver's side and handed the valet a tip.

He followed. "Are you sure you're okay? I would feel terrible if something were to happen."

She took a deep breath and thought about what had just happened to Sierra's mother. "You know what," she said, looking up at him, "I'm not so sure."

"I'll tell you what. Let's just go somewhere quick and get you some coffee."

"Umm, that would work." She felt safe doing that. She got out and went around to the passenger side as he got in the driver's seat.

~~~~~

"Ugh!" Cassie's head fell back on the cushion of her seat at the 24-hour diner.

Bencil grinned. "I don't think I've ever seen you drink."

She raised her head and rubbed her eyes. "Omigod. I'm so embarrassed."

"No need to be embarrassed. Just glad I could make sure you were okay." He folded his large hands in front of him.

"Can I help you?" An older woman with leathered skin put down two menus and silverware.
~~~~~

"I'm not hungry." Cassie rubbed her forehead.

"You need to eat something. You'll feel much better. Promise."

Cassie looked around. "Never ate here before. Wouldn't picture you as a diner type of guy. What's good?"

"Pretty much everything. I've been coming here for years. I know the owners. Nice

Italian folks."

The waitress cut her eye at Bencil as she patted her pencil on her pad. "Do I need to come back?"

"No, no." Cassie looked down at the menu. "Just some toast and juice will be fine."

"I'll have the usual." He winked at the woman. "Oh, and we'll take two coffees."

She waved her hand at him. Then scribbled on her pad. She walked away and returned moments later with two cups of coffee.

"Now, Cassie," he opened a packet of sugar, "How did you end up in Noir? Last time I checked you didn't party or drink. You're one of the good girls."

Last time I checked, I wasn't about to leave my husband. "Just needed a little girl time."

"Uh-huh." He took a sip of coffee.

"What?"

"I know my Godson. He can be a little selfish and hot headed."

Cassie paused. She sensed an opening. On the one hand, she wanted to remain her super private self, but on the other hand, she was about to burst. She literally didn't have anyone to talk to. Her mother would take Grayson's side. She literally had nobody on her side. *Maybe he's not such a monster.* "We just fell out a little. That's all. Over his son."

Bencil shook his head. "You know, I'm no expert, but I know how much that boy loves his son. And if I were really honest, I'd say he'd leave you before he would do anything to jeopardize that kid."

Cassie was about to speak, but the waitress returned with two plates of food. "Let me know if you need anything else." She cracked a smile then walked away.

Cassie paused and bowed her head to bless her food. When she looked up he was staring. "What's the matter?"

"I just think it's so cute how you Christians pray over your food."

She squinted. "You're not a believer."

"I wouldn't say all that. I just think you need more than prayer. I hate passive people, and Christians can be passive. Anyway, I don't go to church and I made out all right. So maybe I more of an agnostic."

"Hmm." She buttered her bread and put a little cream in her coffee. "So where do you think you're going after you die?"

"Not quite sure. So my guess is you are one of those people who believe if you do everything right life rewards you. Like your marriage. Everybody has the storybook in mind when they jump that broom. No such thing. I've been around a long time. Nothing is as it appears."

She coughed and took a sip of her coffee.

He smiled.

"So what are you saying?"

"I'm just saying don't be naive. Successful people find a way to make every situation work for them. Ask yourself, what is it that I want out of this relationship other than the title 'Mrs.'."

Cassie chewed slowly. She was in need of some fatherly advice. It was times like this she missed her own dad. Bencil wasn't the most sensitive person, but she figured he was genuinely concerned. He'd have to do. "I guess I want respect, love."

"That's too general. Is that all you really want? Marriage is like a business. You have to have measurable goals like anything else."

"Really? I'm not so sure I agree." She leaned back. "You know, I thought I wanted the big house and all the perks of marrying into the Grier family but really? I just want a simple life. A house, one car will do and I want a career. I need to start my dental practice and…"

"And what?" He leaned forward.

"If I were really honest, I don't want to be anybody's stepmother. I want a child of my own." *There, I said it.*

"Okay, what if you never have a child of your own? Maybe just maybe you're supposed to be a mother to little Gray."

She paused for a few seconds. "I am. I mean I never mistreat him."

"You're not hearing me. I mean I think his real mother and grandmother are great people, but let's face it, they wouldn't be able to give him what you and my Godson could. I bet if you didn't fight it, you'd actually love being a fulltime mother to little Gray." He leaned forward and lowered his voice, "I could help, you know."

She continued to chew. Her spirit was hesitant. She was no longer feeling where this conversation was going. "You know what? I think it's best that I don't talk about this." She brushed the crumbs off her hands. Then wiped her face with a napkin. "Wow, I really feel so much better. I probably need to get back home. Should I drop you off at your car?"

Chapter 33 – F.E.A.R.

Sierra delayed opening the new pile of mail. She'd been so paralyzed with depression she was unable to do anything productive.

"Time for damage control." She grabbed an armful of envelopes and spread them on the bed. She took a deep breath and began opening the envelopes. Just as suspected, some serious deadlines had whooshed by. In reality, they were bleeding debt. She opened the envelope to the shop rent. It was in major arrears. Her eyes widened at the number. She organized the bills in several piles: *hope*, *no hope* and *no way in heck*. All while trying to keep from breaking down—again.

The phone rang. "Collect call from the Essex County Jail."

Great.

"Do you accept the charges?"

"Yeah, I'll accept."

"Sierra, please don't hang up." Her mother's words were like rapid fire at a gun range.

"Baby, I know you're angry, but you have to listen to me." She pled. "I didn't do anything. I wasn't drinking. You *have* to believe me. Baby, you're all I've got."

It took a few seconds for Sierra to speak. "Mom, I want to believe you. I really do. The evidence, I mean you were driving and a woman's fighting for her life in the hospital. If she dies…"

"Sierra, don't speak it. I know it looks bad. But I have no choice but to trust God." She lowered her voice. Please, look, honey, I gotta —"The phone call cut off. For once she was happy about the bad reception of her cellphone.

Sierra removed the phone from her ear. *God, I don't know what to believe or what to do anymore.*

~~~~~

Maxine sat on her bed; her head was pulsating. If she were at home, she'd knock out her migraine with a BC Powder. She was making it on four hours of sleep, barely eating. She refused to get comfortable. But the heaviness of the circumstances wore on her resolve. She tried to think back on that night. Her mind could only go so far. From the time she got in her car to when she awoke in the hospital was fuzzy. It was like a door was blocking a certain part of her mind. She mentally banged the door until her head hurt. She had millions of questions, no answers. Since her childhood, Maxine was terrified of the law, any system for that matter. *God, please don't you leave me here and don't you let my child give up on me.* She curled in a fetal position and cradled her Bible to her chest.

"Where the spirit of the Lord is there is liberty." She quietly repeated the words as she clung to her Bible until her eyelids grew heavy. *Just any sign, God, please. I need to know you haven't left me.* She finally closed her eyes and dozed off. Several minutes later, she opened them to what looked like writing scrawled on the wall. She focused, trying to make out the words. *F.E.A.R. –False evidence appearing real*
~~~~~

Chapter 34 – Pouring Out

Sierra walked down to the basement. When she reached the floor, she jumped back to the steps. *What in the…?* Her foot stepped in what felt like a pool of water. "That freakin' washing machine!" It had flooded the basement once before, and it was an expensive mess. She placed her hands atop her head the look upward. "God, are you *serious* right now? Ugh!" She grabbed loose hair, then wrapped and tucked it in a ball.

She turned and stomped back upstairs, then heard her cellphone ringing. She was temped the throw it across the room when she saw the name. "What!?"

"Mommy, I miss you. When can I come home? Why are you yelling?"

"Oh Gray, sweetie, I'm so sorry. I thought it was your dad. I didn't know it was you." Pangs of guilt shot through her. "Little Gray?"

"Sierra!"

She cringed at the sound of his voice. "Yes, Grayson."

"What are you doing? All he wanted to do was talk to you. He misses

you."

"I wasn't yelling. I miss him, too. Look, I have a minor emergency. I can't see him right now."

"So what else is new? What's wrong now?"

Father, please help me. "Grayson, you know I don't have anybody over here. The basement's flooded."

"Are you serious? *Another mess I have to cleanup.* He sighed. "What do you need? I guess I can send somebody over."

She sucked her teeth and rolled her eyes. *I need a new house. How about I come stay with you and Cassie? Oh, and a cool $100,000 to save our business, settle our tax bill and take care of the house.* "Look Grayson, you can take your cape off. Just take care of my son for the moment."

"You know it I didn't think it would be so hard on Cassie, I'd keep my son for good."

Sierra felt her chest tightening. "You know what? Never mind."

"Nevermind what?"

"I apologize your son has been an inconvenience. Besides, she knew you had a son when she married you, right? Well this comes with the territory!" She disconnected the call.

~~~~~

Sierra turned the corner and walked toward Deja Reaux. When she arrived, she saw Amber standing outside. As soon as she saw the white piece of paper affixed to the front door, she didn't have to guess.

"I'm so sorry, Sierra. I'm so sorry." Amber grabbed her arm.

Sierra stood there looking at the padlock on the door. She was almost numb at this point. "Amber, there's nothing to be sorry about. It is what it is. I'm so freakin' tired." She sighed. "Grayson Jr. is right."

Amber bit the side of her lip as she searched for some other words of encouragement. "Well, you think you want to maybe pray?" Amber held her breath for a response.

Sierra looked at the door then around. "Is that your answer for *everything*? A little too late for that, don't you think?"
~~~~~

Amber looked at the lady walking by and smiled nervously.

"You tell me, Amber, what's left to pray about?" Sierra shut her eyes and rubbed her forehead. "Sorry, I know you're only trying to help. Didn't mean to take it out on you. Don't know why you've hung in this long."

"Sierra, do you think I'm here for just a part-time job? When you look at me you probably see some college kid from an upper middle class family working just for fun."

"Yeah, pretty much."

"You may not understand, but I'm here by assignment. God's more concerned about saving us than things." She searched Sierra's eyes for a response.

"Doesn't make sense to me. Everybody's tried to help me understand *your* God. My mom, Zoe, you. Know what? Let's just get out of this summer heat. There's nothing else we can do here."

Amber paused looking around, slightly deflated. "Sierra, guess you're right. There's nothing else we can do in the moment, but I just can't leave you here. You hungry? Let's go get something to eat."

Sierra shrugged. "I guess. I need to rest my mind for a minute. I need to figure out a game plan. But I don't have much of an appetite."

At a coffee shop down the street, the pair stepped in and seated themselves. Sierra didn't realize just how tired and hungry she was. As sad as it was, the store closing was one last thing she had to worry about. Nevertheless, she felt as though there was a big "F" for failure stamped on her chest.

Once the waitress brought them water and took their order, Sierra let down her guard a little. "Amber, I don't get it. Why do *you* have so much faith? I mean, what have you really gone through?"

Amber sipped on her water then smiled. "I'm laughing because your question is evidence."

"Of what?" Sierra was getting impatient.

"That I don't look like what I've been through."

Sierra tilted her head. "Huh?" She was always intrigued by Amber's sunny disposition and refused to believe her life had been a struggle. She bounced and shined as much as her honey blonde highlights and ghost white teeth. *She and Zoe must be drinking from that same Jesus jar.*

"The summer after my junior year of high school," Amber began. "I had everything to live for. I'd applied to Montclair State and was looking forward to senior year. A few weeks later, I was barely alive." She watched Sierra's face grow stoic. "My best friend and I were on the way to the beach. A driver was texting and hit us."

Sierra held her breath in anticipation of the rest of her words.

"My friend was thrown from the car and died instantly. The driver lived. I was in critical condition. The doctors told my parents I was going to be a vegetable with no brain activity. But they refused to believe it." Her eyes grew glassy. "They *refused* to give up. I'm here because of their persistent and unwavering faith."

Sierra sat up and leaned in. Shame rose up in her spirit about her insensitivity. *Why do I make assumptions about people?*

"I had countless surgeries. When I finally was cognizant and able to process what had happened, I was devastated, hurt and angry at God. After the physical healing, there was a mental and spiritual healing that took hours, days and months. It was and still is a journey. I refused to forgive that driver. Do you know what it's like to lose a best friend?"

The waitress placed their plates down as she paused.

Yes, I do. Sierra instantly thought of Zoe. She waited for the waitress to walk away. "How'd you get from that place to where you are now? I mean, hopeful and peaceful?" she said in a lowered voice. "Definitely not angry."

"G-O-D, salvation. I mean, I went to church, but I didn't have an intimate relationship with him. It wasn't a cake walk. God had some construction work to do on my heart. I had to let him into my most vulnerable spaces. Each time my flesh entered, the Holy Spirit saturated it with light. The only way to forgive is through Christ." She watched as Sierra's face softened, then Amber grabbed her hands. "Sierra, you can't run from your life. Life is pressing in, but it's for a purpose. This time you have to face it all, without fear. You and you alone are going to be the key to your family's freedom." She squeezed her hand and made eye contact. "I believe your mother is telling the truth."

Sierra showed no emotion. "So what makes you so sure, Amber? I mean, that she didn't slip this once?"

Amber looked down then back up. "I don't have any proof. I just have a knowing in my spirit. Look, I'm a twenty-seven-year-old white girl. I've never been to a jail in my life. But the Lord told me that Deja Reaux was not just some part-time job, but my spiritual assignment. Your mom and I used to talk and pray in that back room of the shop. She'd come to bible study. Our prayer group is praying for her. We've been taking turns fasting on her behalf. We've been praying for you, too."

Sierra swallowed. Guilt and disbelief rumbled within like two gang leaders. "Wow, I had no idea. Honestly, I want to see my mother. I want to believe her, but every time I head that way,

I feel this rawness in my stomach. I mean I become physically sick." She fumbled with her silverware. "I hear you, but all this 'knowing in your spirit' sounds like more spiritual babble. Stuff I never truly understood, stuff that never worked…for me."

Chapter 35 – Put It on the Altar

Cassie and Grayson maneuvered their way out of the sanctuary. Despite her feelings, Cassie greeted and smiled her way through the crowd. She wanted Grayson to cut his after church fellowship short. Although they'd somewhat made up, this season of life had tried her patience. She wasn't in the mood to pretend.

"I'm going to get little Gray from children's church." She didn't wait for him to respond before she took off. The pastor had poured his heart into the sermon, but she was still walking away empty. She was so tempted to get in line for prayer but talked herself out of it. She didn't want anybody wondering what kind of issues she had. She wasn't even sure she could trust the prayer partners.

She darted through the sea of people and reached the designated check out area. She watched mothers and fathers catching their children as they sprinted from children's worship. Cassie smiled at the flurry of little girls in dresses and little boys running out with their projects in hand. Her smiled turned to stoic when she recalled she was picking up somebody else's child. *God, all I want is a child, is that so wrong? My child. Not someone else's. My flesh and blood.* She instantly felt a bump against her head and some arms wrap around her. She looked down and found her stepson peering up at her with a bright smile. She smiled back.

"What do you have there?" she asked.

He handed her a picture he'd colored. "For you!"

"She examined the picture and clearly it was supposed to be her, Grayson Jr. and Sierra. That's Daddy, Mommy and Mommy." He smiled wide.

She ran her fingers through his curls.

She knelt down and gave him a hug. He reached his arms around her neck then gave her a big kiss. "I love you."

"Love you, too." *God, if this is what motherhood feels like, I want it more than anything. I know it is wrong. But please, grace. I need your grace.* She grabbed little Gray's hand.

"Can I take my picture to Grandma today?" he asked as they walked.

"Maybe later. How about we go eat? We can go to your favorite restaurant. Anywhere you want, okay?"

~~~~~

Once they reached the car, Cassie turned to her husband before he opened the door. "Babe, I don't want to fight anymore."

He took a deep breath. "I know. It's been hard, and you've made a lot of sacrifices. If I haven't said it enough, I appreciate you." He kissed and hugged her.

She smiled. "Little Gray needs us. It's not the ideal situation, but he's your son. I'm here for you."

He looked into her eyes. "No, he's *our* son."

She smiled. "Yeah, you're right…*our* son." She instantly recalled her conversation with Bencil.

He took her hand and held it. "You're a really special woman."

Once they were all in the car, she looked back at little Gray. He was fixated on his game with headphones. Her husband turned on the ignition and before he pulled off, she grabbed his arm, "Babe, what if–"

"What?" He kept the car in park.

"Nevermind." Her heart raced.

"You sure?"
~~~~~

"No. I know this sounds crazy, but what if we, we kept little Gray…for good?"

Chapter 36 – Bedfellows and Old Favors

"So does Lydia know you're here?" Maxine sat across the table staring blankly at Grayson Sr. "Where's my attorney?"

"Lydia, well, she has an idea, and I found you new counsel."

Her forehead creased. "I don't know what's wrong with my other lawyer. He seems so vested."

"Maybe." He scratched the bottom of his goatee.

Maxine studied his face, then her lips trembled. She turned her head away when her eyes began to water. "I'm tired, really tired," she said quietly, her voice parched. "Sorry." She took a deep swallow.

Maxine, no, I'm sorry. He clasped his hands in front of him and rubbed his thumbs together. "So are you okay, I mean under the circumstances?" He swallowed.

She shrugged.

He studied her eyes then her face. Her natural beauty preserved like a rose in concrete. "Nobody's messed with you or anything?"

"No. I have a bodyguard." She let out a faint laugh as a tear streamed down one of her cheeks.

His eyes squinted. "A what?"

"Unofficially, her name's Ruth. She's huge tall *and* wide. Scared me at first. Never prayed for a covering so hard in my life! But she's like a gentle giant."

Grayson Sr. cracked a smile then shook his head.

"One day I was in the rec room. All I wanted to do was watch something positive. This loud woman came in and threatened me. Before I knew it, Ruth shut it down. She snatched the remote and decided we were all gonna watch Joel Osteen. It would have been funny if I wasn't here. Definitely can't judge a person by their looks. She's born again, a gazillion tattoos. And no, she hasn't tried anything!"

Grayson Sr. smiled to keep from showing the pity in his eyes. He cleared his throat. "So you should here from the new attorney soon."

She watched him wrestle with his thoughts. "Doesn't look good, does it?"

He sighed. "No, but if Johnny Cochran got O.J. off, anything's possible. Definitely praying for that woman in the hospital to fully recover."

She shook her head. "I'm really worried about Sierra. She won't talk to me."

"Well, she's somewhat okay. My son's been talking to her, but the shop—"

"Yeah, I know. Amber told me. Can't do anything about it right now. That young girl's been more than an employee. She's been a Godsend." She looked off into nothing. "I really miss my grandson. I've never missed his birthday." Another tear crawled down her face. She wiped it. "It's tough."

"He's doing okay. But Sierra, well just as stubborn as you. I'll do what I can for the business and other issues."

She shook her head. "Thanks. Just don't know how I'll ever repay you." She paused as her chest heaved. "Grayson, I may be many things," she looked around, "but I'm *not* a liar. And all I had that night was some coffee. It was late, and I knew I had to get home."

His face softened, and he nodded.

She grew quiet. “Grayson, I need to tell you something. Something I’ve kept to myself for, well, a long time.” She looked down then in his eyes.

“Maxi, you have to tell me, especially if it’ll help your case.” His eyes pled more than his words.

Her words initially drizzled then poured out like a heavy rain. As she continued to talk, he balled his hands into fists, clenched his teeth, and closed his eyes.

“Grayson, please,” she swallowed, her eyes watering, “don’t do anything stupid.”

He nodded as she spoke. “I’ll be back.”

~~~~~

Grayson Sr. made several stops. It had been many years since he had to call up favors but felt he owed Maxine. He knew he had the key to her freedom, and he wouldn’t stop until he got it. He’d let her down before and wasn’t going to make that mistake again. He walked up to the huge wooden door and before he had a chance to knock it opened. He was greeted by two familiar bodyguards that led him down a short hallway to meet his friend. Like old times, the familiar aroma of homemade pasta led the way. After greetings he sat at the table where they broke bread, ate lasagna and sipped on wine. He and his old friend walked the big meal off through the vineyard and shared cigars.

Finally, he had a chance to share the reason he was there.

Grayson Sr.’s friend sat on the concrete bench amid the vines, periodically shaking his head. Years had gone by, and the telltale signs of age were etched in his face. His jowls were more pronounced than Grayson Sr. had recalled. His eyelids occasionally lowered as if he were about to take a nap. But Grayson knew better. He’d heard every word. His mind was still sharp.
~~~~~

Grayson Sr. had made his plea. He'd laid out the details on the mossy floor, waiting for his friend to retrieve them like a game of pickup sticks.

After a yawn and a second of silence, words emerged from his scratchy throat. "I'll get Goodboy on it right away. He'll make a few calls to the judge and find out what's really going on. Won't be hard. They owe me one."

"I thought Goodboy was retired."

"He never retires. He'll find out whatever you need to know."

Grayson Sr. cleared his throat. "Well, can he–."

"I'll get him right on it," his friend said in that eerie way he finished his words. "The only reason he's still living is because of you."

Chapter 37 – Lock Down

It had been a week since the shop closed, and Sierra hadn't left the house. She stopped answering her cellphone. The people came to clean the basement. It cleared her bank account. Exhausted, she resigned herself to the couch in her terry cloth rob where she fell in and out of sleep. Raising her head to watch the television was a chore, so she lay on her side with the remote clutched to her chest.

A thousand images played through her mind while she lay comatose. Everything but solutions popped in her head. In a move of desperation, she tried to call Bryce, but his number had changed. She thought about calling Zoe. The image of her belly poking out from her tiny frame put a faint smile on her face. She imagined Zoe's parents and husband surrounding her in the delivery room and a beautiful shower put on by all her loved ones.

Sierra was resentful her best friend had something so big happening and she wasn't a part of it. Her heart ached. She wanted to talk to her son. But didn't want him to hear or see her so weakened, broke down. She couldn't fake it. He was better off with his dad for the moment.

She focused on her only distraction. Amber once told her if she kept the TV on a gospel channel, it would drain the negative energy out the room. Sierra wasn't sure it was working but felt she didn't have anything to lose. So hence, her Daystar marathon commenced. But she still felt heaviness in the air. When she tried to get up, oppression pinned her down. She finally drifted off. Two hours later, a knock on the door awakened her. She struggled to coherence as the taps came more rapidly. *Oh crap.* She clumsily stood and shuffled toward the door.

"Okay, okay!" she yelled, dreading the possibility on the other side of the door.

"Sierra Sanders?"

"Yes?" She eyed the tall, slim white man with reddish hair curiously.

"Can you sign for this?"

She grabbed the pen and slowly scribbled her signature as she noticed the law firm address. After tearing it open, her eyes grew wide with the words. After swiping her phone from the coffee table, she frantically dialed. There was no answer.

"Are you seriously filing for full custody?" she yelled into the voice recorder.

~~~~~

Sierra jumped up and paced. In the middle of her steps, she rushed to the kitchen. She marched toward her cabinet and pulled out a small bottle. After seeing what it had done to her mother for years, she swore she'd never touch alcohol—ever. *I just need something.* She poured some in a glass and added ice and a little soda. She held her nose and threw the glass back. "Uh, disgusting." She wiped her mouth with the back of her hand. With each drink the taste became more palpable. Before she knew it, she'd passed out on the couch.

She slept straight through until the morning. She'd almost forgotten about the alcohol until she struggled to sit up. Nausea knotted up her stomach, and her head felt like someone was standing atop it banging a metal steel pot. Despite a full night's sleep, her problems flooded to her brain like the water to her basement. She looked over at the brown envelope on the coffee table and the legal petition. She thought about the basement, her mother, the eviction notice on the boutique door.
~~~~~

Screaming, she ran to the China cabinet, threw open the glass door, and tossed an antique cup across the room. Then another, glass splattering across the floor. Before she picked up another, she caught her reflection in the glass door then surveyed the floor.

God, I give up, I give up. I can't fix it. Tell me what to do! Isn't that what you're supposed to do?

She fell to her knees. *Silence.*

She whispered a prayer. *Silence*.

Finally, she yelled at the top of her lungs, "God if you are real, like everybody says, I'm not gonna move until you do! I am ASKING you for help, a sign, *something*!" Her eyes lifted, as if Jesus would manifest himself through the ceiling. When she finally stood, she walked around the room, looking up and shouting. Then the doorbell halted her steps. After several rings, she walked slowly toward the door. She peeked out. A short elderly lady with caramel skin and milk white hair stood at the door fussing away.

"Hello, I hear you on the other side. I need some help."

Sierra stepped back then placed her hand on the door knob. *She's an old lady, how harmful could she be?* Sierra peaked out the window alongside the door again.

"Well, are you going to open the door?"

Sierra finally opened it.

"Well, young lady, it's about time. It's hot as fish grease out here! We most certainly are living in the last days. It's a heat wave." She patted her neck with a monogrammed handkerchief. "Looks like my car stopped in front of the right place. Just can't go knocking on anybody's door these days." When she noticed Sierra eyeing her curiously, she stuck out her hand. "Oh, where are my manners? I'm Queenie Upshaw. Princess Di got a flat."

Sierras smirked. "Princess who?"

"Princess Di, my Thunderbird."

Sierra looked past her, and sure enough a few feet up the road was a bubble gum pink vintage Thunderbird.

Chapter 38 – Divine Connection

"I prayed for God to send me to the right place 'cause I needed help. "Can you help me, sweetie?"

Sierra looked around her. "Well, I guess." Sierra stepped away from the door and let her in. "Apologies, house is a mess."

The woman looked down at the floor at the splattered glass. "Not my business, just need to use the phone. By yourself, sweetie? Cause don't need any more drama today."

"Yes ma'am," Sierra said, a bit annoyed. *She's the one with the drama.*

"My car got a flat. You got a cellphone or something? I don't carry them. Don't believe in them."

Sierra was eyeing her to see if perhaps she might be some maniac, part of some operation or a lure for the press that had been popping up. Then she realized the energetic elderly woman had questions of her own, considering the way the house looked. "Of course. Please, use my cellphone." Sierra handed her the phone.

"Thank you, dear," she said as she grabbed it. "Where's the speaker thingamabob? Can't put it up to my ear. They say it gives you cancer," she whispered as she dialed. "Yes, I need someone to come fix this flat…don't take too long, I pay my insurance on time every month!" she yelled. "Where am I, oh yeah, where am I? Sweetie?"

"Oh, 3965 Orange Road."

While Queenie finished her call, Sierra rushed to get a broom and quickly swept up the glass. Queenie glanced out the corner of her eye. After she finished, she rushed back to the kitchen and put on some tea.

"Ms. Queenie, would you like some coffee or tea while you wait on the wrecker?"

"Well, if you have anything left to drink out of, I'd love to!" Her eyes lit up.

Sierra was about to get mad, but let out a hearty laugh instead. "I have more cups in the kitchen." Sierra went in there and poured her a cup of tea and put a few tea biscuits alongside of the tea cup saucer. "Ms. Queenie, I'm going to run upstairs and freshen up. As you can see, I wasn't expecting company. I'll be right back." She backed up toward the stairs.

"Honey, go ahead, I'm not a thief. Just gonna wait on the wrecker," she said as she blew on her tea.

"Right." Sierra turned, and once upstairs, she brushed her teeth, washed her face and ran a comb through her hair. She threw on a T-shirt and some jeans and a pair of slippers.

"See, everything's still here," Queenie sang when Sierra jogged downstairs. "Again, sweetie, thank you so much for helping me. Not many people would open their door to a stranger, but looks like you needed the company. Good Lord knew what he was doing."

"Well, not so sure about that, but glad I could help." Sierra grabbed some tea for herself and sat down on the couch near her guest. Suddenly Sierra relaxed; it was something so comforting about Queenie's presence. Despite her seasoned years, her youthful spirit was highly energetic and refreshing. It's obvious she'd either taken great care of herself or had great genes. Her silver white hair was neatly tapered into short layers. She sported a jogging suit with matching Nikes.

As they awaited the tow truck, they talked non-stop. Soon Sierra found herself pouring out her heart to her, as if she'd known her forever. As Sierra talked to Queenie, her new confidante shook her head and periodically only said, “But God. My God.” She was patient and never interrupted Sierra. The more Sierra talked, the better she felt. After Sierra got everything out of her system, the woman finally said, “It’s gonna be all right. It is *always* going to be all right, just takes time.”

“That’s it?” Sierra said, astonished. “That’s all you got for me? I just poured out my heart, and that’s the most profound thing you have to say?”

The woman’s eyes widened, and she placed her hand on her chest. She took a deep breath before speaking. “Sierra, when you’ve walked this earth as long as I have, you realize even the worse circumstances turn around. It truly is a matter of time. It’s what you do during that time that matters most. You gotta have patience in the process. I wouldn’t lie to you. I’ve had some heartache, pain, grief, lost it all and got it all back. God is faithful. You just have to believe.

“And even in our unbelief, God gives us grace. He meets us where we’re at. That, my child, is how we grow up in the faith. Sounds like it’s about that time for you. That’s when, sometimes, God allows the enemy to lay it on thick. That way we have to come to Him. It ain’t a pretty process.”

“Here we go again.” Sierra threw her hands up and let them fall to her lap. “Why does everybody think I’m immature? I’m a mother, I finished school, and I’m a freakin’ adult!”

“I said grow up in the *faith.* Sierra, only God knows why all this is happening. All I know is he’s the only way out. Sometimes God doesn’t take us around the fire but makes us walk clean through.” She looked Sierra in the eyes and grabbed her hand. “And like I said, this looks like one of those times, sweetie. And if you don’t want to go around this mountain again, I suggest you persevere.” She gripped Sierra’s hand. “Persevere and pray.”

"Well, I don't know if I can hold on much longer. I mean I need some *right now* answers from a *right now* God!"

She touched Sierra's face. "Honey, God can do anything. If he wanted to answer or do anything right now, He'd doit. We just have to hurry up and wait. He has all power. He can give your mother twenty new stores. He can set your mother free just like that! You're facing the test of your life, and you have to believe. And the one thing you don't want to do is piss him off."

"Him who?" Sierra's forehead creased.

"God. Anyway, I'm gonna pray God gives you an extra measure of faith. I know you haven't given your whole heart to Him. That's probably what he's waiting on. He works best with an open and transparent heart. I bet He's saying, 'Look at MY beautiful daughter. I wish she'd stop fighting me. 'Every time he tries to get in, you keep slamming the door on his toe."

Sierra tried to laugh at the visual then took a deep sigh. "All of this is too hard and too confusing. God hasn't been so consistent either." She felt tears coming again.

Queenie sighed. "It's hard by the yard, but it's a cinch by the inch. No, Sierra, it's not easy. Everybody's path to Christ is different. But God knows what He's doing. The good news? I'm gonna walk with you!" She tapped Sierra's knee. "Now, I'm gonna leave you my number. When you get scared, tired or need encouragement, call me anytime. I don't care what time of the night! I've mentored many young women and some of them, way worse off than you."

"Sure about that?" Sierra wiped her eyes.

"I'm positive, young lady. You do the best with what you got where you are."

Sierra managed a smile. She needed *somebody* on her side right now, and Queenie would have to be it. "Whoa, I feel like I just let a ton of bricks fall off my back."

After about fifteen minutes, the wrecker arrived. They walked outside and before they knew it, Princess Di's was up and ready to go. Sierra was sad to see Queenie go. She felt like an aunt or grandmother was leaving.

As Queenie was about to get in her car, she paused and looked as Sierra's eyes begged. She swallowed. "Sierra, God's able. You remember that. All you need is mustard seed faith." She reached into her purse and handed Sierra a little sealed plastic bag. "These are mustard seeds. See how tiny they are? Every time you look at them, remember that's all the faith you need."

Sierra nodded and grabbed the plastic bag. The tears began to flow despite her best attempts to cut them off. She reached out, grabbed Queenie, and held her tight. When she stepped back, she wiped her eyes, embarrassed. "Ughhh! Didn't mean to do all that."

"It's okay. We all cry. Weeping endures for a night, but joy will come in the morning, and you can take that to the bank!" Queenie opened the door, got in the car and started the engine. Before she pulled off, she reached in the glove compartment. "Wait! I need to give you my info. She pulled out a pen and paper, scribbled and handed Sierra the note, "Now, this is *all* my contact information. Come holla at me. I live in Oaks Bluff."

Sierra stared at the writing. Her eyes grew wide. "Martha's Vineyard?"

"Year round, honey," Queenie quipped.

"That's where, um Dorothy West lived." Sierra was tongued tied. "I've dreamed about going there forever."

"It's a special place. You read a lot?" Queenie put on her aviator shades.

"I used to. As a kid, it was my escape. But The Wedding, my *favorite* book of all time." Sierra said, feeling a wave of enthusiasm.

"Good, when you come to visit I'll take you by her old house. Not Shelby's, Dorothy's." Queenie stared in the distance. "I miss old Dorothy, Isabel, too."

"Isabel?"

"Yes, used to be married to Adam Clayton Powell. Made this Bloody Mary that makes you wanna...oh nevermind." Queenie sighed. "Everybody's gone."

Sierra wasn't sure what to say.

"But you know what?" Queenie said excitedly. "That's why we must live each day to the fullest. God gives us a new twenty-four hours every day. And when you get to be my age, well you're grateful for each hour, minute...second! Even when you get a flat tire!"

Sierra shook her head and smiled. "I guess you're right. Wow, can't believe you live near the oval."

"Sweetie, you do know that was fiction, right? Now you listen to me, when you feel like you can't bear another second of this town, you get on that train and come straight to the vineyard. I have plenty of room, and I love to spoil guests! You're one of *my* daughters now. And from the looks of it, you could use some good old fashioned mothering!" Queenie winked. "Gotta go." She put her car in gear, then turned to Sierra and mouthed the words *mustard seed.*

Before Sierra had the chance to say anything else, Queenie put a scarf over her head and tied it around the neck. She zipped off and threw her hand up as her car disappeared down the street. Sierra stared at the paper and shoved it in her pocket as she walked toward the house. She didn't solve her problems, but she couldn't help to think that God had actually heard her.

Chapter 39 – Strange Fruit

Sierra was clinging to her mustard seed faith for dear life. However, her trips to the mailbox failed to yield much fruit. After sorting through her mail, she noticed a pink envelope with handwriting on front.

Zoe?

She put it aside and decided to open it last. She moved on to an envelope from the mortgage company. She opened the letter and read the first lines. She didn't even bother to read the rest. She went back to the pink envelope. Then realized it was from Martha's Vineyard. *Queenie.* She tore off the envelope and read the card. It was a beautiful thank you note, train ticket and ferry passes. She scrolled down the note to the last line:

The cure for anything is salt water…sweat, tears or the sea

– Isak Dinesen

A week or two will birth a brand new you!

Love, Queenie

Sierra smiled, dismissing the notion at the same time. "Leave now? Right. Makes absolutely no sense!" She sucked her teeth. "Grayson Jr. would love that. It would be the height of irresponsibility." But, as she stared at the note, the words burned in her spirit. She wanted nothing more at this time than to get, no run, away. "What could really happen in a week or two?" The words "Martha's Vineyard" vacillated in her mind until she grabbed her phone. She began dialing Amber's number.

"…Sierra, I know it's not logical, but God rarely answers our prayers in ways we often recognize. Trust me, God is a pretty creative problem solver."

"I get that. But the house, little Gray…" She kept the phone wedged between her ear and shoulder as she grabbed some dirty clothes off the floor.

"What about the house?"

Sierra paused. "Mortgage is behind." She didn't want to tell all their business, but Amber knew about the shop eviction and her mother, so there was little else to hide.

"Well, hmm. Why not ask your father's son for the money? Surely he wouldn't want his son to be out on the street. And honestly, a week or two wouldn't make a difference with anything right now."

Sierra released a big sigh. "That would be a great if he hadn't just served me with custody papers. He's done this before when I've made him extra angry. His father, as much as he doesn't care for me, would force him to withdraw the papers. But that was before he was married."

Amber was silent for a few seconds. "You know what? We can sit here all day and try to figure this out, or we can pray. God's not the author of confusion. He'll give us the clarity 'cause seriously, ain't nobody got time for this!"

Sierra chuckled. "Amber, girl, you've been hanging around way too many black people!"

"That has nothing to do with it, just focus!"

Sierra shrugged. "Okay, go ahead and pray."

Finally, Amber thought. *A breakthrough*. "Dear Jesus, I join my faith with my sister Sierra. Father, we ask for discernment and wisdom concerning every issue before us. We ask that you'd intervene in this custody situation. We decree and declare that Sierra will not lose any custody rights, in the name of Jesus. We take authority over the spirit of lack, darkness, worry and fear. We cancel every assignment working against Sierra and Maxine Sanders.

Everything that is out of order is now in order. Now Father, speak clearly concerning this trip. Please give Sierra, her mother and son strength, rest, provision and a covering. We decree and declare that Maxine Sanders will be set free without record, blemish or stain and all will be restored. The wealth of the wicked will be stored up for this family. In Jesus' name, I pray. Amen."

"Amber! I can't believe all that power is in that little body!"

Amber chuckled. "It's not me, that's the work of the Holy Spirit. Never mind about all that. When I was praying, I saw a vision of you packing with a big bright light surrounding you. Sierra, this may not make a bit of sense, but I believe this trip is God-ordained. You may feel some guilt, but I feel so strongly about this. You need to go, Sierra. It isn't just a trip. Something greater is waiting on the other side of your obedience."

Sierra strained her mind, trying to make sense of what Amber was saying.

"Sometimes, we have to leave our comfort zone for answers. There has been nothing but

Chaos around you lately. Maybe God's giving you a chance to rest, get clarity. Besides you know the cure for anything is salt water—"

"What did you just say?" Sierra blinked rapidly.

"Just something my mother always says. The cure for anything is salt water: sweat, tears or the sea!" Amber chuckled.

"Wow. That's the exact quote Queenie put in her note. Isn't that unbelievable?"

"Nope," Amber said, "that's God! We asked for confirmation and we got it!" She yelled and started dancing.

~~~~~

As Sierra packed erratically, Amber's words swirled through her head, "The answer's in your obedience."
~~~~~

Sierra spun around the room, throwing random items in her bag, pausing every few seconds to ask, "God, I've never done anything like this before. Are you sure?" During Amber's prayer, something weird happened. She felt like fire or maybe electricity was dancing atop her head. She had a burst of energy. Sierra's actions were so fast and frantic over the next twenty minutes, she collided with her bookcase. She hit it so hard she thought half the books would fall down. She sat on her bed a few seconds, rubbing her thigh. Then reached down to pick up the only two books that fell. The Bible and her copy of *The Wedding.* She paused and sighed.

"Okay, okay, God. I got it."

Chapter 40 – Vineyard Virgin

Sierra navigated the train station and finally boarded. At the time the only person who knew her whereabouts was Amber. Once on the train, she quietly and quickly moved to a window seat. She settled and let out a sigh of relief as if she'd made a great getaway. The seat next to her was physically empty, but guilt rode shotgun all the way to Boston. She eventually dozed off. Once she arrived at the bus station, she popped in a shop, grabbed a snack and purchased a large beach hat. She perched on a bench for about ten minutes before a roomy bus drove up. She read the sign above the window. *Woodshole.* She breathed a sigh of relief. She reached in her wallet for the ticket as she awaited an invitation from the metal door.

As soon as her bottom hit the cushy fabric seat, she exhaled as her head fell back. The bus pulled away and she silently declared, *I'm no longer Sierra Sanders, just Sierra for the next two weeks. I'm going to forget about all my problems for two weeks.*

After a few miles on the road, she rehearsed her narrative, "I'm from a good home, a great family, and I'm visiting a relative." The Griers were known all over and Martha's Vineyard was fertile ground for people like them. She was going to be careful not to raise any suspicion. She reached in her bag for something to read, deciding to get reacquainted with her favorite protagonist. After about fifteen minutes, the book rest upon her chest as Sierra closed her eyes. She envisioned riding a bike in a gingham sundress, chatting with the neighbors on the oval and laying *on* the beach, just like Shelby. Soon, the vibration of the bus lulled her into the sweetest slumber.

"Woooodshole," the bus driver yelled as he pulled up and parked near a pier. Sierra opened her eyes, stretched, yawned and peered out the window. The ferry to Oaks Bluff was front and center. She smiled then eased out her seat, feeling weightless. She grabbed her belongings and headed down the steps. The bus driver extended his hand to help her and winked. "Hope your day's as beautiful as you are."

Sierra smiled, and scurried by without any further conversation. She'd noticed him staring when she first got on, but ignored him. *I'm not here to make any friends.* Her small piece of luggage was sitting on the ground awaiting her. She placed her hat on her head, slugged the tote on her shoulder and rolled her luggage toward the ferry. She handed the checker her ticket. He smiled then tore it in half. She followed the rest of passengers up the ramp as if she'd done it many times.

Sierra was about to rush to a seat, but instinctively paused at the rail. She focused on the stillness of the water. She drew in the light and crisp air. As the ferry pulled away from the pier, a reverent hush fell over the boat. Something magical was about to happen. Sierra remained at the rail as several people joined her. This was clearly some ritual, a peaceful rite of passage.

She watched as they floated past the cluster of boats docked along the pier. Sierra gazed downward as the liquid carpet ushered the gentle giant along. Her linen sundress fluttered in the wind. She removed her hat, allowing her ringlets to catch the breeze.

As the boat got underway, the foaming waves sliced through the waters. While the orange sun meld in the distance, Sierra didn't know if it was the water, air or the purity of the moment, but she suddenly felt permission to leave her guilt and worry behind on the pier. The moment was too serene, too surreal and too perfect to surrender to anything less.

Chapter 41 – The Inkwell

"Oaks Bluff!" Sierra's spirit leapt. She squinted at the cluster of people at the pier. She tried to find Queenie, but the boat was still a little too far away. *If she's not here, I'm totally messed up*, Sierra thought. Her heartbeat suddenly quickened. *What am I doing? What have I gotten myself into?* She stood still as the ferry slowed, then closed her eyes and breathed deeply. Her heartbeat slowed. Once the ferry stopped and the ramp lowered, she was one of the first ones to get off. She paused for a moment and her eyes darted frantically through the people hugging and greeting. *Do I even remember what she looks like?* She spun around when she heard a voice.

"Sierra sweetie! Here I am!" Queenie walked toward her with arms open and her crown of silver hair.

"Queenie!" Sierra moved quickly with her luggage rolling behind her.

"Come here, dear, I'm so glad you're here!" She wrapped Sierra in a warm hug.

Me too. I don't know what I'm doing here, but me, too.

~~~~~

Sierra took in the beautiful trees, shingle style houses, screened-in porches, and bike riders on the narrow road. They eventually turned on a road and continued along the shoreline in Queenie's old red pickup. "That's The Inkwell over there to the left."

"Oh, like the movie."

"Yeah, I guess," Queenie said and rolled her eyes. "We'll come out tomorrow morning and swim with the Polar Bears."

"The Polar who?" Sierra was still looking at the beach.
~~~~~

"The Polar Bears. We swim at the crack of dawn. You can swim, can't you?" she said, not taking her eyes off the road. Nina Simone was blaring through the car.

Sierra was about to cut her eyes "Yes, ma'am, I can swim. So, *how* early in the morning? Is the water warm at that time?"

"So full of questions. Trust me, you'll love it!" Queenie said, driving slow as molasses up the shoreline.

Must be pretty early in the morning, Sierra thought as she noticed the beautiful mosaic of purple and blue hydrangeas on most of the lawns.

They turned right down a street and passed a few Victorian houses and finally pulled up to a pale yellow cottage. As they got out the car, Sierra noticed two older women sitting on a wraparound porch at the larger house next door. Queenie lifted a hand.

"Hey Queenie," a woman in her rocking chair next door said with a smile.

"Hey Cora, how's it going?" Queenie didn't look her way until they got Sierra's luggage out the back of the truck.

"Well, going well. Why, what a beautiful young lady. Family?" The woman stretched her neck.

"My niece." Queenie smiled then kept walking to open the screen door. Sierra smiled at the sound of the word niece. Sierra paused to notice the children riding by on bikes and other children running around seemingly without supervision. Across the street in a similar flag-draped cottage, a man was napping on his porch. Sierra paused as she drew in the slow, easy, regal air.

"Well, come on in. Got enough flies in the house as it is," Queenie chastised.

"Oh, yes, yes, ma'am." Sierra stepped inside. It was light and homey with hardwood floors, built-in bookshelves that held lots of old books. She could only catch a glimpse of the vintage stove and colorful cabinets in the quaint kitchen.

"Okay, let's get your stuff upstairs. You can rest for a little while, and I can give you the grand tour," Queenie ordered. "And please, don't ever call me ma'am! You can call me Queenie, Queen B., anything but ma'am."

"Oh, okay." Sierra followed her up the narrow steps. Once upstairs, it was just as she imagined. The room was decorated in pastels with two twin beds covered in lace trimmed spreads and quilts. A set of towels were folded and placed on her bed. Across the hall was a bathroom with hexagon tile, a shower and a small sink. A little basket of toiletries awaited her. She had a porch off her bedroom and loved it. "Wow, this is beautiful. You stay here by yourself?"

"Sometimes, but I love guests." Queenie winked. "Most of the time, it's just me. I crochet, swim, cook me a nice breakfast. But you're never alone on the island, plenty of company. Why don't you freshen up while I fix us a snack?"

She left Sierra to go downstairs.

Sierra washed her face and hands and put on some lip balm. She changed into shorts and a T-shirt. She quickly wrapped her hair up in a ponytail and slid on some flip-flops. When she came outside onto the porch, she saw a spread of fresh fruit, yogurt, bagels, pasta, fresh lemonade and a few sandwiches. "Oooh, this looks good, I'm starving." She eyed the rocker on the porch and couldn't wait to sit there after making her plate.

She turned around, and a little boy ran up the stairs. "Ms. Queen-ie."

Queenie came to the edge of the porch and stared at his big freckled face. "Chad, what's wrong with you?" She noticed the little boy holding his arm.

"Fell on my bike." He poked his lip out and held up his fresh scab.

Queenie looked on the lawn where he'd thrown down his bike. "Uh-huh."

"See," he said, still holding his elbow up. His two other rough and tumble friends joined him.

"He hurt," one of them said.

She stepped down and looked at it. "No blood, you'll live. How about one of my homemade oatmeal and raisin cookies?"

He nodded. His two friends looked at each other as if they'd hit the jackpot.

She placed her hand atop his head and shook it. "You want a sandwich, too."

"No, ma'am, just cookies!" They ran up the stairs, grabbed a few from the plate and took off running.

Queenie shook her head. "They get me every time! Only reason I keep sweets." She looked at Sierra. "Now help yourself, I won't be waiting on you at all."

Those little boys made her think of her son. *I can't wait to bring him here*. Before the panic and guilt consumed her, her growling stomach took over. She finished loading her plate and sat in the rocking chair. She chewed while discreetly wiping a little water from her eyes. She rocked, feeling as though the chair had been meant for her. It soothed her.

"This was about the best sandwich I've had in a while," she said as she finished off the last bite, wiping the crumbs from her hands. She let out a huge sigh. "Wow, didn't realize I was so hungry." She looked around. "It's beautiful out here, so peaceful."

Queenie grabbed a plate and sat in the chair next to her. "Yeah, that's why I retired here."

"Did you buy this house or was it passed down? Oh, sorry, maybe that's too personal."

"Sweetie, it's okay. Bought it. Used to come here and stay with friends every summer. One summer, I declared I was gonna buy a house and that's exactly what I did. Sierra, if you never learn anything, understand the power of words. Anyway, I loved my job, but it was time to move on. I worked hard, saved, invested. Now I enjoy the fruits of my labor." She looked at Sierra. "When you sow good seeds, you get good harvest. But I sure miss my girls." She watched two teenage girls pass by laughing and talking.

"What girls? I thought you didn't have children."

"I was a college dean. They were *all* my girls. I used to love the fall when I'd see those beautiful, smart girls in every hue coming. Some ready to leave home, others clinging to their parents. College is the best time in a young woman's life."

"Wow that sounds wonderful. My best friend…" Sierra caught herself, "I mean, this place seems so different, special. Everyone seems so friendly and free. It's like the chocolate Mayberry!" She laughed. "Do parents just let their kids run all day like that?"

"For the most part. We look out for each other."

Sierra looked into the street and at the surrounding houses. She listened to the giggle of the children and the lone car driving by. "Well it's a little different than what I expected."

"How?"

"Well, I thought it was going to be like that Oprah Winfrey movie with Halle Berry, I mean you know…"

"Oh that. We do have some Shelby's around here." Queenie chuckled. "The island's a really good place. It's one of the few places you can run into politicians, relatives of civil rights leaders, or writers at the coffees shop. The island's rich with history and culture. It's *ours*. You can learn a lot, just keep your eyes and ears open."

Sierra was listening but couldn't help but see a man pull up at the house next to theirs in a BMW SUV. Queenie noticed she was clearly distracted.

"Oh, *that* one." She smiled.

"What?" Sierra said as she instantly tuned back into what Queenie was saying.

"Hey Carrington." Queenie lifted her wrinkled hand, then discreetly rolled her eyes.

"Hey Queen Elizabeth!" He hadn't looked up on the porch, but locked eyes with Sierra when he did. "Uh, hey, how are you doing?"

"Queen Elizabeth?" Sierra whispered.

"Yes, that's my first and middle name, and I only let a handsome gentlemen call me both! My father thought it was a good idea. It grew on me."

And handsome he is, Sierra thought. He was tall, built, clean cut and had the most perfect teeth Sierra had ever seen. She was done with his type. Grayson Jr. had spoiled her on the suit and tie guy. And she recognized one of those when she saw him. But the artist formally known as Bryce soured her on the whole Eric Benet vibe. Carrington's quiet eloquent voice had a subtle powerfulness. It intrigued her. But it was his looks that truly had her hypnotized.

"Carrington, this is Ms. Sierra, my guest for the next two weeks." Queenie noticed she was caught between the electricity of lasers flowing between the two of them.

Carrington rushed over, and his long legs climbed up on the porch. Sierra jumped as he reached out to shake her hand. She clumsily dropped the plate, and the remaining chips and a few grapes fell to the floor. She couldn't decide whether to reach to clean her mess or shake his hand.

"Sorry." She smiled. She reached down and picked up the plate. "Um, Hi."

"Nice to meet you. Is this your first time on the Vineyard?"

Sierra turned to Queenie.

"Yes, it's her first time, and why are you concerned?" Queenie raised her brows.

Carrington smiled.

Sierra quickly spoke up, "I guess you can say I'm a vineyard virgin." Sierra laughed a little too loud.

Carrington raised his brow. "Wow, I guess that's one way to put it." He grinned.

The ladies next door whispered to each other behind their hand fans.

Sierra was instantly embarrassed. She smacked her forehead. "I mean, this is my first time on the island. That didn't come out so right."

"Don't worry, I know what you meant." Carrington eyed the homemade cookies sitting on the covered table.

"Go on over," Queenie said as she caught the lustful look on his face. "This one eats all the cookies before the kids."

His smile lit up his face. "You make the best!" he said as he grabbed a few cookies off the table. "Well, Queenie, I gotta go." He leaned down to give her a quick kiss on the cheek. "Oh, Sierra, maybe I can take you on a tour of the island in the next couple of days."

Before she had a chance to answer, he bolted from the porch and hurried next door, the screen door slamming behind him.

Sierra immediately turned to Queenie. “Who was *that*? *He’s* staying next door?”

“No, that’s a friend of the family that stays next door. His house is a huge Victorian that actually sits facing the beach. His family’s been here for decades. “That’s my Carrington.” She shook her head. “He’s a good one.” She winked. “But a little confused.”

Chapter 42 – Morning Dip

Sierra thought Queenie was kidding when she woke her at the crack of dawn. As much as she adored the beach, she couldn't ever recall taking a swim at the crack of dawn. "Isn't the water a little chilly this time in the morning?" Sierra said, wrapped in a towel as she followed Queenie up the road.

"Yep. You'll get used to it!" They both marched steadily toward the beach.

Before Sierra could protest, she was there, especially since Queenie's house was minutes from the beach. A group of ladies of all shapes, sizes and shades of brown were already waiting.

"Morning!" Queenie said brightly and threw her hand up.

"Hey Queenie," they chorused and went back to stretching and chatting.

"Ladies, this is Sierra…"

Several of the women came over and gave her a hug. "Welcome!" a lady with salt and pepper dreadlocks said. "Another daughter, Queenie?"

"Something like that. You know I have a million children and never gave birth to one!" Queenie's infectious laugh rose up from her belly.

Sierra was still trying to get the sleep out her eyes.

"Now don't be shy, you're gonna love the water. This isn't time to be cute. You have to be open to enjoy it." one of the other ample ladies chimed.

"Open to what? And what is a Polar Bear?" Sierra said in a low voice.

Another lady passing by heard her. "The Polar Bears are a tradition, and you're about to become an honorary member," the woman with a short salt and pepper 'fro said.

"Really, how?" Sierra yawned and smacked her lips together. "Oh sorry."

The woman placed her arm around Sierra. "My dear, you show up and swim. Bam, that's it! You're a member. Well, and you're with Queenie."

Sierra tucked away her protests and followed the group on the sand. She removed her flip-flops, feeling the coolness of the sand beneath her feet. The sand felt so good just walking in it would have been enough for her. Then she looked up out at that sun. It was calling her name.

She continued to trek slowly as the ladies sped past her. They first formed a circle on the sand. Sierra looked around at the women. They were queens, clearly comfortable in their own skin. Not worried about their hair or how their swimsuits fit. Their common bond was only one of positive, joyful spirits. Sierra felt their energy. They all radiated a powerful beauty, radiance and confidence. Sierra removed her towel and got in the circle.

Soon several women took turns praying. The rolling waves provided the worship music with an occasional seagull chiming in. Sierra's body felt lifted with every word, every song.

"Amen," they all spoke, then headed for the water.

Sierra clearly wasn't ready. Queenie grabbed one of her hands, and another lady grabbed the other. Queenie winked. "It's only water."

Sierra walked slowly, her lithe body shivering. She cursed her iron poor blood. *Okay, you can do this.* Once far enough in the water, they all began to sing, repeat affirmations, stretch, and praise. Sierra released her fears and soon felt a connection that was therapeutic and powerful. Once they finished, she broke away and just floated. With her back in the water, she looked up at the clouds then closed her eyes. *God, cover me like a blanket.* The water washing over her cleansed her from the inside out. She felt a wave of light consume her as she buoyed in weightless wonder. She focused only on the ebb and flow of her own breathing.

Gazing upward to the sky, she could only utter two words, "Thank you."

Chapter 43 – Good Gifts

Sierra sat on the couch in the living room. Queenie made her feel at home, but that peace she felt on the ferry floated in and out. A little fidgety and restless, she eyed the bookcase, home to tons of novels and textbooks. She walked over scanned the shelves. She grabbed a book just as Queenie walked in with some iced tea.

"Zora Neale Hurston."

Sierra examined the spine. "You have so many of my favorites." She reached up and grabbed another. "The Living Is Easy," Sierra said quietly and smiled. "Alice Walker."

Queenie smiled back. "Okay, we'll do the African-Heritage Trail before you go. I'll take you by Dorothy West's old house."

"Really? I would love that," Sierra said as she looked back up at the wall. "You have a lot of books. What college did you work at again?"

"Well," Queenie began as she walked over and handed Sierra the glass of iced tea, then dropped in a wing back chair, "I worked at many. But I retired from Spelman."

"Wow, "Sierra said as her eyes widened. "That makes sense, I mean when you say you have lots of daughters." Sierra swallowed and grabbed her arm. "My best friend…" Sierra took a deep breath. "I mean, I heard it was a really special school."

"Loved every minute of it. Mentored many a young woman like you." Queenie smiled.

I doubt if they were anything like me. Sierra sat on the couch. "Do you have any children of your own? Where are you from, I mean so many things I don't know about you, and I'm staying in your house. You are literally a stranger."

"No children. And, for your information we're family not strangers. God brought us together, and ain't nothing you can do about it! "Queenie let out a hearty laugh. "Now do you plan on going to school? What's your calling, my dear?"

Sierra shrugged. "Calling? Not sure about that. I love jewelry. I mean I design it. I get lost in it for hours. Honestly, it's the only thing besides books I've ever loved. The only thing I think I'm good at." She folded her arms. "Shoot, I don't know."

"You do know. And a calling is what you were brought here on this earth to do."

"Well, I don't think jewelry is a calling."

"Nonsense, if you're good at it, and you love it more than anything else, it's part of your life's mission. God is creative, he loves beauty. He's the one that gets your fingers to working." Queenie spoke like a teacher expecting her student's response.

"Wow, never thought about it like that. Something happens to me when I create something beautiful from a few stones, metal and whatever else inspires me. It's like God's working through my hands."

Queenie smiled from her chair. "Did you say God?"

Sierra smiled back. "Guess so."

"You recognize your gift is from God. That's a good thing. Once you acknowledge it's His gift, God can do the supernatural. One thing's for sure. Plenty of creative folks on the island, all sorts of writers and painters. Did you bring any of your jewelry?"

"Yes. I left so fast I didn't bring all the clothes I wanted, but I don't go anywhere without my jewelry!" Sierra could hear the excitement in her own voice. "And believe me I've been thinking about all that. I've made vision boards. I believe Saks and Barneys and every boutique will want my jewelry collection. I have a website, too."

"Wonderful. I want to see it all. And don't worry about having lots of nice clothes. No one really dresses up here. People come to the island to relax, swim and run around. Do you see anybody dressed up here?"

Sierra shook her head.

"Now show me some of those jewelry pieces. It's time for the world to see your gifts, and we might as well start here at the island!"

Sierra could not contain herself. She was excited because finally she had someone who believed in her. Finally, somebody got it. Finally, somebody was not trying to talk her out of her dream.

Chapter 44 – Like Riding a Bike

Sierra mentioned to Queenie she wanted take a bike ride. A day later, a bicycle showed up near the shed in the back of the house. So after about three days of staring at that bicycle in the yard, she finally got on it. She waved to the women on the porch next door as she clumsily backed the bike out into the street. She'd thrown on a seersucker sundress and pulled her hair into a ponytail. She didn't quite know where she was going, but Oaks Bluff didn't seem that big. She headed up her street and over to the only main street she knew how to get to, Circuit Avenue. She peddled along the shore and cut over a number of streets bypassing the gazebo sitting in the middle of Park Square at Seaview and Ocean Avenue.

She passed a group of little girls playing in their swimsuits headed toward the beach and a few joggers. Everyone raised a hand to say hello. She kept peddling until she reached the carousel near Circuit Avenue. A few feet over she noticed an old movie theatre. She jumped off the bike. She peeked inside and saw all the children yelling and bouncing with excitement as they danced around their parents in line to ride. *My little Gray would like this.* She instantly blocked out his face. *Nope, I can't. Not until I know why God brought me here.* Soon she replaced his image with the colors of the carousel. She had instant inspiration for a new jewelry line.

Sierra wheeled her bike up the side walk. She paused for some ice cream. It was the best ice cream she had in a long time. She felt like a kid. She was free, almost happy. She was determined to leave Montclair behind while in the Vineyard.

As she walked up Circuit Avenue, she peeked in some of the little shops. She spent the longest time in C'est La Vie. Maybe it was the cute little gifts, but Sierra was more drawn to the handsome owner with the French accent. She kept going until she paused at a narrow pathway to her right. She was curious, so she took it. She came upon the most beautiful whimsical display. She looked on a sign and she realized she'd reached the Gingerbread houses. She'd seen them on postcards sitting outside on a stand at one of the little souvenir shops. Then she saw a huge tabernacle with stained glass on its roof. She went and sat there. She meditated. She took deep breaths.

A short time later, she stood and turned her bike around. She walked a little ways and headed back toward Circuit Avenue. She paused to look into the window of an art shop. Then she read the words on the entrance: Cousen Rose Gallery. She parked the bike outside and went right in. An author was signing his book. She smiled and passed the few people standing in line for a copy of the book. She walked over and looked through the prints. She flipped through until she saw one with two little girls with sun hats on the beach. She smiled.

"You like that one?" She quickly turned around in the direction of the male voice. "Didn't mean to sneak up on you, how you doing? See you're finding your way around the island."

Carrington. She swallowed. "Um, hey. What, what are you doing here? I mean, not what are you doing here. Well, you know what I mean." She smiled.

"The author's a friend of mine. We both went to Brown."

Ugh. Sierra felt small again. She put her head down.

"You okay?" He grabbed her arm. When he touched her arm, she felt a warm sensation go through her body.

"Oh, yeah. Great." She forced a smile.

"Well, how about I give you an official tour of the island tomorrow? We can even head over to Vineyard Haven and the Aquinnah cliffs. And then perhaps a picnic lunch." He smiled. His large brown eyes searched her face. Sierra was tall, but he towered over here. He was so clean cut with a white T-shirt, khaki shorts and

Tod's boat shoes. She recognized the shoes because Grayson Jr. had several pairs.

Okay, I need to get a grip here, she thought, mesmerized by his woodsy and slightly sensual cologne.

"Well," she stuttered, shaking her head, "I'd love the tour. I'll see about the picnic."

"Well I'll take what I can get. Come on, I'll introduce you to my friend. He wrote a book about the island."

Sierra smoothed her dress with her hands.

"Don't worry. You look beautiful, "Carrington said, winking.

~~~~~

When Sierra made it back to Queenie's cottage, she was winded but invigorated. Dinner met her on the porch. The wooden table was covered with a gingham tablecloth. Plates were stacked and Sierra smelled apple pie. Queenie greeted her at the door.

"Whatever it is smells fantastic," Sierra said.

"Well," Queenie said, walking out with a crockpot, "look who's all smiles. Never seen somebody so happy after a bike ride."

"I'll go wash my hands."

"I don't think it's the bike ride," the lady who sat on the porch next door said as she swatted flies.

"Cora, mind your business," Queenie yelled over next door. They all giggled.

~~~~~

"That was so good!" Sierra plopped in her chair and extended her feet. "Is this all people do here? Eat, laugh, swim and rock on the porch?"

"I guess pretty much," Queenie said as she swatted flies.

"Well, I'm not complaining." She watched several kids ride by on their bikes. "This *is* a special place." Sierra leaned back and smiled.

"Yes, it is. So, you gonna to tell me about that bike ride?" Queenie's chair slightly creaked in motion.

"Oh yes. I went to Circuit Avenue and by the marina to see the boats. It was so relaxing. I took some pictures. It looked like a postcard, just beautiful."

"And…?"

"Okay," Sierra swat Queenie's arm with her fan, "I ran into Carrington. That's his name, right?"

"You know that's his name."

They both let out a laugh like two schoolgirls.

Chapter 45 – Island Tour

Sierra wasn't sure what to expect from Carrington, but she'd made up her mind to say as little as possible. And she was definitely wasn't reading more into their outing than necessary. He'd picked her up at noon, and she was riding shotgun in his SUV. He looked over occasionally and smiled.

"You okay? You seem a little nervous." His eyes faced the road and he waved at what seemed like every other person.

"I'm okay." *Ugh, he noticed.* "Wow, you know a lot of people." Sierra looked out the window. She'd smoothed a loose strand blowing wildly in the wind. She'd pulled it back with a fabric headband. *Something Shelby would do*, she reasoned. *Maybe I should have worn shorts?* She felt cool and comfortable in her maxi linen sundress. She wore simple pieces from her own jewelry. Small mother of pearl earrings and a matching lariat.

"People on the island are just friendly. But I guess you can say I do know quite a few people. You look great, by the way." He looked her way again and smiled.

"Thanks, you too." She instantly regretted her choice of words, "I mean, you look nice and casual. I mean—"

"I know what you meant." He laughed. "Sierra, relax okay? I'm not that kind of person. I'm stress free."

Yeah, okay, Mr. Ivy League.

"So, how long have you been coming to the island?" Sierra asked.

"Umm, since I was a kid. Our house has been in the family for generations."

"Nice, you're really lucky."

"I guess you can say that. But the truth? This house almost broke up our family."

"Really? How?" Her forehead creased as she listened.

"Well, there was some ambiguity in a will. Ultimately, my dad won. But he and my uncle stopped speaking for years. My uncle passed before they had a chance to really mend the relationship. Kinda sad. My cousins and I are still close."

"Wow."

"Yeah, unforgiveness is a poison to the soul."

Sierra took a deep swallow. His words landed with a strong thud in her heart. "Yeah, it is," she said slowly.

"Anyway, enough about me. How do you know Queenie?"

"Oh, well, she knew, well knows my mother." She cleared her throat. "From a long time ago. She came to Montclair, then invited me here."

"Oh, that sounds just like Queenie, that house is an open door. I love Queenie. She always there for everybody and so much fun. Never heard her say an unkind word about anyone. And believe me, in a place where the gossip sometimes runs rampant that's tough! Feels like you've known her forever the instant you meet her. You'll have a good time. Lots of good childhood memories for me."

Sierra could see the little boy in him come alive as he shared more of his memories. Before Sierra could get too comfortable, they drove through an area with trees and pulled up to a little red building. They didn't get out right away.

"That, my lady, is Shearer's Cottage. People think African-American people had money when they initially settled on the island. But many of the people who purchased homes took care of other families."

"I have to admit," Sierra said, "I had my picture of Martha's Vineyard. I thought it was a bunch of bougie people walking around. So far everyone has been so nice."

"Well, that's partly because you're with Queenie. She knows everybody. We do have families that hold the island sacred. It's like a hidden treasure. We share but we are a bit protective."

"Sooo, what do you do for fun, any hobbies?"

"Well, I dabble a little in writing. Working on a mystery."

Sierra sat up. "Like The Emperor of Ocean Park?"

"Whoa, Stephen Chambers, now that brother there is a true writer! I'm just playing around, nothing serious."

"You never know. Might be your calling."

"Maybe. Actually I'm fascinated with any kind of writing: screenplays, plays—all of it. It's something magical about inventing characters and bringing them to life. There are several film festivals that come to the island."

"Sounds like more than a hobby, sir. But I get the creative part. That's how I feel about my art, well designs."

"You paint?"

"No, no...I sketch a little but design jewelry. Actually, the sketching is usually to flush out my designs."

He shook his head and grinned in a way that revealed that cavernous dimple. "Very cool."

Sierra smiled back. "So about this Shearer's Cottage, I want to know more."

"I'll do better than that, let's go inside and meet the current owners."

~~~~~
~~~~~

Sierra was amazed at how much history Carrington knew about the island. She'd enjoyed every morsel of history and insight.

"So, worked up an appetite yet?"

"Maybe, a little. But can I ask one thing?" Sierra said with hesitation.

"With a face like that, how can I say no?" He glanced her way and quickly focused back on the road.

"I, well Queenie told me that Dorothy West has a house here, and well, I really would love to see it. You know, the book. It's my favorite."

He let out a big smile. "Oh, yeah I know. You want to see *the Oval*. Although I have to tell you, it's not as big and grand as they portrayed it in the movie."
"It's not a real place?" Her voice sounding as if she were six and someone told her Santa wasn't real.

"Um, yeah, but it's fiction, babe." He reached over and grabbed her chin.

"I know it was fiction, but there's such thing as the oval, right? Please tell me. I have to know."

He kept smiling and started to hum. He made a quick turn onto another street. He turned off on a road and was driving up a narrow road with several houses littered around it. They parked in front of one of the houses and got out to walk. As soon as Sierra stepped on the lawn, she felt this weird spirit. The area was simple, but still she felt honored to walk the ground. She noticed a simple swing on the oval patch of grass. He grabbed her hand as they took a few more steps.

"Okay, madam, here it is…the house where *The Wedding* was born."

Sierra stood, staring. She couldn't move. Dorothy West was her shero. For decades, she imagined the oval. She'd imagined a place she'd summered every year. Shelby was rich, beautiful and marrying the love of her life. Sure she had her share of problems, but Shelby was the Black American Princess Sierra wanted to be. The closest thing to Shelby was in front of her. A simple cottage with a lot of history. She let go of Carrington's hand to bend down and read the metal sign that marked the house.

"I used to come by and see her from time to time," Carrington said. "She was a feisty something. Did you know Jacqueline Onassis was the one who helped get her book published?"

"Yes, I know."

"Now, who is this pretty little thing you got with you, Mr. Carrington Carver?"

The both looked on the porch next door.

"Oh, hello, Ms. Mable," Carrington said.

A lady who looked like she could pass for white stepped outside, eyeing them both up and down through her black rimmed bifocals. "Never seen her before. Come here and say hello. Don't make an old woman yell." She waved her old church fan.

Carrington grabbed Sierra's hand again and ushered her over slowly.

"Carrington dear, isn't it about time for you to settle down? When are you going to make up your mind? Every summer you have a new one," the lady said, still inspecting Sierra. Carrington shifted his long legs. "Ms. Mable, I just want to make sure I'm only going to do this thing once."

Sierra smiled nervously.

"Well, this one looks like a good one. Just pick one. She'd make some pretty babies and they'd have some beautiful hair.

Who's your family?" She looked over the top her glasses and wiped her mouth with a handkerchief.

"Uh, Ms. Mable, we really need to go. We're starving." Carrington wrapped his arm around Sierra's waist.

She waved at Carrington. "Go on and tell your mother not to be a stranger, okay?" She patted the moisture from her forehead.

"Yes, ma'am," he said, walking backwards and pulling Sierra toward the car.

Sierra didn't say anything until they got inside.

"So what did you think?"

"About what?" she said with folded arms.

"The Oval, the house?"

"Oh, you were right, it wasn't like the movie, but it still felt special. I appreciate you going out of the way to bring me here," Sierra said dryly.

"Well, let's go get something to eat. I'm starving." He cranked up his truck.

"Maybe I should just go back to Queenie's."

"Nope, I'm kidnapping you."

Chapter 46 – Lobster Fest

Sierra and Carrington left Myrtle Avenue headed toward what she thought was Queenie's place.

"So, you like lobster?" Carrington turned to her and flashed an infectious smile. He refocused on the narrow road, awaiting her response.

Sierra's stomach replied before she did. "Yes, love it."

"Great."

After about fifteen minutes of driving past more beautiful homes, they came upon another beach. She noticed a sign that said the Aquinnah Cliffs. Carrington parked and jumped out to open the door for Sierra. He grabbed her hand to help her down. Soon they were walking on the beach. The potential of a romantic walk on the beach excited her, but she dared not show it. All of a sudden she heard voices.

"Here he is…finally."

A fire burned in the distance as they hiked further up the beach. Several people were laughing, chatting. It looked like a party. Anxiety took over Sierra's insides. Now that she'd spent a little time with Carrington, she felt safe, but he had no clue of her social phobias.

"Over here, C.C.!"A young lady in a bikini top and sarong waved in the distance.

Carrington waved, and then grabbed Sierra's hand.

"Are you okay?" he asked as he felt a tremble in her hand. "Don't be shy. It's just friends and family." They continued until they reached the group.

"This one, always with a beautiful lady." A guy who favored Carrington came over and playfully slapped his back and grabbed his neck. "Eh-em, introduction?" he said, finally eyeing Sierra.

"Hi," she giggled, "I'm Sierra." She kept a tight grip on Carrington's fingers.

"Everybody, this is Sierra," he yelled.

They all smiled and said hello. Three women who looked to be about Sierra's age waved and smiled, but one whispered in the other's ear. Another broke from the pack and ran over to kiss Carrington on the cheek. "Hi, Sierra, I'm Chloe, C.C.'s cousin." Her fresh, makeup free face was sprinkled with a few freckles. Her smile was natural, and she bounced with energy as the ocean breeze lifted her ponytail.

"Hello," Sierra said and smiled back. Her spirit was as warm as the highlights in her sandy brown hair.

"That's Gracelyn my sister, Grace for short and our friend Layla." She pointed in the direction of the two young women coming toward her.

"Hi, what a pretty name." Grace hugged Sierra. "I'm a hugger."

"Oh," Sierra said, caught off guard at the slight embrace. She admired Grace's nutmeg skin glistening from the small droplets of water. Judging from her sand covered legs, she'd been tussling with some of the guys.

"Hi I'm Layla," she offered with a tight-lipped smile; she was always hesitant when new people came around. Her textured mane was pulled away from her face with a wide headband. Her Howard University T-shirt knotted at the waist exposed her taught stomach.

Two guys who had been throwing a football rushed over, almost knocking down Carrington.

"Where you been, boy?" one of them asked. He was a strikingly good looking guy with his shirt hanging on his belt. Dark skinned with coal black hair and a chiseled jawline, his confidence overflowed.

Sierra tried not to stare at his defined chest.

"Oh, I see why you were late!" he said. "Hi, I'm Christian."

Sierra blushed. "Hi, Christian."

Christian's football partner rushed into Carrington and air boxed him. "Uh, punk. Where you been all day?" He barely looked at Sierra.

"Man, you can't speak? This is Sierra."

Sierra shifted her weight from one leg to the other and bit her lip.

"Oh, my bad." He nodded his head. "Nice to meet you."

"Don't pay his rude arrogant behind any mind. That's Tristin." Chloe slid her arm through Sierra's.

"What? What'd I do? Uh, C.C. where's Fallon?" he asked as if Sierra was invisible.

Everyone all of a sudden paused and looked at Carrington.

"Just kidding, dog. Just kidding." Tristin was the only one laughing.

"Look, the food is ready. Those lobsters have been in the fire." Chloe pointed toward the large pot atop the fire. "I'm starving waiting around on you! Sierra, hope you're hungry. We've got so much food!"

Sierra fumbled with her necklace. "Yeah, I mean yes, I am, um hungry."

"Good." Chloe threw her arm around Sierra. "Let's go eat!"

Sierra looked over at Carrington, afraid to leave his side. He winked at her. "You're okay."

~~~~~

"That was the best lobster I've ever had in my life!" Sierra said as she leaned back on her elbows. Her stomach was about to burst. She looked out on the water; the sun was settling in the distance. For a minute, she convinced herself this was really her life.

"Sierra?" Chloe called her name. "Sierra, did you hear me?"

"Huh, oh, I'm so sorry. I was so full on food and lost in the scenery. I got relaxed. I'm sorry. What did you say?" Her eyes fixed on the water hitting the rocks in a distance.

"I was admiring your necklace. I love the combination of the stones. Where'd you find it?"

"Oh, this? It's nothing." She shrugged. "I made it."

"Really?" Chloe's eyes focused in on the necklace. "It's *gorgeous*."

Carrington burst in their conversation. "Sierra's way too humble. She's a jewelry designer. She went to Parson's."

"Wow, really? That's fantastic. I love creativity!" Chloe said, still eying the necklace. "Hey where can I find your jewelry?"

Sierra, not wanting to reveal too much, paused. "Uh, well, I have a website."

"Great, you'll have to give me the web address so I can check it out."

"It's beautiful," Layla said, eyeing the necklace from her beach chair. "Can you do that full time and make a living?" She reached in a beach tote for her magazine.

Grace cut her eyes at Layla.

"What?" Layla said once she looked up. "I'm just curious. I mean some things are meant to be a hobby."
~~~~~

“It’s not a hobby, “Carrington said as he moved closer to Sierra.

“C.C., I was talking to Sierra. Nevermind.”Layla rolled her eyes and started flipping pages of the magazine.

“So, where’s your boy Rob? Can’t believe you let him roam free.” Carrington smirked.

“Funny. Anyway, you know where he is, on lock down prepping for the bar.” Layla still focused on the magazine.

“That’s what he’s telling you,” Christian chided.

Everybody laughed.

Layla slowly raised her head. “Sierra, if I were you, I’d watch that one.” Her head nodded toward Carrington.

He shook his head. “Really? I just met Sierra, she’s not thinking of me like that. And second, everyone knows you don’t take advice from a woman scorned.”

Everybody burst out laughing again.

“Man, ease up, you starting to act like me now,” Tristin said. He slid over to Layla and whispered in her ear. She winced and giggled.

Carrington stood and grabbed Sierra’s arm. “Let’s go for a walk.” She was happy to escape.

“So, what do you think so far?” Carrington said as he picked up a rock and threw it into the water.

“About what?”

“The island.”

“Oh, it’s beautiful. I’m enjoying myself.” She paused to remove her sandals and allowed the granules of sand to soothe her feet. She wanted so bad to ask him about Fallon and other comments but didn’t. *None of my business, I barely know him. And let’s get real. I’m only here for another week.* What she did know was she hadn't felt attracted to a man since Bryce and despite her logic, Cupid had other notions. She couldn't ignore little butterflies doing the wobble in her stomach. She broke free from his hand and walked closer to the tide. He followed behind her. She allowed the tide to cleanse and relax her feet as she listened to the waves.

She closed her eyes for a moment, and immediately Zoe's face appeared. She wanted so much to call her best friend. Share all the little tidbits about her trip. She would have described Carrington from his facial features to the little way his legs slightly bowed and the little traces of hair on his bulging calves. She would have told her how tall and lithe he was and mocked his perfect diction. She would have told her about Queenie and the beautiful room with the arched double windows that opened to the balcony off her bedroom. But she couldn't because they weren't speaking.

I miss her.

Carrington eased over and placed his hand on her shoulder and gently squeezed it. She jumped at his touch. "Deep in thought?"

She shook her head. *You have no idea, Mr. Chambers.*

He eased his arms around her from behind and placed his head on the area between her chin and shoulder. "Hope this is okay."

She smiled and closed her eyes. *More than okay.* "Yeah, it feels pretty good."

Chapter 47 – The Wings of Forgiveness

Sierra got up early to jog along the shoreline. *Why did I stop running?* It wasn't like she was a marathon star, but on some mornings, she had liked to get out and release her stress. The sea air and emerging sun were a bonus. For the first time in a week, her head was clear, and she wasn't sure that was a good thing. Her son, Zoe, her mom and the feelings she'd associated with them bombarded her thoughts. She couldn't shut them out any longer. She pumped the music louder in her headphones. After about a half a mile, her frustration and guilt dissipated. It didn't hurt to have a handsome man alongside her. She and Carrington were jogging in sync. Despite her nagging feelings, one thing was for certain, a shift was happening. She felt stronger, maybe even strong enough to face everything she'd left behind.

Amber was right.

Sierra shuffled her playlist. Old school Mary J. Blige blared in her ear, providing momentum for her Nike clad feet. Her vision of training for the Olympics lasted as long as the song. The infectious beat prompting her to mouth the words. Suddenly reality set in as she felt a little pain in her knee. She glanced at Carrington. Despite her pride, she knew a detour to the nearest bench was imminent. She signaled to Carrington and veered off.

He grinned then followed her and continued to jog in place once she stopped.

"Ha, ha, okay, so I was a little overly ambitious today. But this felt good." She dropped her hands to her knees and bent over slightly to catch her breath.

"That's okay, I'll let you slide. But you did say five miles, we barely did three." His mouth curled to an irresistible smile.

God he's even fine in the morning.

She removed her earphones, dropped to the bench and stretched her legs in front of her.

He sat next to her and smacked the brim of her hat. "I thought with all this running gear you had the power! I mean all that stretching and warm up you were doing, I'm just sayin'."

She looked at him and rolled her eyes. "Okay, all right, enough! I'm a little out of shape. It's been a minute."

"I'm kidding. Got to be consistent with running." He paused to speak to a family walking by. He winked at the little boy trailing behind. "So Sierra, got something to ask you."

"Yeah." She pulled out a water bottle from her belt and took a sip.

"I think I mentioned my parents are having their anniversary party next week. Would you like to come? I mean, it's not a big deal, but I think you'd enjoy yourself."

"Oh." *I hate parties, I don't have a dress and if his people are anything like Tristin or Layla, no thank you.*

"Is that all you can say? I mean, you can come meet some more of my friends, get some good food and just hang out. And it's another excuse for me to see you."

"Well, what's the attire?"

"All white. I mean sort of dressy casual. I don't know. I'm a guy but it's not formal."

"Ohh, okay. Yeah, I guess I'd love to come. But you probably figured it out. I'm not a big fan of groups or parties." She looked down at her running shoes.

"That's okay, you'll be with me. Promise you'll feel at home. Queenie's invited, too. She knows my parents."

"This isn't one of those Martha's Vineyard who's who soirees, is it?" She raised her brows and searched his eyes.

He squeezed his fingers together. "Maybe just a little bit, you'll be fine, my family's good people."He smiled and bumped his leg against hers. "Besides, you don't have to do much, you're already beautiful.

Lord Jesus.

"Why do you make it impossible for me to tell you now?" she said as her mouth burst into a smile like fireworks.

He shrugged, then leaned back against the bench. They sat quietly for a few moments.

"This is like a little paradise. Another world," Sierra said, looking out on the water.

He thought for a few seconds. "Paradise is in your mind."

She smiled and shook her head. "Where did I hear that before?"

"India.Arie."

They both laughed.

"So now that I have a yes on the date, eh-em I mean invite to the party, do you mind if I get in my five miles, my lady?" He placed his hand on her knee.

"Oh yeah, sure. Sorry I couldn't hang." She chuckled.

"No worries, call you later?"

"Definitely."

~~~~~

Sierra removed her sneakers and walked down to the sand. "I can't wait to tell Zoe—" She caught herself once again. It wasn't long before reality tried to stick its big ugly toe into her current fairy
~~~~~

tale. Despite suppressing all the negativity, problems and pain, she finally let the cork escape from the bottle.

God, what's really going on? I miss my son, my mother and my life. God, seriously, why am I here, why? She yelled internally. She knew Zoe was about to have her baby any day if she hadn't already. Sierra thought of the many times Zoe had been there for her. She leaned down and picked up a shell. She wiped off the sand. *The chance to share the one thing we could was ruined over a stupid fight.* She sucked her teeth. For once in her life all that God babble, as Zoe used to call it, was starting to make sense.

She continued to trek down to the beach until she was at the end of a jetty. She looked out at the sea, watching the sailboats in the distance. Staring intently, waiting as if the ocean had some answers.

God, are you gonna fix all this or not?

"The power to change your circumstances begins with YOU. You just need to get out of your own way. Stop holding on to all this stuff. I can bring your mother home, restore everything you think you've lost. But I want you first!"

"Huh?"

The voice was loud audible. She turned around. She was still alone. She steadied her feet on the rocks.

Until you stop blaming everyone for your problems, you'll get more of the same.

"Whoa," she whispered.

You have everything you need to create the life you want.

She stood several more minutes, looking around. She expected to hear more, but that was it. "Wow, was that the holy spirit?" She waited for something else, some instructions. She waited for another ten minutes. She was about to turn and walk back.

One last thing.

Her head went up like periscope and she paused.

Forgive.

~~~~~

When she reached Queenie's cottage, Sierra burst through the door "Queenie?"

"Up here, sweetie."

"Where are you?"

Sierra saw her step down a small wooden staircase. "What's up there?"

"Attic, well, I sort of transformed it into a craft workroom. So, how was your run, dear?" Queenie was wearing a smock and looking fresh and vibrant.

"Good, well great!"

"I see, what a little Carrington Chambers will do for you in the morning."

Sierra noticed the paint splattered on her jacket. "Wow, I didn't know you painted."

"There's a lot about me you don't know. I'm full of surprises! Now for you, what's this glow about?"

"The run helped. Weirdest thing afterwards. I walked out on a jetty. It was only me and God, I guess it was him. He started speaking. At least I thought it was him. That's never happened. People try tell me what it's like to hear his voice. All these years I've tried to imagine what it was like and all of a sudden like bam!" She hit the wooden stairwell. "I hear him."

Queenie jumped. "Oh my."

"Sorry, did mean to scare you, can't explain it. But I think you get it."
~~~~~

Queenie's eyes tried to follow her. "Yeah, I know what you mean, dear."

Sierra was bursting with enthusiasm as she tried to articulate the tumble of emotions inside.

"Well, I don't know what happened on that beach or on that run, but you need more of it."

"Yes! I need more Jes—us!" Sierra said before she realized, shocking herself.

"Well!" Queenie said as she placed her hands on her hips. "Did you all stop by the tabernacle on the way in?"

Sierra grinned a little. "No ma'am, just can't quite explain it…"

She gave Sierra a hug. "You don't have to."

Chapter 48 – Surprise Guest

Queenie loved cooking and singing. She brushed past Sierra and headed out the screen door and onto the porch. Sierra inhaled the aroma of catfish and hot water cornbread. She hurried and washed her hands in the kitchen sink and dried them with a linen towel.

"Need some help?" she yelled.

"Just grab the sliced watermelon," Queenie replied.

Sierra looked around and saw a plate of fresh ripe watermelon sliced and covered with plastic. She grabbed it and scurried out the door. Sierra was definitely getting spoiled and in the back of her mind wished she and Queenie were really family.

"Well, you look refreshed," Queenie said. "My guess is you met the Lord out on those jetties."

How does this woman know…nevermind. She stretched. "Queenie, I *feel* brand new."

"By the way," Cora said from her rocking chair, "a certain tall glass of water by the name of Carrington came through looking for you. Claimed he was taking a walk, but I know better."

My, she doesn't miss a thing, Sierra thought. "How long ago?"

"About an hour."

"Okay thanks." Sierra smiled. You know you're at home once the neighbors start to get in your business. She made a plate and dropped in a chair. "You know I need to cook for you one day. You've been taking such good care of me."

"You don't have to do that. I love to cook. I love to make people feel at home, and I love my daughters."

Sierra paused. It's something about the way she said the word "daughter" that made her feel nurtured, wanted. She instantly thought of her mother.

Queenie was cutting up a few tomatoes for a salad. "Sierra, your mother is going to be all right. I put my God on it." She wiped her hands on her apron.

Sierra paused. Queenie always seemed to know what to say in the moment. But despite Queenie's confidence, she seriously doubted her mother would be okay.

Queenie turned around. "I know it's hard, but remember what I said about mustard seed faith? And I'm going to join my faith with yours. So it is already done. Now back to this event with Carrington Chambers. You got something to wear?" She bit into a slice of watermelon.

"Not really. It's an all-white attire or something fancy smancy like that." Sierra rolled her eyes.

"I think you should go. Get out, meet some other young people." Queenie picked a piece of cornbread and started to bite it. Then she brushed the crumbs off her hands.

"So why do you think I need to go?" Sierra rocked as she savored her food.

"Well, it is supposed to be *the* affair of the summer. And you never know. The Chambers are connected to a lot of people. You got to be in it to win it, my sister! Successful people know how to network."

Sierra paused from chewing. "Hmm, never thought about that. A lot of business contacts?"

"Suppose so," Queenie said.

"Since you put it that way, I *guess* I could make an effort. I mean, anything could happen, right?" Sierra twisted her mouth to the side as she looked to Queenie for more assurance. "But I really didn't bring anything like that to wear."

"There are some shops on Circuit," Queenie quipped.

Sierra didn't want to say she didn't have extra money to spend on a dress and some shoes. "Maybe I'll head up there and look."

"You better get to moving. The party's next weekend."

Chapter 49 – Wynter in Summer

It was late, but Sierra felt like someone placed two quarters in her eyes. She tossed and turned. Threw off her cover, opened the window and still couldn't get to sleep.

"Forget it." She sat up, and threw on some yoga pants, a sweatshirt and flip-flops. She eased downstairs, not trying to wake Queenie, and warmed up a cup of milk and cut a slice of pound cake. She headed outside and dropped in a chair. It was quiet with the exception of a few chatty crickets. She barely rocked while savoring the butter saturated cake. *God, why can't I have a house here?* She closed her eyes and took in the stillness. In that moment, she remembered the words Zoe used to utter all the time. *You need to give your words an assignment.*

"What do I have to lose?" Sierra whispered as she rocked. "I decree and declare that I will never have to worry about Grayson Jr. taking my son again. I declare my mother is physically, mentally and spiritually free. I decree a home for myself and my mother here on the island. We are completely restored."

Initially, she didn't feel any different than when she initially sat down. But slowly something stirred on the inside. She had some kind of knowing in her spirit. She began to envision herself happy, smiling, running on the beach with her son. She saw her mother with a boutique on Circuit Avenue. It felt so real.

Suddenly the images went away and she felt a knot in her stomach. She closed her eyes and whispered, "God, whatever is standing between me and the life I desire please show me. I need a breakthrough. I know I desire something better. I'm supposed to be happy." She took a deep breath and laid her head back against the headrest of the chair.

Then suddenly, she formed the words: "Father, I forgive. I forgive Bryce, Zoe, Mom, Grayson Jr., and most important…myself."

After about a half hour, she went upstairs. She felt a ton had been lifted from her shoulders. She lay across the bed, and her eyelids relented. She instantly fell asleep. Two hours later and close to dawn, she felt the message alert go off on her phone. She rolled over, grabbed it and checked the text. The words almost caused her heart to leap from her chest.

Sierra Wynter Reed– 7 lbs. 4 ozs.

She clicked on the picture and saw a tiny brown princess curled up with closed eyes. Sierra placed her hand over her mouth, and the tears flowed…and flowed.

She's perfect.

~~~~~

"Sierra, omigod, she's so gorgeous! I mean I never thought I'd be this in love with anything," Zoe screamed into her ear.

"I can't believe you named her Sierra," she said with a mixture of joy for the occasion and sadness that she couldn't be there.

"I always loved your name. Zoe is so plain." She laughed. "Besides, when I looked at

Her, she just said, 'I'm Sierra and that's it.' So you're a Godmother. One good turn deserves another!" Zoe's words were quick and punched with enthusiasm.

Sierra dropped down on the bed. "I, wow, I'm so happy for you, Z, so happy. I know your husband is over the moon. And your parents, man, I know they have her spoiled already. She just looked like a little princess in the photo."

"Yeah, you know that. We're back home and well, everything is just beautiful."
~~~~~

The line was silent for a few minutes. Sierra could not help but to think of the less than perfect circumstances in which her son came into the world. She was happy for Zoe nevertheless.

"Sierra, how's your mom? I heard, well I know. I'm really praying."

"She's, okay I guess." Sierra hated to taint the occasion with her issues.

"What do you mean, you guess?"

Sierra went on to tell her everything that had happened. She didn't want to, but it all just poured out.

"God led you there? Sierra, I never thought I'd hear those words out of your mouth. Wow, He's up to something big. Sierra, from the day we had that fight, I never stopped praying for you. I mean every morning I've been calling you out. Sometimes I fasted just for you. If I couldn't do food, I'd fast from social media." She laughed.

"I knew somebody was praying for me. Zoe, I'm sorry. You were right. It's time for me to stand on my own two feet. I realized I'm not cursed. God does not love me any less. I know things look bad, but for some reason I have hope. Things are going to turn around for good. I mean, coming here has been a total faith walk and none of it makes sense. But I have to say, I'm getting the courage to face everything."

"I'm sorry, too, Sierra. You weren't all wrong. It was hard for me to stand in your shoes. Seems like you've had more than your share of trials. But I believe God is getting ready to break through and for good this time! So now on to the important stuff, tell me about this Carrington. He sounds like a nice guy."

"Ugh, on the one hand he reminds me of Grayson Jr., but more mature. He does seem like a decent guy. But then again, so did Grayson. Anyway, he invited me to some White Party for his parents' anniversary. You know how I am about stuff like that. Besides, I don't have anything to wear."

"Sierra, life is about showing up. You are beautiful, gifted and smart, and it's time the world knows it. If you think it's going to be a terrible time, then it will be. Don't give him a hard time based on the way Grayson turned out. Just keep an open mind and have fun. Now about an outfit..."

Chapter 50 – Vineyard Friend

"Hey," Sierra said as she reached the bottom of the stair and opened the screen door. "Right on time."

Chloe stepped inside. "Hey Queenie," she yelled as she noticed her buzzing around in the kitchen. Queenie popped out the kitchen. "Oh, hey sweetie. Coming to get my Sierra?"

"Yeah, thought we'd go hang out over at Vineyard Haven and maybe catch a movie."

"I think that's a great idea. I have a book I want to sink my teeth into. Y'all have fun."

Remember, don't talk too much, Sierra reminded herself on the way out the door.

"I already purchased a bus pass for us. We can just jump on. It should be here any minute," Chloe said as she adjusted her headband. "It'll be fun, something different. While you're here you might as well see everything."

Once they got off the bus, they headed toward the shops then stopped for lunch.

"Okay, I have to confess. I need to pick your brain," Chloe said as she bit into her hamburger.

Sierra stiffened. "Um, 'bout what?"

"Well, I have this dream. I want to start my own design firm. I mean I love to decorate. I have this fantasy, to be the next Design Star."

"So what's stopping you?" Sierra said, somewhat relieved.

"I went to school to be a financial analyst. Exciting, right? My passion is interior design. Our family is all about the academics, not creative stuff. We support the arts, but don't have careers in them." Chloe sipped on her lemonade.

Sierra was somewhat offended but held her tongue. *But how can I judge? Fear is fear. Whether you are afraid to pursue your dream, love or face your problems*. "Chloe, all I can tell you is everything's a risk. You might try to enter some contests or do it part time until you're ready to fully commit."

"Actually, between you and me, I auditioned for a television show. I'm a finalist! I haven't told my parents. I'd have to take a leave of absence from my job. But I have a plan. I mean life is too short, you know what I mean? Look at you. You are throwing everything you have into your dream. That takes courage." She was about to burst with excitement.

Sierra shrugged. "I mean, I just don't know anything else I'd rather do. My son and I—" *Crap, didn't mean to say that*.

"You have a son? You're a mother? Wow." Chloe chewed slowly on her fries.

"Yeah," Sierra said dryly.

"How cool is that? I love kids. I'm so glad I met you, Sierra. I mean I get tired of the same friends talking about the same thing." She laughed. "So where's your son? What's he look like? Got a picture? You look so young to have a kid."

Sierra wished she'd stop asking so many questions. "Oh, he's with his grandmother." Sierra drummed her fingers and looked around. "Now, I have something to ask you."

"C.C. Yes, he likes you. I can tell." Her eyes smiled.

Sierra sighed. "Now how did you know I was going to ask you about your cousin?"

"Because most women do. He's not a ladies' man like you might think. Everyone's always trying to marry him off. He's my favorite cousin and a really good guy. You should give him a chance."

"Give him a chance? I just met him. But he *is* extra easy on the eyes and he has a very sweet personality." Sierra laughed. "So what about this Fallon chick?"

"Uh, she is irrelevant. They've been friends forever and honestly, he'd been crushing on her forever. She never gave him the time of day. I think something went down last summer, but it fizzled out. I'll let him tell you what happened, but he's pretty much done with her. Besides, none of us really like her."

"Oh." Sierra wanted more information but kept quiet.

"Anyway, are you coming to my aunt and uncle's anniversary party?"

"I, I'm not sure," Sierra said.

"You have to! It's gonna be really nice. I know C.C.'ll be disappointed if you don't and so will I."

"Um, well I didn't bring anything to wear."

"Nonsense, we can find you something at one of these shops."

"No! I mean, I can find my own dress," Sierra said, not wanting to feel like a charity case.

"Sorry, didn't mean to offend you. So is that a yes?"

"I guess. Layla and Fallon will show up, too?"

"*And* so what? Sierra, you must not look in the mirror often. You are much more beautiful than either of them. I wouldn't worry about them or their crazy mamas."

Sierra's brow went up. "So what's up with them?"

"Honey, let me tell you. Layla's mom is always high on some nerve medication, and

Fallon's mother has slept with all her help, the lawn man, plumber, you name it.

"Wow," Sierra said.

"Everybody's got drama in their lives. Some people hide it better than others. We can't ever compare our life with someone else's highlight reel."

Sierra was caught off guard about Chloe's candor, but it made her look differently at

Layla and any perceived power she'd given them. It almost made her feel better about her own situation. *Almost.*

~~~~~

Sierra came back from hanging out with Chloe and headed up to her bedroom.

She couldn't understand why social events caused her to have a full blown anxiety attack. She always felt people were watching the way she held her fork, whether she wore the appropriate outfit or...belonged. *One day I'm not gonna worry about any of that stuff. I'm gonna have the confidence to walk into any room.*

When she came into the bedroom, she noticed a large cardboard box sitting on her bed. *Who could have sent this?* It had been shipped overnight. She looked at the return address and instantly knew. *Zoe.* She carefully opened the box and pulled out a white strapless dress with beautiful draping.

Dear Sierra,

I miss you. Just wanted to send you a little something and to officially say I'm sorry. And because of you I realized I love designing clothes more than anything else. I talked it over with my husband, and I'm not going back to work. (Happy wife happy life – lol) After the baby gets a little bigger, I'm going to start a fashion blog and start sewing again. Enough about me, Sierra, just want you
~~~~~

to know I love you. P.S. please find enclosed a "Zoe original" and a pair of glass slippers ☺ Love you much, Zoe & Sierra Wynter

Sierra sat on the bed and reread the note. Her heart leapt. *I have my friend back.* She immediately pulled the dress from the box and tried it on. It hugged all her curves in the right places. It was elegant, tasteful and looked beautiful against her coppery tanned skin. She looked down at the ankle wrap sandals. They were more expensive than any shoe she'd ever worn. Most of hers came from the vintage shop or Marshall's. They felt different and hugged her arch to perfection. She did a half turn, then ran over to her luggage and sorted through a smaller bag. She unwrapped one of her necklaces and put it around her neck.

Now I look like a daughter of the King.

As Sierra took off the dress and hung it up, she felt such a spiritual high. Somewhere deep in her spirit, she felt God was hearing some of what she'd been saying. Nothing could bring her down—until her phone rang. When she looked at the number, a familiar dread consumed her spirit. She knew she couldn't put it off any longer. She'd been running and she knew the longer she took to answer his calls the worse it would be. But she had to have courage. Sierra pressed the button and put the phone against her ear.

"Where have you been? Gray's been crying and asking about you. What kind of mother are you?"

She closed her eyes and paused before she spoke.

"Grayson, I need to be honest and I don't need you judging me. Truth? I was two seconds from a nervous breakdown. I had a chance to get away for a minute. So I did. Might not make sense 'cause everything's perfect in your world. I knew as long as little Gray was with you he was fine." She braced herself, hoping and praying for some type of grace.

"Sierra, maybe you just need to get on some medication. This is life. There's gonna be good, bad and horrific days. You can't run from everything. Because guess what? It follows you wherever you go. Nevermind. His birthday's next week. Think you'll be around?"

"Grayson, I know when my son was born, I was there, remember? I won't miss it."

"Your son wants to speak to you." Before she had a chance to protest, little Gray was on the phone.

"Hey Mommy, I miss you. Where are you?" His voice was bright and bubbly.

The moment Sierra heard her son's voice, she almost broke down. Her emotions went from defensive to conviction in two seconds. "Hey, little Gray, how are you? Mommy's not far, I just needed to go away for a little bit, but I promise I'll be home soon and I won't miss your birthday, okay?"

"First Grandma, now you, how come everybody had to go away?"

She felt a stab in her gut. "It's only for a short while. Are you having fun with your dad?"

"Y-e-a-h, we went to Great Adventures and to the safari and Mom Cassie's taking me roller-skating."

The sound of Cassie's name pierced her heart. "Oh, sweetie, that's nice. Can you give me a kiss?"

"Ma, on the phone? That's for babies."

"Please? For me, just this once."

She heard a quick smack on the phone. "Love you, baby."

"I love you, too."

She waited for Grayson Jr. to get back on the phone.

"Sierra, look," he said, his voice lowered, "if you're not back home in a week, I'm keeping my son. I'm not playing this time."

“The pot calling the kettle,” she muttered. “*Who* ran away from their son, Grayson? *Who* didn’t keep *his* word?” she yelled louder than intended.

He was quiet for a few seconds. “Sierra, I meant what I said.”

Sierra felt the tears coming. *How could someone who once claimed they love me be so evil? What happened to his heart?*

Chapter 51 – Back to Reality

Sierra ran downstairs, and once she hit the floor, she started to pace and ramble. “Queenie, I need to go right now.”

“Whoa, what happened, dear?” She put her crocheting aside.

“It’s my son, his father. I just have to go.” She threw her hands up, hoping Queenie would not press for more.

“Look, calm down. What just happened?”

Sierra continued to pace the floor with her hands atop her head. “I can’t believe I was that out of my mind to jump on a bus and leave my son. He’s right. I’m a horrible mother.”

Queenie stood and grabbed her. “Sierra, calm down and tell me what happened.”

“A week on some island isn’t gonna solve my life. He’s right. I can’t run from my problems.” She hit her forehead with her hand.

“Sierra, come here and have a seat,” Queenie said with a calm reserve. She walked her over to the couch, and Sierra followed. Her head dropped as soon as she landed on the couch.

“I don’t know why I let him have so much power over me!” She looked away as her eyes watered.

“Are you finished?”

Sierra quickly turned toward Queenie, stunned at her apparent lack of compassion.

“Sierra, let me tell you something about the Graysons of this world. They don’t have a monopoly on what’s right and wrong. Now judging from what you told me about him, he’s got some maturing to do himself. You need to stop letting him intimidate you.

As long as he can affect your emotions, he's got control. The only person who should have control over your life is God. You're not super woman. Sometimes you have to put the oxygen mask on yourself before you can save anybody else. Trust me when I say it's gonna be all right."

Sierra took a deep breath as she massaged the area of her heart. "Wow, that's the first time somebody didn't make me feel crazy. I realize I'm not perfect, but I need a little support right now."

"Think about it. Until you talked to him, you were doing fine. God's doing a work here. He's s giving you mental, physical and spiritual rest. Surrender, Sierra, let everything go." She grabbed Sierra's hands. "You, my dear, are a daughter of the king. You are going to get off this mountain once and for all. You are not powerless. Your past is a place of reference, not a place of residence. And every knee has to bow down to Him. Let Him fight your battle."

Sierra smiled a little. "Sounds easy in theory, but as soon as I make a little progress…"

"No! Sierra, that's it. It's time to change that stinkin' thinkin', as Joyce Meyer would say."

Sierra smiled. "I've watched her and read one of her books."

"Good. Sierra, change is hard. I believe God has sent me into your life to walk with you. This is your final breakthrough, and you're gonna have to fight for it. God loves you so much he arranged for this crazy old woman to get a flat and show up on your doorstep!"

Sierra smiled. "So what's going to happen when I have to go back? And face everything?"

She grabbed Sierra's face. "Girlfriend, God's already gone before you. I've got your back and so does God. We'll fight through this together." She shook Sierra's hands.

"You'd do that for me?" Sierra's face lit up. "But why?"

Queenie took a deep breath. "One of my greatest regrets was not having children. In spite of all my titles, ministering to the young women who came across my path brought the most joy. You think you're the only one who has secrets, problems or shame? No, there are hundreds of Sierras in every zip code and income bracket. One of the enemy's most successful tactics is to rob women of their worth or keep them in mediocrity. Why do you think women spend millions dollars on hair weave, designer bags and them red bottoms?

"Don't get me wrong, ain't a thing wrong with having fine things. But you can't be empty on the inside and dressed up on the outside. I've seen gorgeous women like you running around in jeans and a T-shirt because they are shining from the inside. There's a time to wear your finest, but you've got to put as much work on the inside as you do on the outside."

Sierra's eyes widened. She instantly thought of Cassie, the tons of designer bags, shoes and outfits, but she never seemed quite free to be herself. "I really know what you mean. All my life I felt there was more, something greater. Oh Queenie I want to be free, I want the best that God has for me. I want to feel his power, his love. I don't think I've felt it yet." Sierra was amazed at her own admission.

"Well, it's not all about feelings but once you experience the Holy Spirit, that light consumes you. You'll never be the same. Honey, you got it on the outside. You're gorgeous but you let people steal what rightfully belongs to you. No one is better than you. Understand me? God's prequalified all of us for something special." She got up and grabbed her bible. "I have proof. Don't take my word." Queenie flipped the pages. "Read it."

Sierra grabbed the Bible and read slowly, "Before you were formed in your mother's womb I knew you. Wow. I've never seen that scripture before."

"When I read that scripture for the first time, man it was like something just went through me. From that point on, I realized no matter what anyone says about me or who fails to acknowledge, God is the one who holds my fate! Before you were born, God said you know what, I'm going to design this child, my daughter Sierra and she's a masterpiece. But what happens? The world comes in and starts to plant all these negative seeds. God's got a plan for you, and it is for good and not harm. So you tell Grayson Jr., that depression and the devil himself that ain't nobody got time for that! Stop shrinking back."

She grabbed Queenie's hands and laughed but soon she fell into her arms and cried. But this time, they weren't tears of sadness; they were tears of release.

Chapter 52 – White Night

Sierra completed the finishing touches to her makeup.

"You look beautiful. You are going to have a fabulous time, and that Carrington is going to pass out!" Queenie said, standing behind her.

"Thank you. When are *you* getting dressed?" Sierra asked, noticing Queenie was in her terry cloth robe and slippers. "Wait." Sierra turned around and walked toward her. She grabbed her hands. "You okay?"

"Not feeling too good, sweetie. Just a little upset stomach, but I think I better stay and get some rest. I know I promised I'd go, but I just don't think I'm up to it." Queenie fanned herself.

"Wow, well I need to stay here. You need somebody to look after you."

"No!" Queenie barked. "I mean, I'll be fine. You *have* to go."

Sierra squinted. "Why? What's so important? It's just a party. Why do I need to be there?"

"Because, well you just do. You need to break that spirit of intimidation, and this is a start! Maybe God's got a divine connection waiting for you. Anything can happen. Ninety percent of life is showing up!"

Sierra studied her face. "Queenie, now you're just acting weird. Nothing's waiting for me at that party except a bunch of bougie folks!" She was about to continue her protest, but she was interrupted by a knock at the door.

"That must be Cora," Queenie said. "I called her to come and watch out for me while you were gone. C'mon in, Cora." Queenie headed down the steps. "I'm here."

Sierra, irritated, followed her.

Cora had let herself in.

"My, my Sierra, you are *beautiful*. That dress, that necklace, those chandelier earrings…and your hair. So elegant!" Cora paused before she sat next to Queenie on the couch.

"Thank you, but I—"

"Sierra, isn't it time for you to leave? Take the keys to Princess Di and go."

She'd forgotten about transportation. She would have had Carrington pick her up, but she and Queenie were supposed to ride together. She looked at Queenie then Cora both standing there grinning like they were in cahoots.

"Sierra, you will be fine. Don't worry about me. Cora will look out for me."

"Yeah," she said as she grabbed the remote, "time for R & B Divas."

Sierra rolled her eyes, grabbed the keys and walked out the door, letting the screen door slam behind her.

Queenie looked at Cora, and they both laughed. "She'll thank me later."

~~~~~

Sierra's heart was beating double time until she finally found the street. Queenie's directions were a bit sketchy, but she managed to get the navigation system on her phone to work. Once she arrived, she took a deep gulp. The house was even bigger than what she'd imagined. *No wonder his family was fighting over it. This is beautiful.* She was frozen in her seat. *What am I doing here?* She
~~~~~

watched as couples and people her age walked by chatting. When she managed to make eye contact with a few, they smiled and spoke. She thought she was a little overdressed yet felt good in her outfit. *It's now or never*. She said a quick prayer and was about to get out the car when she heard someone calling her name.

"Sierra!" Chloe called from a few feet away.

Thank God. Sierra stepped out the car and waved at Chloe.

"Omigod, you look gorgeous! And your hair, I love how you put it up. And that necklace is gorgeous! You'll have the whole room buzzing." She grabbed Sierra's hands.

Now I'm definitely nervous. "I'm not overdressed, am I?"

"No, not at all. It's perfect. Sometimes you have to show folks what you're working with." Chloe winked and they both laughed. They walked past the entrance, and Sierra felt like she'd been ushered into a new world. People were scattered on the lawn. They went around the back where slip covered couches were arranged on the lawn and a large tent with chandeliers was in the middle of the yard.

"It's beautiful out here, "Sierra said, looking around. She spotted Carrington in the distance talking to a tall and slender woman. He looked toward Chloe then looked away then looked back again. His eyes fixed on Sierra until she came closer.

"So who is this beautiful young lady?" a man said as he kissed Chloe on the cheek.

"Oh, Uncle Gavin, this is Sierra, C.C.'s, well our friend. She's here visiting Queenie."

He nodded. "Ah, any friend of Queenie's is a friend of mine," he said with smiling eyes.

Sierra smiled. "Congratulations on your anniversary."

"Thank you, dear."

Carrington stepped up a few feet alongside his father in white linen slacks and a wheat colored blazer. “Sierra, so glad you made it.” He leaned in and kissed her on the cheek. “Wow,” he shook his head, “you look, just wow…*stunning*.”

She blushed.

“Oh boy, he’s at it again.” His father shook his head. “Bea, come get your son.”

Sierra didn’t quite know how to respond. But what she did notice was how Carrington could not take his eyes off her.

“Where’s Queenie? Thought she was coming?” he said as he grabbed her hand and led her through a few of the floral arrangements.” He grabbed two glasses of champagne as the waiter passed by with a tray.

“For you,” he said.

“I really don’t drink.”

“C’mon, it’s a celebration.”

She grabbed the flute from his hand. “Okay, maybe a little.”

“I want you to meet a few people,” he said as he grabbed her hand.

She looked at Chloe as he pulled her away.

“Go on,” she mouthed. “You’re in good hands.”

As he wrapped his hand around her waist as if claiming her for the evening, Sierra took a big gulp of champagne to calm her nerves.

Lord, please don’t leave me, she thought as they eased toward a group of people.

Chapter 53 – Island Belle

"Carrington, I really need to go to the ladies' room, "Sierra whispered after mingling for about an hour.

"Oh, sure the nearest bathroom is inside down the hall to the right."

Before Sierra was a few feet away, several people swarmed around him like bees.

He was laughing and enjoying the conversation.

"So, who is your new friend?" a young woman in a white halter dress and shoulder length hair asked.

"Her name's Sierra. She's here visiting Queenie, but I know you got the scoop already."

"Why would you say that?" She grabbed his hands and moved to the Charlie Wilson song the D.J. had just put on.

"Because I know you, Fallon. By the time you finished with Layla and your crew, you probably know more about her than I do."

"Funny. It's not that serious." She wrapped her arms around his neck then whispered in his ear. "C'mon, one little dance won't hurt."

He looked around. Not wanting to make a scene, he obliged. He swayed, keeping a distance. "Fallon, give it up. I'm done, you know why," he said through clenched teeth.

She ignored him and moved closer. "You've been waiting for a chance since we were kids. I finally gave in and this is the way you want to treat me?"

"Yeah, that's the point. You knew I was feeling you for all those years. Every summer I waited. You played me, slept with my boy." Just when he was about to pull away, Sierra spotted him on the floor.

She wasn't sure what to do. Chloe happened to see Sierra out the corner of her eye and rushed over. "It's nothing."

"What? I'm not tripping. I barely know him." Sierra looked around and smiled at an older lady passing by. She looked everywhere but in Carrington's direction.

"Yeah, okay, I know that look," Chloe said.

Sierra took a deep breath. "I have no idea what you mean." She started swaying to the music.

Carrington left the dance floor as soon as he spotted Sierra. "Hey you," he said after making his way over.

"Hey," Sierra said less enthusiastic. She rubbed her bare arm with her opposite hand. "Well, I promised Uncle a dance," Chloe said as she eased away.

Sierra smiled as she watched Chloe walk off.

"It's a beautiful night," Carrington said. "Like to go for a little walk?" He slid his arm through hers. "C'mon…"

"Okay," she said, feeling a little lightheaded from the champagne.

They walked across the grounds toward the back of the house. As they moved further away from the party, the sound of the tide slowly replaced the music

"Wait." Carrington bent down and slowly removed her shoes. Then slid out of his own. As they proceeded to step down the few wooden steps to the sand, Sierra almost lost her balance. "Uh-oh, I got you!" Carrington said.

"Wow, embarrassing."

"It's okay, I won't tell anybody."

They both laughed. Carrington was happy she'd finally relaxed.

"I told you I didn't drink," she said as she steadied herself.

"I get it. So, you having a good time?"

"Yeah, you were right. Your parents are very nice people. I'm actually enjoying myself. I thought everyone was going to be all stuck up and stiff." She felt the coolness of the sand beneath her feet. She held on tight to Carrington's arm as they took slow steps.

"Please, these people know how to party. Any minute the strobe light's gonna come on and I wouldn't be surprised if they won't be chanting the roof is on fire when we get back."

"I don't know about all that." Sierra giggled. A few seconds of silence passed. Her ears tuned into the waves. "Wow, isn't that the most peaceful thing you've ever heard?"

"Yeah, sometimes, I admit, I take it for granted."

"If I lived here or came every summer, I'd never do that."

Carrington turned and gently grabbed her face before kissing her forehead and slowly moving down to her lips. "You have such an infectious smile."

She stood completely still, and her body went limp.

"You taste way too good," he said.

"Uh, yeah, that's enough of that." Sierra fought all the bells and whistles going off in her body.

He leaned in once more and kissed her softly. "Can't help it. You are adorable." They walked a few more steps, and he removed his jacket then placed it on the sand. "After you."

She paused then eased down on the makeshift pallet. He walked over and sat beside her. They both stretched their legs out in front of them and looked up at the moon. Sierra leaned on his shoulder. "Now this is heaven. I could stay here forever."

"Doesn't take much to make you happy, huh?" he said, staring at the water.

She shrugged. "I wouldn't say all that. What's happy anyway?"

"This." He turned to look at her, then placed his finger under her chin and kissed her

Lord, I'm in so much trouble. So much for the coy role. Give me something else! "So, who were you dancing with when I came from the restroom?" Sierra pulled away, abruptly cooling the atmosphere.

"Fallon. She's nobody."

"Well 'nobody' was pressing up on you pretty hard. I'm just sayin'. I wouldn't be asking, but a few minutes ago you were all over her on the dance floor, and now you're kissing on me."

He paused a few minutes. "I wasn't all over her. And trust me when I say, she's nobody significant. We went out before and nothing came of it. She's the type of person who wants what she can't have. Now if you don't mind, I don't want to waste the little time that I have with you on something that's irrelevant."

"If you say so," Sierra said, unconvinced.

He grabbed her hand and kissed it softly.

Why Sierra thought that was a good enough explanation she had no idea. Before she knew it, she was laid back. Her arms stretched overhead as granules of sand massaged her skin. Carrington lay alongside her tracing her neck and area above her strapless dress with his fingers. His light touch caused her senses to heighten.

Carrington had aligned his body next to Sierra. He slowly massaged her face as the kisses progressively lingered. His hands gingerly massaged her bare arms, and she instinctively wrapped her arm around his waist. He slid in close to her until there was no space between him. He began to ease atop her when he felt her gentle push.

"Carrington," she whispered.

"Okay, I'm sorry. Really sorry." He broke away. "I would never want to offend you. It's just that you are so beautiful and well everything just kind of felt right. Like I've known you a lot longer."

"Yes, it feels really nice, but I don't want to get carried away. Besides, the truth is you really don't know me." She sat up and smoothed the back of her hair and brushed the sand off the bottom of her dress. She folded her arms.

"Sierra," he grabbed her arm, "I'm really sorry." He stared at her face until she looked his way.

"Look, Carrington, it's not you. I just well have a lot going on in my life. It would only confuse you."

"How do you know? Want to talk about it?"

She sucked her teeth and laughed. "I appreciate your concern, but I'm not sure you could handle everything."

"Why don't you try me?"

She released her arms and slid closer to him. "Well, for one thing, it's been awhile since I've dated someone. The last person broke my heart. And, I come as a package, well, I have a son." Sierra held her breath, waiting for his response.

"Is that all? So you think having a child is some disease? Do you think I'd be turned off by that or something? I love kids. This isn't 1965."

"Have you ever seriously dated someone with a child?"

"Well, no, but I have been in a few serious relationships with childfree women and you see how that worked out." He smiled.

"That's a nice safe answer." She jumped up. "Just forget it, I have to keep reminding myself I just met you."

"This is true, but I think the feelings I have are mutual." He stood and grabbed her hand. "Am I wrong? May sound corny but love at first sight doesn't just happen in the movies. It's just something about you."

She rolled her eyes. "Please. The last time I just went with my feelings, I ended up with a son. Don't get me wrong, he's the best thing that's ever happened to me, but well, I wish the circumstances would have been different." She bit the side of her lip and tried to figure out what he was thinking. "Look, I hate to cut this party short, but there's a great party going on, and I don't want to waste a great dress." She leaned in and kissed him softly on his cheek.

He winked. "And a great dress it is."

~~~~~

As soon as they came back to the party, Sierra rushed to go freshen up. Once in the restroom, she felt a rush of anxiety. She paused then found herself staring at her reflection as she ran her hands under the faucet. *Wow, I look stunning.* She rarely lingered in the mirror, but that night she truly felt a glow. She was beaming from the inside out. She took a few deep breaths and relaxed. "I guess a little while longer won't hurt."

As she made her way back from the restroom, Carrington waved toward her. "You okay?"

She nodded. "Yes, I'm fine." She smiled. "Just a little warm." She patted her lips and forehead with a cloth handkerchief then placed it back in her purse.

"Okay, no more champagne for you." He broke into a grin.

She softly punched him in the arm.

"Carrington! I have a bone to pick with you!" A middle-aged woman with a short afro and gorgeous skin rushed over and stood between them. "Now, who is this stunning young lady? And where
~~~~~

did you get that gorgeous necklace? I've been staring at it for a while now! You are simply gorgeous, dear."

Sierra was caught off guard. "I, well…"

"Sierra, this is Mrs. Jamison, she's an old family friend. And, well I'll let Sierra tell you about the necklace." He grinned.

Sierra felt her neck. "Actually it's one of my, my designs."

"Are you serious?" Mrs. Jamison said, her eyes moving back and forth between the necklace and Sierra's face. "You must give me your information because I have to have one just like it. I love jewelry."

"Sierra, if I were you, I'd follow instructions," Carrington chided. He moved in closer to her like a proud husband. "She doesn't take no for an answer."

"Well, the thing is…"

"Okay my dear, I don't have time for this, here's my card and I'm expecting to hear from you." She raised a hand at a man across the room and wandered off as quickly as she wandered in.

In seconds, before Sierra could catch her breath Chloe, Layla, Fallon and Christian circled them.

"And where have you two been?" Christian said. "They're about to make a toast and you missed your parents' dance.

Carrington rolled his eyes. "No, I didn't. I saw them rehearse and I was saving myself from embarrassment." Chloe hit his chest. "Girl, stop playing."

Fallon stood there with raised eyebrows and her hand on her hip. She tapped her foot as she stared at Sierra. "Forget it, I'm Fallon." She reached her hand toward Sierra.

"Hi," Sierra said, not feeling the need to say more.

"So, Sierra where are you from?" She sipped slowly on her drink.

"New Jersey."

Fallon nodded as Carrington cut his eyes toward her.

"What part?"

"Why?" Sierra asked.

Fallon was taken aback. "Oh, just curious, making conversation."

"Montclair." Sierra felt increasingly uncomfortable. "Hey, you know I'm getting really tired. Carrington, do you mind? Queenie wasn't feeling well when I left, and I just don't want to leave her too long." She grabbed his hand.

Fallon stared at Sierra and squinted, "You know you look *really* familiar. I'm trying to figure out where I've seen you before. I go to Montclair to shop occasionally. I have a cousin that lives there. It's bugging me, I know I've seen you before."

"Car-ring-ton," she said through clenched teeth.

"Yeah sweetie…"

She smiled. "Can you please walk me to my car?"

"Yeah, yeah. No problem, if you're really ready to leave."

"Yes, I'd like to if you don't mind. It was nice seeing you all again and nice meeting you, Fallon." She knew in her spirit it was time to go home. Although she'd miss Queenie she knew the visit had served its purpose. As much as it would hurt, she didn't want to answer any more questions or much worse get close to some random guy. *What was I thinking? Eventually these people will know who I really am.* She was headed out on the first ferry smoking. She felt strong and ready to go back and fight…for everything.

Chapter 54 – Ferry-Weather Friends

Sierra refused to let Carrington know which ferry she was leaving on. She had too much going on in her world. The trip had served its purpose. She felt strong and ready to face the mess she had left behind. She was more than ready to see her son.

"So, you going to stay in touch with boyfriend?"

Sierra looked over at Queenie and rolled her eyes. "Really? I've only known C.C. for what, two seconds?"

Sierra watched as the houses along the shore flew by. She felt like she was leaving old friends.

"Oh, it's C.C. now?" Queenie kept her hands on the steering wheel and kept her eyes ahead. "C'mon, Princess Di, we gotta get my daughter to the ferry. Since she just *has* to leave.

Sierra smiled. "You know I have to go. Can't stay here forever."

Queenie turned up the radio and blasted an old Salt-N-Pepa rap and knew every word. It made Sierra laugh all the way to the ferry station.

As the car reached the curb, Sierra felt melancholy. Right before she stepped out the car, Queenie grabbed her hands. "We're gonna pray."

Sierra nodded. She knew the power and the anointing on Queenie, and she figured the two of them could definitely get a prayer through. As Queenie prayed, she felt light. Her spirit rose higher, and she knew whatever was on the inside of Queenie had transferred to her spirit.

"How can I ever thank you?" Sierra asked.

"You don't have to thank me. That day when I stopped in front of your house, I just finished asking God to send me somebody that really needed me. It was a divine connection. God loves you so much that He made our paths cross at just the right time. Anybody else would have cursed old Princess Di, but I knew better. It was a divine assignment."

Sierra leaned over and gave Queenie a kiss on her warm ample cheek. "So I'll let you know how everything turns out."

"You better." She pulled her Jackie O shades off her head and slid them on her eyes to hide the tears. *God, this is always the hard part*, she thought.

Sierra was about to step out when her door opened. She looked up.

"Now, you didn't think I was going to let you get away that easy, huh?" Carrington held a bouquet of flowers and reached for her hand. She wanted so bad to say something mean but couldn't. Her heart was beating so fast she had to steady herself.

Queenie looked at them standing their together and winked at them both.

"I'll take it from here Queenie," Carrington said and grabbed Sierra's bags.

"I bet you will."

Chapter 55 – Home Again

Sierra finally made it home. She held her flowers the entire time and put them in water when she hit the door. As persistent as she was, she left things open ended. The last thing she wanted to do was bring Carrington into the mess she left behind.

If it's meant to be, she thought, *it will happen.*

Miraculously, the house was still intact. Despite the abrupt ending to her trip, she'd returned rested and with resolve. Amber had been right. All the way home, she thought about her mother, and for the first time, empathy replaced her anger. After taking a hot shower, she called Amber, then her son. And finally she was determined to go see her mother.

~~~~~

Grayson Sr. didn't plan on staying but had to stop in on his grandson's birthday party. The screaming kids were not a welcome distraction to his roaming thoughts. He looked on as his mother and Cassie doted on the children. His wife saw him walk into the backyard and flashed a smile. He smiled and nodded.

Grayson Jr. walked up behind him. "Hey, Dad. Look at your grandson. He doesn't know what to do with himself, "he said as they both watched the little boy opening gifts.

"Yeah, glad he's having a good time." His eyes roamed to Cassie. "So, I see Cassie's getting used to having him around."

"Yeah. She's been great. It was rough for a minute. He threw a few temper tantrums, which is so unlike him. I blame it on his mother."

They both were silent again. "Dad, I filed for permanent custody of little Gray. I mean it this time. He needs some stability
~~~~~

and whether Sierra wants to admit it or not, it's not looking too good for her mother. Gray deserves a good home."

"Come over here." His father motioned him away from the people littered in their backyard. "Whose idea was this?"

"Dad, what are you talking about? Yeah, Cassie and I discussed it. She is in agreement."

"Of course she is. Son, you need to withdraw the petition. You're doing it out of spite."

"You know, Dad, this is my *son*. I should be able to make decisions about him."

"Son, it's just some things…nevermind. And why does Cassie all of a sudden want custody? You need to really think about this."

Grayson couldn't figure out where his father's head was. "Why all of a sudden are you the moral police?"

Because I'm tired of living lie after lie. Grayson Sr. looked out toward the garden. "Son, you know sometimes life is complicated. Just don't do anything you'll regret."

His forehead creased. "Dad, what are you talking about?"

"Look, son. I wouldn't be so hard on Sierra. She's still little Gray's mother, and honestly, she's under a lot of stress."

Grayson Jr. sat down in the patio chair. "I'm really confused right now. What's up with you, Dad? The first four years after little Gray was born all you did was badmouth Sierra. You berated me for getting her pregnant. I took it. I did everything you said, including marrying Cassie. Now I want to get custody of my son so I can raise him in a stable environment, and you're on Sierra's side?"

"Son, I get it. But things change and people change. I'm not always right. We'll talk some more about it, son." He put his hand on his shoulder. "I didn't want to miss Gray on his birthday. I'm headed out on a short run with your Godfather. We'll talk some more when I get back."

Grayson eyed his father, not understanding his ardent need to go on this fishing trip. In the past, he had to beg his father to go.

Chapter 56 – A Mother's Love

"I'm taking my son home."

Sierra turned and looked Grayson in the eye.

"It's no longer up to you. You run off like you're twelve and expect to come back and just take him home."

She watched as her son broke away from the other kids when they locked eyes. He ran over, screaming, "Mom-my!"

She reached down and hugged him tight. Then kissed all over his face. "I missed you!"

Cassie watched as something stirred on the inside. "Excuse me, I need to go and get some more cupcakes." She pulled the sliding door and raced to the restroom.

"Where are you going?" Her mother said as her daughter sped by. She'd been in the kitchen getting together more goodie bags.

"Not feeling well."

Cassie's mom smiled nervously at Lydia. "Excuse me." She put the bags down and followed her daughter.

They both went into the restroom. Cassie sat on the toilet and broke down in tears.

"Oh no, sweetie. What is going on?" She rubbed her daughter's hair.

"Mom, how did we get here? Was I so desperate, so scared I'd never marry I had to lie to Grayson?"

Her mother continued to stroke her daughter's hair and look up. "Honey, I get it. But what's done is done. He doesn't need to know. We just have to keep believing."

She looked up at her mother. "Mom, just stop it. We're no better than them. I can't anymore. I don't have peace. This is my husband. I should have told him about my surgery. I was about to take some other woman's child because I was so desperate. I can't do it. I feel sick. Literally sick."

She looked up at her mother with a tear-stained face. "How do I ask God to bless this mess? I didn't want to believe it at the time, but Mom, it was about the money, wasn't it?

Her mother shook her head. "No, no."

"So what kind of mother would tell her daughter to lie about something so serious?" She looked up at her mother, her face saturated with tears.

Her mother grabbed and pulled her toward her waist. "Shh, sweetie. I don't know I just didn't want you to be alone. I wanted you to marry into the right family. Maybe I'm selfish, but it makes a difference. And well your father, when he died he didn't leave us much. I was thinking about you."

Cassie pulled away and stood. "Wow, you know until this moment I didn't want to believe we were like them." She wiped her eyes with her hand. "The first thing I'm going to do is tell Grayson Jr. to remove that custody petition. Then I'm going to pray and ask for God to go before me when I decide to tell my husband the truth. If he decides to leave me because I can't have a child, so be it. If he stays, by God's grace this marriage is truly meant to be. But Mom, no more lies."

Chapter 57 – Justice Is Among Us

Grayson Sr. scratched one of many items off his to-do list. He followed up at a routine stop with his financial planner. He thrust his overnight bag in his back seat and headed toward Bencil's house. He turned to the old school rap radio station and was in route. He was calm, focused and had a plan. After about twenty minutes, he pulled up to Bencil's gate and eased into his driveway minutes later.

"What's good? You ready to hit this?" Bencil said after he loaded his bags and jumped in Grayson Sr.'s Hummer.

"Yeah, let's get it. Can't wait to get to the lake."

"So how's Lydia?"

"She's cool. Just finished celebrating the grandson's birthday." He adjusted his mirror, avoiding eye contact.

"Wow, time flies." Bencil settled in for the less than hour ride. He slid down in his seat and soon his eyelids closed. Minutes later he was snoring.

Grayson Sr. kept his eyes focused on the road. Forty-five minutes later, they were the lone car on a private road to his lakehouse. Lush greenery lined the road that led to the secluded area.

Bencil woke up just in time to catch a glimpse of the woods. "Man, I love this place." He yawned and stretched his arms.

Grayson Sr. pulled up to the gravel driveway and parked. "Yep, let the mancation commence." He jumped out and unloaded the cooler and headed toward the back where the boat was docked. They immediately headed out to fish. After a few hours, they'd caught several bass.

Insides, as always, Grayson Sr. cleaned the fish while Bencil sat drinking his premium beer. "Man, I've been thinking."

"'Bout what?" Grayson said as he coated the fish.

"I think you finally got me ready to settle down."

Grayson laughed. "Where's this coming from?"

"Man, I'm tired. I can't keep up with these young women. I figure I need to get settled down before nobody wants my old behind. Who wants to die alone anyway?"

"May have a point there, partner." Grayson Sr. turned over the fish and scooped out another and put it on the paper towel lined plate. Once he was finished cooking, he joined Bencil at the table. He watched as Bencil helped himself to the food.

"Man, remember when we first met?" Grayson asked. "I was green, so naïve."

"Yeah," Bencil said as he stabbed the fish with his fork. "You were so green. Strictly by the book. Then you turned street hustler in a suit." He laughed.

Grayson nodded and spat out a laugh. "Guess you can say that. The one thing that it took me years to realize…" His smile wiped away like a smudge, "You had every advantage, all the pedigree but couldn't make it work without me."

Bencil spat out a bone. "Well, my friend, you had it all too, but didn't have a clue about what to do with it. You were hungry. Hungry and naïve." He shook more hot sauce on his fish.

"Yeah, I guess I was the perfect protégée." Grayson sucked the meat out of his crab claw.

More like an experiment. Bencil grinned, exposing his gap. "By the time I finished, you had a new identity, a brand new life and we made millions. Insider trading was the come up. Then when we pulled in the Italians, man, we made a grip."

"Right!" Grayson Sr. lifted his bottle of beer. "Bencil, you are a strange dude."He kept eye contact. "But for the most part, I think I have you all figured out. Except I could never figure out why you hated Maxi. You knew she was the only family I had."

"Family, huh? You're tripping. The only thing I never liked was how she made you lose focus. I could tell the exact moment she showed up. Talking that ying yang about the past, you had a weakness for her."

"Well, it all makes sense now."

Bencil stopped eating. "Man, where you going with this? Something you need to ask me?"

"Something you need to tell me? I mean about you and Maxine?" Grayson Sr. took a sharp knife and stabbed the wooden table with it.

Bencil jumped. "Man, I don't fool with trash. I was simply trying to protect us."

"That so. How, by sleeping with her? It all makes sense now. You couldn't have her, so you tried to destroy her."

"Man, you don't know what you're talking about. Yeah, I slept with her. But you need to wipe your conscience. She was in love with you. She came after me! I went along with it because I needed to know how much of our business she knew. She sang like a bird! You should have left that trash back in Louisiana."

Grayson Sr. clenched his teeth. *Stay calm.* "Bencil, it's over. It may have started as a game, but she turned the tables on you. You fell for her. And I know you are Sierra's father."

Bencil stopped in the middle of sucking a slice of lemon. "Man, you done lost your mind. Where could you have possibly gotten that information? She told me some other dude was the father."

"You knew Sierra was your daughter. You never wanted it to come out. You were still afraid of whatever damage she could do to the both of us. Maxi never wanted anything. But you continued to torment her. It was you she was with the night of the accident. You did something to her."

"You gonna believe some trick over me? She's crazy. You know she's always wanted to get back at you." He pounded his fist against the table.

Grayson Sr. stood and walked over toward Bencil, never breaking eye contact.

"Man, you need to chill out," Bencil said, his voice as cold as death.

"Don't worry about me. You're the one with the problems. You put something in her drink that night. I don't know who you got to, but you know what you did. Now, you need to make it right."

Bencil stopped smiling. "Okay. Man, something had to be done. You think I built all this to let one person have the power to destroy it? I needed her out the picture."

Grayson Sr. narrowed his eyes as he shook his head. "You're sick. If she would have done something, or even knew enough to do something she would have done it by now."

Bencil jumped up and grabbed Grayson by the T-shirt. His eyes darted back and forth then stared into Grayson's. His breathing heavy, he laughed then released him. "Man, we need to just calm down, it's me, Bennie remember? How about we work this out?"

Grayson Sr. didn't stir, his face frozen like the figures on Mt. Rushmore. "No, my brother, this is your mess. How about you fix this? Whatever you did, undo it. Do right by her and do right by your daughter. This is it. Bencil, I want out. There's no more business. I don't owe you anything else." Grayson Sr. reached in his fishing vest, and in one motion, he pulled out a gun and put it to Bencil's temple. "This is your fault. It's personal now."

Chapter 58 – Iron Lady

Sierra felt as strong as the iron security doors at the prison. She waited patiently until her mother quietly eased in. Sierra almost gasped at the sight of her mother's frame as she sat at the table. She'd definitely dropped a few pounds.

Maxine's eyes lit up at the sight of her daughter. "Sierra, you don't know how much I've been praying to see your face. Baby, I miss you." She stared blankly. "I feel like I'm seeing a ghost."

Sierra couldn't hold back her tears. "Mom, I'm here. And I'm so, so sorry. I, I tried but I just didn't have the strength–" She swallowed as her eyes begged forgiveness.

Maxine shook her head. "No, no, Sierra, you *are* strong. I know you have every reason not to believe me. But I needed to tell you in person. Sierra, I didn't go back on my word. I promise you as God as my witness I did not go back on my word. When I said I quit drinking, I meant it."

"I believe you." Sierra sucked back her own tears. She studied her mom's face. "Mom, you are still beautiful."

"What 20 years of Dove soap will do for your skin. All these people using anti-aging, serums and Botox. Good old fashioned Dove's kept me!"

Sierra laughed. "Guess you're right."

"My attorney came to see me and told me about the woman I hit. She's in critical but stable condition. It makes a huge difference."

"So when and how'd you get a new attorney?" Sierra's eyebrows knitted.

"Grayson's father."

Sierra looked puzzled. "Mom, why is he helping you so much when his son is being such an A-hole?"

Maxine shifted. "I don't know, getting soft as he gets older I guess. What's going on with Grayson Jr.?

Sierra hesitated. "You know, the usual. Just threats. Says he's going through with the custody hearing, for real this time."

"Really, I don't think his father would support that."

"Says he doesn't care what his father thinks. Going rogue I guess." She shrugged. "I don't know, Mom. What I *do* know? I'm not afraid anymore." She sat up taller. "God's in control. Amber and I are fasting…"

Maxine's eyes bucked; she couldn't believe what was coming out her daughter's mouth. "Whoa, whoa a fast? You?"

Sierra laughed. "Well, it's the Daniel Fast. I'm a newbie. But every morning we've been on that phone praying with the other ladies from your Bible study."

"Huh," Maxine studied her daughter's face.

"Mom, I'm not running from anything ever again, not even myself. We just studied David and Goliath. I've got my stones!"

"Baby, you didn't run. You were tired. God will use just about anything to get us where he needs us. I don't always understand it, but guess we don't have much say so." Maxine looked up and around and shrugged.

"Yeah." Sierra sighed. "Guess you're right."

Maxine suddenly broke down and the tears started to flow. "Baby, I'm so sorry. For everything. I've made your life miserable for so long. But I tried, I tried so hard."

"Mom, please don't. It's not your fault. None of it's your fault."

She shook her head. "Not true, I've made some bad choices. Things didn't have to be that way. I made things so hard on us."

"Mom, Mom, please. Stop okay. Listen, I talked to Zoe."

She wiped her eyes. "Oh sweetheart, that's good. That's so good. You know it's hard to find a good friend in this life. Did she have the baby?"

"Yeah." Sierra's eyes watered. "She named her Sierra Wynter."

Maxine put her hand up to her mouth. "Really? Oh, that's so beautiful. So beautiful."

"Yeah." She looked away then in her mother's eyes. "Mom, I just want to say I'm really sorry. I've should have come sooner. I just didn't know how to handle it. I mean, I was afraid. I was on the verge of a nervous breakdown. If it wasn't for Amber…well I'm not sure what I would have done." After a pause, Sierra added, "If it wasn't for Queenie and Amber, I wouldn't have ever had the courage."

"Who's Queenie?"

"I would say she's a stranger, but she's like family. She just, just, showed up when I was just ready to give up.

"Well, I don't know who she is, but I guess I have to thank her and God. Sierra, I'm so proud of you. We have to just keep praying. I know our breakthrough is coming."

Chapter 59 – Who's Afraid of the Dark

After the incident at the lake house, Bencil went to work as if nothing had happened. That week he sat in meetings with Grayson, Sr., who also gave no signs as to what occurred at the lake house accept the occasional steely and lingering glare. It had been an unusually long day.

Now that Bencil was home, all he wanted was a good meal and a warm bed. He'd picked up some Thai food from his favorite restaurant. He never ate in his bedroom; he decided to skip the rule tonight. He changed into pajama bottoms and a T-shirt and sat up in his huge four poster bed. After watching the first ten minutes of his favorite cable news show, he couldn't get into it, so he switched channels looking for some lighter fare. The political bickering he once loved vexed his spirit. He finally landed on The Cosby Show. He mustered a laugh here and there, but the show only reminded him of the emptiness in his own house.

If I died right now, would anyone even care? He had family, a sister and a brother. But the more money he made, the more he'd alienated himself. He became the family's money pot. Soon he was paying for college, giving loans and fixing financial failures he hadn't created. He finally put a stop to it years ago. It caused a lot of strain. *They never cared about me, they cared about the money. Who comes to see me? Who has ever said thank you? So what I blew up and cursed everyone out? Does that mean they need to stop speaking to me? What about everything I did before that?*

His food half-eaten, he placed his plate on his nightstand and took a deep breath. After a little more channel surfing, he landed on Ghost. He never watched the entire movie, but he watched Demi Moore and Patrick Swayze at the potter wheel. *That kind of love costs your life.* Then he watched the scene when Patrick Swayze's character was shot. Bencil wondered about life after death. He never let himself think of what happens after he dies. He slid further under his comforter. His eyelids crawled close, but he could not fall asleep. Bencil never got cold. He was too hot natured. But tonight his body shivered in intervals. It wasn't just his body, but the room felt cold. For all the money he spent on the generous bed, imported linens, marble posts, expansive and headboard, it still felt empty.

Forget this. He shut off the remote as if it it'd do the same to his racing thoughts. But the opposite occurred. As soon as the room went black, the scene from the lake house began to roll. He turned on his side and curled his large body in a ball. *He's bluffing. How's he gonna threaten me? I brought him in the game.* Finally, he jumped up and raided his medicine cabinet. He popped a Tylenol PM as a last resort.

It wasn't long before his body was coaxed into a slumber. Shortly after, a series of random dreams forced their way through. Grayson Sr.'s, Maxi's and Sierra's faces spliced through nocturnal vignettes. Then he felt this heavy, persistent evil presence. He felt something pressing down on his body then what felt like a pillow over his face. He screamed loud, but no voice escaped. He fought tirelessly, clawed, pushed. Then he was transported to a gravesite. He was naked, exposed to all the elements. He could barely see his way as the rain mercilessly drenched his body. His toes sunk in the muddy grass as he inched toward the headstone. He didn't see a name but before he knew it, his body dropped seven feet into the grave. He yelled, cried out, but piles of dirt continued to cover him.

Bencil shot up. He looked around in a panic, trembling. He rubbed his arms and noticed his T-shirt was soaked. His heartbeat thumped against his chest like a bass drum. He swallowed hard as he grabbed his remote and turned on the television. He sighed in relief. *Just a nightmare.* He watched a little more TV then closed his eyes. But the same dream reoccurred, magnified with dark images, the likes of which he'd never seen before.

~~~~~

Bencil set out on a morning run. He plugged in his earphones and headed for the normal trail. The morning air was a direct contrast from his experience the night before. Fifteen minutes into the run, he already felt revived. His endorphins released, he felt an instant energy boost. As he ran the trail, out the corner of his eye he spotted a shadow. He brushed it off. The trail was surrounded by trees. It was easy to see things that didn't exist.

But then he saw it again. The shadow appeared to move in sync with his steps. He abruptly stopped and looked around.

He removed his earphones. "Hello, anybody there?" As he dropped his hands to his knees, he slightly bent over to catch his breath. Outside of the leaves blowing, it was silent. He put his earphones back on and continued to run.

After a run, shower, bagel, and a quick read of the Wall Street Journal, Bencil felt as good as new. He dismissed the looming deadline with a scoff. *Grayson Sr., the man I made threatening me?* He laughed.

He headed for his walk-in closet to pick out his outfit for the day. He pressed the button and a round of suits circulated. He hit the button again to pause at the navy gray suits. He touched one or two of the jackets. "I'm feeling this one right here." He pulled the hanger off the revolving suit rack and hung it on the back of the closet door. He then went over to his shoe closet and picked out a pair that would complement his suit. He was about to get dressed when he heard wind. Howling whistling wind. He frowned as his brow furrowed.

He backed out into the hallway and followed the sound. Three large windows in the bedroom were open. The wind caused the curtains to lap like heavy breathing. *I don't recall opening any windows.* He looked around and slowly went to his top dresser drawer where he stored a handgun.
~~~~~

“Who’s there?” he said as he quietly retrieved it. The house was eerily silent. He went from room to room. He contemplated calling the police but left it alone. Although a bit shaken, he finished getting dressed.

Looking good from head to toe, he went downstairs to get in his car. He jumped in, pushed the garage opener and noticed a red envelope in the passenger’s side front seat. He looked around, slowly then grabbed the note. He pressed his lips together as he opened it. It was a single note card with one word typed on it.

REPENT.

Chapter 60 – Paranoid Partner

Bencil threw open the door and marched into Grayson Sr.'s office without knocking. He was on the phone and coolly continued speaking. Bencil stood there glaring at him, waiting for him to acknowledge his presence, his nostrils flaring.

Grayson Sr. gingerly placed his phone on the hook then clasped his fingers together. "Yes, my friend, how can I help you?"

Bencil leaned over his desk. "Knock it off," he said with a coarse whisper.

"I have no idea what you're talking about." Grayson removed his glasses and examined his face.

"You know *exactly* what I'm talking about." Bencil didn't blink. "The window, the note, the man following me in the park."

Grayson's forehead creased. "Ben, man, you all right? I have no idea what you're talking about." He leaned back and pressed the tips of his hands together. "Maybe it's your conscience."

Bencil slapped a legal pad off his desk. "Don't play with me."

Grayson didn't flinch. After a few seconds, he stood up and grabbed his iPad. "Look, I'm late for an appointment." He brushed past Bencil. "Maybe you should swing by your therapist on the way home. You camlet yourself out." Before he placed his hand on the door knob, he paused. Then turned around and tapped his watch. "Three more days. Clock's ticking."

~~~~~

"Am I losing it?" Bencil checked his rearview mirror repeatedly on his way home from his frustrating day. After about twenty minutes on the road, a notification beeped on his phone. A
~~~~~

name flashed that used to give him chills. He instantly knew what it meant. He clicked and waited.

"Fix it," the grainy voice said on the other end.

He wasn't bluffing. Bencil held the phone for a moment as he swallowed his own saliva, then hung up. Since his car was the only one on the road, he did a swift U-turn. He loosened his tie, cleared his throat and attempted prayer. Seconds later a huge white light flooded the road, impairing his vision. A large horn blared and he swerved. He continued to move the steering wheel back and forth and the car felt as though it was riding on two wheels. It did a 360-degree spin and abruptly stopped. He placed his head on the steering wheel to catch his breath.

"Thank you, Jesus," he repeated in between heavy breaths, afraid to look up.

~~~~~

Bencil awoke. He tried to lift his head, but fatigue forced it back to the pillow. He slid out of bed, took a step, and stumbled over his shoe. A bit disoriented, he realized he was fully clothed. He'd gotten three hours of sleep at the most. As he schlepped toward the bathroom, he removed his shirt. Water poured out the faucet the instant he slid his hands underneath. He splashed his face, and then paused to examine his reflection. His cold hands traced the jowls and cursed the enlarged pores the most expensive treatments failed to fix. His fingertips touched the sagging skin beneath his eyes. *A carrot juice and I'll be good as new.* He instantly recalled the text he'd sent to his attorney. With a 7:30 a.m. appointment, he only had time to strip, throw off the rest of his clothes, and jump in the shower.

~~~~~

"So, that's it?" Bencil signed the last stack of papers and slid his Mont Blanc inside his suit pocket. He leaned back in the leather wing back chair.

His attorney pushed his glasses up his hawkish nose and released an exasperated sigh. "Hope you know what you're doing." He stared at Bencil.

"Sy, you've known me for a long time, right?"

He nodded as he placed the tips of his fingers together. "And got me out of some really sticky spots."

He nodded slowly again.

"You're the best. But sometimes the only way is the right way."

Sy spun the mini-globe on his desk. "'Right' is subject to interpretation."

Bencil smiled at him. "Spoken like a true lawyer."

~~~~~

Bencil walked out the building. He felt like someone had removed dark shades from his eyes as he looked up at the New York skyline. He still missed seeing the twin towers, but he could appreciate the way the clouds danced around the top of the buildings. He loved New York. He'd come, conquered and in the words of Sinatra, made it there. Although he'd never admit it, he'd never be half as successful without the brains and boldness of Grayson Sr.

It's all business; the end justifies the means. He took a deep breath. Too bad he was never comfortable with that. The valet brought his car around, and he headed for his meeting with Grayson Sr. a gentleman always admits when he has been outmaneuvered.

He started his car and headed back toward Montclair. In the midst of all the day's activities, he'd hadn't eaten since the morning. His stomach growled like a lion. He'd wait until he got to Montclair to stop at his favorite restaurant. It was late, and he was tired, so he wasn't his most alert self. He paused at a stop light, and somebody smashed in the back of his car.
~~~~~

Leaping out of the car, Bencil yelled, "Man, what the hell you are doing?"

"Apologies, sir, it was all my fault, I have all my insurance information, and I'll take care of it."

Bencil walked toward the back. "Yes, you will." He examined the damaged rear of his Mercedes. "Damn." *This is what I get for doing the right thing.*

"Sir, one minute, I'm going to get my insurance card. Just wanted to make sure you're okay."

Bencil was still staring at the damage. "Whatever, man, but we're not moving these cars until..." He felt a cold metal object against the back of his bald head.

Chapter 61 – Wrong Place at the Wrong Time

"Are you sure?" Grayson Sr. rubbed the top of his bald head. "Okay, I'll be there shortly." He paced, not sure who to call or what to do first. Suddenly he realized he didn't have a choice. He felt cold and anxious. He walked downstairs as the driver pulled his car around. He thought long and hard on the way. He felt a weird sense of fatigue mixed with relief.

~~~~~

The walk to the morgue was the longest walk Grayson had ever taken. In spite of some of the hate in his heart, this was someone who was like family. The closer he got to the area where the bodies were kept, the heavier the knot in his throat became. The only sound to be heard was his Ferragamos as they hit the tiled floor. There was stillness and a finality hanging in the air. He was guided to a cold area and finally he heard the heavy metal slide and the body emerged. There's nothing to remind a man of his own immortality like staring at a listless body void of breath.

He stared at the face that looked frozen. He didn't flinch. The damage from the lone bullet didn't force his eyes away for he was staring at his friend. He pressed his mouth together as his eyes rolled upward. Then he nodded at the attendant. "That's him." The attendant nodded the same way he'd done a thousand times before. He scribbled on his clipboard and handed it to Grayson Sr. He stood there with arms folded as he waited. Grayson Sr. paused, noting the rudimentary protocol the attendant exercised. Wondering what type of education was required to exempt oneself from any emotion at the sign of a corpse. He scribbled his signature. In some strange way as soon as he placed the pen down, he felt remorsefully…free.

~~~~~

"Maxine Sanders."

She heard the clop of boots headed toward her cell. Then keys, locks at her door.

She had her head in her Bible and looked up.

"You have a visitor." The guard shook her head. "Everybody meets Jesus in the cell."

Maxine looked puzzled then scurried toward the door.

"C'mon, we don't got all day."

As soon as she walked in, her eyes fell on Grayson Sr. Her heart fluttered. In her spirit, she knew it was something positive. "What's going on?" She hesitated, not knowing whether to hug or sit, so she chose the latter.

"Something's happened."

"Sierra? Little Gray, what's going on?"

"No, no. Bencil. He was shot. Random carjacking."

"What? I mean," she swallowed, "Omigod. Last thing I expected." She tried to process her emotions. The situation was so complicated.

"I had to go down and identify the body."

She could tell he was struggling with a range of emotions.

"I'm not sure what to say."

He looked around. "Maxi, there's more. We have some evidence that may have a major impact on your case."

"May? What do you mean may? What is it?" She leaned forward.

"I mean, get you out almost immediately."

"Omigod! Omigod, what, how?"

"Maxi, you were right. I should have believed you."

She gasped then placed her hand over her mouth.

"Maxi, right now I can't tell you everything. But there is a strong indication you were drugged that night, and somebody tampered with some critical evidence. We're going to arrange for an emergency hearing."

She leaned back and took a deep breath. She held her eyes shut. Then wiped her eyes with the back of her hand. "Please tell me this isn't a joke."

"It's not a joke, we're going to get you out. The attorney will arrive here soon." He smiled.

She smiled back then broke down in tears.

Chapter 62 – Cleansing

Grayson Sr. sat in his study waiting for his son. For years he'd dreaded having this conversation. He heard the knock and jumped.

"Hey Dad, what was so urgent? Cassie and I were getting ready to go to brunch."

"Son, close the door. Lock it behind you and have a seat."

He obeyed, realizing his father was extremely serious. Grayson Jr. swallowed hard. "Okay, Dad."

"This morning, I went and um, son, Bencil's dead." The last few words trailed off.

Grayson Jr. shot up. "What? I mean how?"

"Please, son, calm down. It was an extremely random situation. Carjacking. We haven't released a statement on behalf of the business. But when we do, it's going to be a media frenzy for a while, and I just want you to be prepared."

"I can't believe it, my Godfather. Dad, I'm so sorry." He dropped his head then looked up. "Wow, I just can't believe it." He rubbed his forehead. "I mean what, how?"

"I know, son. Somebody backed into him. It looked like a setup by the driver." Grayson Sr. walked toward his window and clasped his hand behind him. "Son, these next couple of days are going to be rough. We just need to be careful about how we handle everything, and there are some things I need to say or share rather concerning your Godfather, the business. What I tell you should not leave this room."

Grayson Jr. eyed his father curiously. "Things, like what?"

“Wow, this is really complicated.”

“Look, Dad, just say it.”

He gazed out the window, wondering how much of the truth to tell. “Bencil and I had a long history. And truthfully we didn’t always do things the right way. We compromised a lot of things. I mean the way we did business and well, that was a long time ago. I mean we did business, well some things just weren’t legal. Thankfully those days are over, but I wanted you to know. I’m just not so sure those things didn’t come back to haunt him.

“I don’t know, son, when I left Louisiana, I never wanted to live that way again. I never wanted to be hungry or feel like trash, and well, I was willing to compromise. And once you compromise a little, you find yourself compromising a lot. Bencil manipulated a lot of people and truthfully, he was jealous. Jealous of what I was able to do for the business. He felt threatened.” He sighed.

“Dad, why are you talking about him this way? You two were close. That’s my Godfather.”

“We were son. We *were* close.” He grabbed the stress balls on his desk and fumbled them in his hand. “I was determined to erase everything about my past and Bencil knew it. So he took me under his wing. He knew I had talent. We did big things together. Your Godfather had ties with some unsavory people. But in the end, they didn’t trust him. But they trusted me.”

“Dad, can you just say what you need to say? So you weren’t a saint. That’s business.”

“True, but we stretched the legal boundaries as far as possible. We had lots of powerful people looking out for us. Mob people, dirty cops. I was so naive. I never questioned things until we were knee deep and I wanted out. It was too late by then.” He watched his son’s face. He was void of expression. “And well, Maxine, Sierra’s mother got caught in the crossfire. She knew more than she should, and it was my fault.”

Grayson Jr. sat there, dumbfounded. “What does she have to do with this?”

“Well, she and I knew each other long before she came here. We were in the same foster home. And when she came here many years ago, I promised I take care of her.”

“Take care of her? In what way?”
“I mean at first it was very much like an older brother, but then…”

Grayson Jr.’s forehead creased and his eyes narrowed. “Dad, you are not going to sit here and tell me that you were in a relationship with Sierra’s mother? Please don’t tell me that.”

“Son, yes, I was in a relationship with her. I loved her.”

“You know what?” He stood and paced the floor. “This is really sick. Why are you fessing up now?”

“Because Bencil and Maxine had an affair. It was all my fault. He’s Sierra’s father. She was angry and hurt when I married your mother. It’s all a big mess. It’s going to come out. His lawyer left instructions.”

“So all this time, you acted as if you hated Sierra. You talked me out of being with her. You self-serving son-of-a…” He rushed toward his father. Before Grayson Sr. could react, his son grabbed him by the throat. “You are a liar! Your entire life is a lie! You don’t love my mother or me!”

“What are you doing?” His mother stood frozen in the doorway before rushing to her son to grab him from behind.

When he realized what was happening, Grayson Jr. released his father. His father gasped for air as his body fell forward. He tried to utter a few words in between gasping for air.

His mother ran to her husband’s side and wrapped her arms around him. “Don’t talk. Shhhh.” She rubbed his back as he continued to gasp. He finally was able to calm down.

"Mom, I wish I would have killed him. He is the scum of the earth. If you knew what I knew, you wouldn't feel sorry for him." His arms dangled with his fists balled up.

His mother slowly looked up. "Son, whatever it is, I already knew."

He stood a few seconds, looking back and forth at the both of them in disbelief. Part of him wanted to run over and embrace his father and the other wanted to run and never look back.

"You know what? You two deserve each other." He turned and walk toward the door.

"Grayson Jr.," his mother said, "if you walk out that door, you'll regret it."

He turned around. "Why, Mother?"

"Because your father's, well he's dying."

Chapter 63 – Ashes to Ashes

They all stood still on the yacht as Bencil's lawyer released the ashes into the ocean. The sea breeze quickly swept his remains into the air. He didn't say many words based upon Bencil's instructions. He didn't want any whooping and hollering. It was an eerily calm and quiet event, void of emotion. The only people present were the Griers, Maxine and Sierra. He'd left a huge portion of money to other family members but didn't want them present. He'd considered those on the yacht his family.

Grayson Sr. stood against the side of the boat, whispering a quiet prayer over Bencil's soul, while quietly praying for the rescue of his own. Lydia came over and lay her head on his shoulder as she grabbed his hand. "Guess it's all over. We're all free." Her face stoic.

"I guess. But, my son hates me. Still not speaking to me." He glanced over at him but Grayson Jr. looked away.

"He will."

"Lydia, I'm sorry."

She turned to him and grabbed his hands. "Shh, no apologies." After a moment, she added, "That Bencil. Came clean with everything."

"He must've known in his spirit something was going to happen." He gazed out onto the water. "I just pray his spirit is at peace. He may have confessed his sin, but we'll never know if he accepted Christ."

"He did." The lawyer walked toward them.

Grayson Sr. turned and looked at him, puzzled. "How do you know?"

"It happened in my office. He asked me if I knew Christ and if I truly believed in God. I told him yes and offered to pray with him. I called my wife from the receptionist area, and she led him to Christ right there. After she left, he wrote the letter under a sworn testimony and redrafted his will. That's all I can tell you about that day."

Grayson Sr. nodded, then cracked a smile.

Cassie walked over to Grayson Jr. and grabbed his hand. "You have to forgive him you know. If you can forgive me, you can forgive him."

"Maybe," Grayson Jr. said. He noticed Sierra on the other side of the boat.

Cassie took a deep breath. "Go talk to her. She needs you."

He brushed her hair away from her face then kissed her on the lips. "I'll be right back." He slowly walked toward Sierra.

"Hey you," She embraced him.

"Hey." He whispered back. "You okay? It's a lot to take in." He stepped back and examined her face."

She shrugged. "Just wish I'd known." She looked in the direction of his father. "Gray, you still have *your* father. He may not be perfect, but he loves you." She poked him in the chest. "Don't let bitterness and unforgiveness steal your blessings. Your Dad would do anything for you."

He lightly touched her arm then gazed at the water. "Gonna work through it." He paused, then faced her. "Sierra, I'm sorry, for everything. For not being a man when I needed to. For mistreating you." He turned his mouth to the side. "Truth? I well, I always loved you. But I wasn't mature enough to, anyway we were just kids. "

She grabbed his hands. "I get it. What we had was something special. But, well you're right. We were just kids. Can't change the past," She glanced toward Cassie's direction. "Time for us both to move on. Your wife's a beautiful woman, and she loves your big head. I'm not sure why but she does." She laughed then took a deep breath. "Grayson, I'm leaving Montclair. I need to be happy and, well I think it's best." She bit the side of her lip and turned to faced him.

He paused then nodded. "When? Where?"

"Soon as we can sell the house. Martha's Vineyard. Always dreamed of living there, and well God's made a way. We already have someone that may be interested in buying it. A couple that loves fixer uppers. I know this is all God."

"Wow. Martha's Vineyard." He smiled. "I'm not sure what happened when you went there but you've been different ever since."

"Sometimes you have to go away to get free. You're right. Something *did* happen. I found me. Anyway, it'll be great for Gray. I want to raise him in a small community. Around art, culture and history."

"Sierra, I get it. I'm good. It's not too far." He reached in to hug her. "Well, at least money won't be an issue. My Godfather, I mean, your father did right by you."

They both laughed a little.

"Yeah," Sierra said, "I guess he did."

Chapter 64 – Goodbye for Now

"Well, guess that's it."

Sierra took one last look at the house. She wanted to miss it but couldn't muster up any emotional attachment. She was excited about the new chapter about to unfold in her life. She smiled at the sold sign sitting in the front yard. Her mother had sold or given away most of the furniture, and buried all the ugly memories of their old Victorian house. It sold for much more than they thought it would, and the new couple was willing to pour money into it to fix it up. Turns out the realtor knew they were waiting to purchase a house in the area, and the house was sold in less than thirty days.

Sierra closed her eyes and pictured the ocean and quiet life she'd envisioned awaiting her. *I can't wait to raise Gray on the island. I can't wait for Zoe to visit, and I can't wait to see Carrington!* So much had happened she hadn't mustered the nerve to reach out to him. She'd left so abruptly she was going to have to work up the nerve to explain. She'd reached out with a text and he was receptive. But she still had some making up to do.

Her mother came out the house and shut the door behind her. She walked down the steps and turned to face her house one last time. "So you ready for this new adventure?" she asked as she faced Sierra.

"Definitely. I thought it was going to be hard to leave this place, but it felt so good just to get rid of everything."

Although Sierra had her moments of disbelief in God's grace, she couldn't deny the fact that when he comes through, he comes *all* the way through. Not only had he enabled the house to be sold quickly, but he aided in her and Maxine being able to catch up on the shop's outstanding debt *and* buy out the rest of the lease.

Amber was given the reins of the shop, and she was ready to put her spin on it.

God had made sure his daughters would start with a clean slate.

Maxine hugged Sierra to her. “Let’s go.”

“Let’s.”

They jumped in their brand new SUV and headed toward Grayson and Cassie’s house to pick up her son.

~~~~~

Sierra walked up the steps and rung the bell. Grayson Jr. came to the door.

“Come on in, you’re early. Cassie, get Gray!” he yelled upstairs.

“Yeah, we moved pretty quickly. Sort of anxious.” She smiled. “Grayson, I just want to say thank you for being so understanding. You could have made this difficult.”

“Sierra, it’s okay. I love my son, and it’s not like you are moving across the country. Time for you to live your life.”

She winked. “Thanks. So have you thought about what I said?”

“It’s taken some real soul searching and prayer, but my Dad and I are talking. I need to be there for him. They were here last night.”

“I’m proud of you.” She reached in and kissed him on the cheek.

“Besides,” he said, “I have a lot to be thankful for. I’m not trying to block any blessings.” Cassie came downstairs and walked toward them. “Hey Sierra.” She reached out and hugged her.”

“Okay, where’s the little guy?” Grayson Jr. asked Cassie.
~~~~~

"He's coming. Wanted to pack up his own bag." Cassie winked at her husband.

Seconds later, he sprinted down the steps with his backpack.

"Finally!" Grayson said, kneeling before his son. He looked him straight in the eye. "Remember what I said."

"Yep, I'm the man of the house and need to take care of my mom," little Gray said.

Grayson kissed him and grabbed him for a hug. "Love you, boy." He ruffled his curls.

"I love you, too."

He stood then kissed Cassie on the cheek as she beamed. "Should we tell her?"

Sierra looked confused. "Tell me what?" Cassie's face lit up with a smile. "We're pregnant."

"Really!" Her eyes widened. "Omigod. I'm so happy for you." Sierra hugged her. "So happy!"

"Yeah, it's pretty great news."

"See, I can keep a secret," little Gray said. "I'm going to be a big brother, Mom! And the man of the house."

Sierra rubbed his hair. "Yes, you are. So how you feel about that?"

"I'm all the way up!" He started dancing.

They all looked at each other and laughed.

Epilogue – Vineyard Haven

Sierra held on to both her men as they walked up Circuit Avenue.

"So what time is Grayson, Cassie and the kids coming?" C.C. asked.

"They'll be in on the 6:15 p.m. ferry tomorrow," Sierra replied.

"So looking forward to hanging out."

"Yeah, me too." They continued to walk as little Gray shot ahead.

C.C. took off after him. "What I say about running off?" Although he didn't really worry too much. They knew everyone on the island. They'd moved into a house around the corner from his parents.

When they reached *Re-Deaux*, her mother's shop on Circuit Avenue, they walked in and saw her mother straightening up.

"Hey, you two. Glad the Fourth of July rush is over." She walked over to Sierra and placed her hand over her belly. "How's my other grandbaby? So excited to have a girl."

"Mom, please." She beamed, "Have to admit we're so blessed." She placed her hand over her mother's.

She looked at her daughter and son-in-law. "God's grace."

"Sooo, what time's the barbeque?" C.C. asked.

They all turned toward Amir, an artist on the island and Maxine's husband. Sierra was still tickled by the love that shone between the two. He was tall, muscular and God fearing with a crown of salt and pepper locs. He made her mother very happy and was a great with her son. “Well I’m getting ready to head out now. Had to help your mother with the inventory.”

“Those college kids cleaned this store out.” Maxine added.

“I guess the Inkwell’s the spot again. Oh, before I forget Sierra, the sweetest lady came in today,” Amir added. “Your mother was gone on an errand. I was here by myself. Think her name was Queenie? Said she knew you. Was in a rush.”

Sierra eyed him curiously. “Did she wear a scarf? Jackie O sunglasses, was she driving a vintage Thunderbird?”
“Yes, she was driving a Thunderbird. Don’t really remember what she was wearing.”

“That was her! Mom, mom I know it! I so want you to meet her!”

“Well, she left a card.” He offered.

“Where is it, where is it?” Sierra was jumping up and down her heart, about to burst out her chest.

Amir went over to the register and scattered a few papers. “Oh, here it is. Well, I thought it was a business card.” He flipped it over and back.

C.C. rubbed his forehead. “Wow, Queenie. No one could understand why she’d packed up and left so quickly. It was strange,” C.C. said as he kept his eyes on Sierra. “Shortly after you went left for Montclair she had this urgency to head back to her hometown. Said it would be temporary. But this is the first anyone’s heard of her after three years!” C.C. was just as anxious to find out if this was their Queenie.

“See I’m *not* crazy,” Sierra mumbled. She grabbed the card. “That house has been empty since. No forwarding address.” She read the card and frowned.

“What?” they all asked waiting for her to speak.

She slowly raised her head. Then read the words on the card, “Do not forget to show hospitality to strangers, for by so doing some people have shown hospitality to angels without knowing it. Hebrews 13-2.” She shook her head and smiled. *Naw, couldn’t be.* Until she knew different she was going to believe that God had loved her enough to send help in the form of one beautiful, witty silver-haired anointed angel named Queenie and she would be forever grateful for it.

Norma L. Jarrett, J.D. is the award winning author of the Randomhouse novels, *Sunday Brunch*, *Sweet Magnolia* (*Essence* magazine National Book Club Selection) and *The Sunday Brunch Diaries* (*Essence* Bestseller) and additional titles: *Bridal Brunch, Brunchspiration, Christmas Beau*, *Love on a Budget* and *Valentine's Day...Again???* Her work has been featured in *Ebony, Essence, Kirks Reviews; Publisher's Weekly, Rolling Out, Southern Living, Upscale, USA Today* and other media. Ms. Jarrett is a graduate of North Carolina A & T State University and Thurgood Marshall School of Law. Norma is also a member of Alpha Kappa Alpha Sorority, Inc., The Junior Service League and one of the founding members of The Anointed Authors on Tour. She is married and resides in Houston, Texas, where she attends Lakewood Church. She blogs at www.lolamae.co you may also visit her website at www.normajarrett.net.

Made in the USA
San Bernardino, CA
12 December 2016